And Then There Were Five

Celestial Series Book Two

Lillith Carrie

LILLITH CARRIE PUBLISHING

Words from the Author

To all my amazing readers, this one's for you.

When you feel like your world is falling apart, remember that you got here this far, and everything you have gone through has made you the strong-willed person you are now.

When one door closes, it isn't because it's over. It's because another door has opened, and you simply have to walk through it.

There is more to life than being mundane, take risks and thrive in the adventure.

Never stop pursing your dreams. One day you will see the world as I do and you will never look back.

Only you can make the change you want, stay strong and don't be afraid.

Know that I'm there with you all.

Love Always,

Lillith Carrie

Prologue

Three months after the claim

Ivy.

Three months. That's all it had been, and yet life couldn't get any better. Sure, things were different now, but that was to be expected, right? Wrong. God, how stupid could I be to think everything was normal?

One moment I'm a normal college student expecting to go to a new place and finish my degree. The next, I'm some fucking goddess shifter thingy, and my life is being turned upside down by four men who are amazing, but also very fucking annoying.

"Damn it, James!" I screamed from the kitchen as I stood with the refrigerator door opened, searching for the Snickers I knew I had hid in there. "Did you eat my fucking candy bar?"

Laughter erupted from the living room, and I had no doubt it was the twins finding my hormonal cravings to be the center of their amusement.

Did I find it funny, though? Of course I didn't and if one of them didn't produce a fucking Snickers bar in the next five seconds, someone was going to get their ass beat.

"Calm down," James sighed, rushing into the kitchen with a smile on his face. "I just put it in a safe place so it didn't get lost behind all the groceries I went and got."

Watching, he reached into the fridge and pulled out a small pink container with the words 'Ivy's shit' on the top of it. The small sentiment was enough to bring tears to my eyes James quickly hugged me for.

"Please don't cry," he whispered, not wanting to get yelled at by Damian again for bringing me to tears.

Since I found out I was pregnant, I had started going through weird changes. One minute I was happy, and the next, I was crying. You would think it was only me that would be going through these changes, right? Wrong again.

It seemed my mates were each having their own version of sympathy pregnancy symptoms, and on more than one occasion, Damian had to feel the wrath of my sadness.

Which in turn made him start crying, and we all know... Damian isn't that kind of man.

"It's just sweet," I said, forcing back the tears as he opened the container and handed me the Snickers. "Just next time, tell me."

"Of course, sweetie. How are you feeling today?" he asked, and a sigh escaped me.

"Like a freakish monster carrying children who could potentially destroy the world."

Rolling his eyes, he shook his head, "I don't know why you keep saying that."

"Uh—maybe because that's what everyone thinks." I shrugged my shoulders.

"Not everyone thinks that," he groaned. "All that was said is we have no idea what traits will be passed down."

"Uh—and that you're worried about what could happen. Come on now, I'm not stupid and I can read between the lines, James."

He couldn't argue with me there. The more and more they tried to sugar coat shit with me, the more annoyed I became. I just wanted the truth when it came to shit and over the past few months, they had gotten better at telling me things.

Yet, part of me still couldn't help but wonder if what I was doing was right.

I was the Luna of the pack. The matriarch and mother to all… or so I was told.

Yet, everyone seemed afraid of me in a way and I couldn't understand why. I had never given them a reason to fear me and with everything that was going on now with the pregnancy, I didn't want to be looked at differently.

"Look, you just have to give things time. I mean, look at Rosa. She was a little unsure of you at first, but now you guys are like BFFs." He said, crossing his arms over his chest.

"James, she is the midwife. Of course, we fucking get a long." I turned from the kitchen and made my way towards the living room.

I knew he was just trying to be helpful, but in all honest—he fucking wasn't.

I had to face facts. I'm a freak with unknown supposed powers, and every day I sit here, I find myself to the point of losing my mind. "I need a hobby."

"You have one, gorgeous," Hale commented, putting down his book as he made room for me next to him on the sofa.

"Oh yeah, what's that?" I said in a flat tone while stuffing into the delicious chocolate treat I had been craving for the past few days.

"Us, of course."

Smacking him on the leg, he, James, and Talon broke out into a fit of laughter. "Just because my sex drive is through the roof doesn't mean it's a hobby."

"True, but it's a great way to stay in shape." Talon pointed out as he scrolled through his phone. "I mean, look at me… I haven't been in better shape in a long time."

"I'm being serious guys," I groaned in frustration. "I think I want to start going back to school. I need something to focus on, and I can't just sit around here forever."

All three of them fell silent at my statement. Damian and I had spoken about it before, but every time we did, he always shot it down.

Not long after I went to enroll again, people started asking questions about Caleb. The guys had formulated something that made it look like he just moved out of town, but the friends he left behind questioned it all.

They were humans, and it wasn't like we could tell them what really happened. Humans weren't supposed to know our kind existed.

"You know what Damian said," Hale sighed, shaking his head. "He isn't going to allow it... at least not right now."

"That isn't fair, Hale. I want something to do, and there is only so much learning I can take with Priscilla. I love her to death, but if I have to sit through one more meditation session with her, I'm going to scream."

"What's going to make you scream?" Damian said as his voice drifted in from the front door.

Jumping from my seat, I skipped towards him and wrapped my arms around his neck. He had been gone for the past week, and I was glad to see him home.

Business overseas hadn't been going the way he liked and now that the drama was over, he had taken his roll back within the company on a more serious note.

"You're back," I smiled, kissing him gently. "Welcome home."

He smiled down at me, pulling me into his arms before letting his hand rub against my stomach. Things between Damian and I had gotten entirely better since my Luna ceremony and finding out that I was pregnant.

Instead of the cold, demanding and asshole-ish person who he was—he became an Alpha everyone respected.

We had all agreed after the ceremony he was still going to be Alpha. With him taking that position, Talon and James took over training, and making sure the borders were protected.

Hale, on the other hand, worked more with me. He helped out tremendously in the pack hospital and on more than one occasion; I had told him he should have become a doctor. It just wasn't what he wanted to do, though.

Instead, he managed the pack hospital and oversaw the pack school.

There was an intelligence about him that stumped even me, and with everything else going on, I was glad to know I had them close.

"I want to go back to school, Damian," I whispered softly. "The guys even agree.. don't you?" The glare I gave them had their eyes wide and their mouths parted.

"I mean—"

"Uh—well..."

"I didn't say shit," Talon finally piped up as a gasp left my lips.

"Talon, seriously?" I asked in disbelief.

Standing to his feet, he shook his head, "look, honestly, I don't think it's safe. Especially considering you're pregnant. Outside of the pack territory, I can't keep you protected like I can when you're in it. Your pregnancy isn't a secret anymore, and everyone now knows about what happened at Sanctum. Who knows who wants you..."

I knew he was right, but I couldn't believe he would be so against it. It was like even though my life had become amazing. I was a prisoner.

Fear enveloped those who didn't understand something, and with me, there was so much people didn't understand. Every day, though, I tried to help people see I was normal.

It just wasn't always possible.

"I will be safe," I begged, looking at Damian with the biggest puppy dog eyes I could put on. "Please let me... I mean, technically I don't have to ask permission, but I'm trying to have you agree and be supportive."

"Look," Damian sighed. "I will agree that you can go back to school, but I would prefer it be after the baby is born. Can you at least agree with that?"

It wasn't the answer I was hoping for, but understanding his concerns, I smiled.

"Okay, deal." I replied, leaning up to kiss him.

In the end, I won the situation somewhat. Now the only thing left to happen was to get through the rest of this pregnancy in one piece, and pray nothing crazy happens with my pregnancy.

The last thing I wanted was to turn into a Godzilla wife, because honestly, that would be my luck. I would have something insane happen, and then watch... the world would literally depend on something completely bizarre.

Like the last piece of pizza that always seemed to disappear when I try to save it.

Life wasn't easy, that was for sure, but as long as I had my guys, anything was possible.

"Ivy!" Priscilla called from the front door as she walked in behind Damian. "Oh, Damian, you're back!"

"Yes, it's lovely to see you again, Priscilla. I hope those classes for Ivy are coming along well?"

"Yes, they are, but she still has a long way to go." She turned her gaze to me and smiled. "Are you ready?"

"Yeah, as long as this baby lets me actually get some peace." I giggled, rubbing my hand over my small protruding bump.

"Don't you mean babies?" Priscilla said with a grin, causing my eyes to widen.

"You're fucking joking..."

"Twins!" Hale laughed. "I fucking knew it!"

"You don't know shit, Hale." I scolded as I watched James and Talon fork money from their wallets and handing it to Hale. "I haven't even gotten the ultrasound done yet. Don't count your chickens yet."

I knew what Priscilla said was true. Over the past month, I wondered if it was two, and something inside me told me it was. I just had been avoiding the ultrasound for this particular reason.

How the hell was I going to deal with Twins?

Oh, wait.. I have two grown ass one's standing in the living room. Goddess, help me.

CHAPTER ONE

History Lesson

Twins.

They confirmed it quicker than I had expected. One day I was listening to Priscilla tell me there were babies... and then the next day I was on an ultrasound table watching as the pack doctor used cold jelly and a magic wand to scan my stomach.

"Oh, look... right there, Luna. There is baby one... and there is baby two."

The doctor's words didn't comfort me. I was excited, yes, but extremely scared.

"Thank you," I replied, not knowing what to say.

I had grown up an only child, and had no clue what it was like having a sibling or raising more than one child. Granted, I wasn't alone. I had four incredibly sexy mates who stood over me as if on guard twenty-four hours of the day, but it still didn't ease my mind.

"There is no need to thank me. I would like to see you back in two weeks. That way, we can get another scan and determine the sex of the babies."

As soon as the doctor finished cleaning my stomach, he stood to his feet and made his way from the room. My eyes cast towards my four mates, who had excited faces as they looked at the photos of my ultrasound that had been given to them.

It shocked me none of them cared to determine who the father of the children was. Instead, they shared in the duty as if all four of them helped in creating the children to come.

Which, honestly, was a sweet notion. I was glad the paternity of the children would not be an issue for them. Then again, they never had a problem sharing me.

"Are we ready to go home?" I asked as their eyes lifted to meet mine. "I mean, we can stay here if you want, but I was kind of hoping for pizza and a movie."

Pizza and movie were two words triggering all their attention.

It wasn't a Netflix and chill kind of situation.

They literally ordered pizza, and we watched movies. It was the one time I let them surprise me with both toppings and genre. Even though I often questioned their choices, because, I mean, who doesn't love pineapple on pizza... cue dramatic eye roll.

"Pizza! You keep saying those sweet magic words to me, and you may end up pregnant for the unforeseeable future, Ivy," James replied as he moved towards the door with me right behind him.

Laughter escaped me, "pizza and movies turns you on and makes you want to have kids?"

James wrapped his arms around me and leaned in, kissing my neck. "With you, yes."

James was definitely the most affectionate of the four men and seemed to always have me laughing and smiling, no matter the situation. My life with them was far from dull, but at least communication was better, mostly, now.

"So, are you wanting to design the nursery, Ivy? Or did you want to have us do it for you... hire someone, maybe?" Damian asked as we climbed into the car.

"I don't know," I sighed. Designing a nursery was sort of the last thing on my mind for the time being. While they thought about things like this, I was still worried about someone coming to challenge us.

Yes, I was a bloody Sølvmåne werewolf, but I was pregnant.

What the hell was I seriously going to do when I would eventually be as big as a house?

I hadn't exactly thought things through when I started letting them fuck my brains out.

However, we didn't know what I was either, so there was that, too.

"Are you okay, Ivy?" A soft touch to my shoulder from Hale pulled me from my thoughts and slowly I nodded with a smile.

"Yeah, sorry, just a lot on my mind," I mumbled, trying to clear my confusion. "I don't mind about the nursery. We can look at some things."

All four of them hesitated for a moment, staring at me before I pushed a smile upon my face. "Seriously, I'm fine."

"Is that why you cut us off from linking you this morning?" Talon asked with confusion.

I wasn't sure what to say. It was the truth, but I suppose part of me didn't tell them, hoping they wouldn't notice.

"Kind of," I finally admitted. "There is just so much going on, and I can't help but wonder if having babies right now is coming at the most unrealistic of moments."

"Ivy... babies never come when they are needed. They come when they come, and everything else just gets figured out around it," Damian replied with a smirk.

"That's easy for you to say, Damian. You're not pushing two fucking watermelons out of your hoo-ha." I was trying not to freak out. Honestly, I was trying.

However, the more I thought about the fact I had two lives growing inside me, and I was going to have to push them out of a hole that shouldn't stretch like that big terrified me.

Their dads were giants among men, and there was no way two big ass babies were going to be able to come out of my cooter. It just wasn't possible.

Silence descended over us for a moment as the car pulled up to the front of the house. My mind reels with the future I have been given. No matter how much time had passed, I could never get used to my current situation.

Stepping out of the car, the guys' laughter consumed the surrounding air.

"Come on now, Ivy. It will not be that bad. Women have babies every day."

Talon's words did nothing but aggravate me further. They had no idea how I felt and with my hormones all over the place, I couldn't control the emotional rollercoaster I was feeling.

Slamming the door behind me, I stormed off towards the house, tired of their bullshit. I loved them dearly, but right now, I wanted to smother them all. They had a tendency to be complete assholes when they wanted to be.

A few hours later, and a tub of chocolate cake frosting, I was in a much better mood.

"You know, I think the only real reason I like these movies is so that I can watch Aquaman's sexy ass," my muttered comment caught the Hale's attention, and quickly, I felt the jealousy he had for the actor on tv.

Suited him right for pissing me off.

Pizza and Marvel movies were my calling. The guys were more than thrilled to not be stuck watching some sort of chick-flick and even though I enjoyed them, I was in more of an ass-kicking mood lately.

I felt as if this calmness surrounding me was only the calm before the storm, and deep inside me, I felt something was coming.

I just wasn't sure what it was.

Looking at Hale, who sat on my left, I found myself curious about the information he had searched about his history. Priscilla had told me there were things he and Talon knew only they could tell.

Even as a seer, she couldn't see everything and if I wanted answers, I would have to go to the source, eventually. "Hale. Can I ask you something?"

"Of course. What's on your mind?" he said, casting a small glance and a smile my way.

Looking down at my hands, I hesitated for a moment while I gathered my thoughts. "I wanted to know what you learned about yourself. You told me you had done research on what the ancients were, and while Priscilla is helping me learn some things, there's still so much that I don't understand."

Hale stared at me for a moment, as if he wasn't quite sure what to say. Every time I mentioned it in the past, he avoided the conversation, but I knew deep down that was because he was scared. I just wasn't sure why he was scared. We're mates and shouldn't hide anything.

"What do you want to know?" He cast he gaze towards the window as if unable to look at me while we talked about it.

"I don't know... anything, really."

To see Hale like this made little sense.

"If it makes you uncomfortable—"

Turning to me with a wide grin, he shook his head. "It's not. It's just that honestly none of it makes sense, but I supposed I can tell you what I do know that will."

Adjusting myself, I stretched out over his legs, making myself comfortable as I continued to attentively listen to him. His hands instinctively going to my feet as he started to rub them. I tried hard to stay focused, but the deep circled motions were more than distracting.

"Our mother was a regular werewolf, but she came from a very long lineage. Her bloodline went as far back as the nomadic Vikings, and possibly even further."

"Vikings?" I giggled. "Like plunder the land kind of Vikings?"

Nodding his head, he nudged me with his elbow gently and smiled. "Yes, those."

"Makes sense now why you and Talon love to throw me around and make claims on me so much..."

At the moment I said that, laughter from the open doorway behind me echoed through the room, and to my surprise James and Talon stood there with popcorn.

"I thought we were watching a movie?" James said as he plopped himself down onto a chair near me, and Talon took the floor below me.

"We were, but Ivy wants a history lesson," Hale said pointedly, causing me to roll my eyes.

"Will you continue, please?"

"Of course... nowhere was I." Taking a moment, he smiled. "Oh right, so our mother was this descendant of a long lineage and at one point, she was supposed to marry this other Alpha from a neighboring pack. The idea of mates had slowly faded back then, and many just married in for power or wealth. Except, our mother ignored new notions and was determined to find her mate."

"What a mate he was," Talon chuckled, popping his snack into his mouth.

"Who's telling this story? Me or you?" Hale replied with an irritated expression.

Gesturing with his hand, Talon let Hale continue. However, there was something in Hales' eyes that made me unsure if telling this story was a good idea.

As Hales eyes met mine, he sighed. "Our mother met our father in the darkest parts of the woods. It was said to be off limits and cursed, but something drew her there, and according to diaries we found of hers in the attic a few years ago, she felt like he watched her for weeks before she let him claim her."

"So he knew that your mother was his mate, then?"

Nodding his head, Hale looked off with a heavy breath and stared out the window as if expecting to see something no longer there.

"He knew, but no one else knew what he was. Except for our grandmother, and she cursed the relationship because she said it would bring hell upon the world with the creations they would give life."

My heart all but dropped into my stomach after hearing him. Those words sounded so oddly familiar, and as much as I wish I could remember why, I couldn't.

The creations they made were my mates, and I knew each of them. They wouldn't hurt anyone who didn't hurt them first.

"She was just scared—"

"No, Ivy. She wasn't a normal wolf. She was a hybrid herself, and Priscilla's twin sister."

Holy fuck... say what?!

CHAPTER TWO

Dreams of Darkness

Running.

It was all I ever seemed to do, and every time I closed my eyes, the darkness cascaded over me like a blanket.

Welcoming me home.

But it made me feel terrified if I stepped forth into that darkness, I would be lost forever.

Taking a deep breath, I pushed past my own fears. The calling sound of a woman in the distance made me move further. I wasn't exactly sure what I was going to find, but something deep inside me told me to keep going. As that darkness finally cleared, I found myself in a valley of light seemingly to never end and within the light stood a beautiful woman with long red hair and glowing crystalline eyes.

She looked familiar to me, but then again, she didn't. Was I back where I met Frigga?

"Who are you?" I asked softly, watching as the woman's gaze turned to me as she gently tilted her head.

Plump red lips and razor-sharp teeth formed into a wide smile as she stared. "Who am I? I am you. Do you not recognize your own flesh and blood?"

What the hell?

"You're not me..."

"Am I not, mother?" Every breath in my chest escaped me at her words.

Mother? Was this the vision of my future daughter? Was I to have a daughter?

For a moment, I stood still and contemplated the woman's words. But before I could say anything, a baby's cry caused me to turn my attention quickly to something in the darkness behind me.

Confliction. Utter confliction filled the core of my soul, and as the crying grew, the higher my anxiety climbed. "If you go, mother, it will end as it was planned."

Turning to look back at the creature, I shook my head in disbelief. "What are you talking about? What is planned?"

The crying grew louder and more restless with every passing second. Instead of waiting to hear what she said, I turned from the woman and ran towards the child. If there was a babe in trouble, I would be the one to save it.

The closer I got, the farther away the child seemed to be, and to make matters worse, a roar of endless terror echoed through the darkness, setting the panic within my soul I did not even know existed.

If there was something dangerous within the darkness, I had to hurry. Not just because I was in danger, but there was a baby in danger too.

It wasn't until I saw the soft pink and blue blanket upon a lush bed of grass I realized I had finally made it. However, the sudden feeling of being stuck captivated my attention to the ground beneath me.

My feet were stuck to the ground, and no matter how much I tried to free myself, I couldn't. It was as if someone had super glued my feet to the ground, and there was no way to escape. "No..." I cried out softly. "Hold on, baby, I'm coming."

As I searched the surrounding area for something to help, I glimpsed something in the shadows ahead of me.

Bright, red eyes gleamed through the darkness and as those red eyes stepped forth, I saw the face of a monster with a hunger dripping from its muzzle that terrified me. Its eyes darted from the baby to me as its tongue reached out, sweeping across its mouth.

"No!" I screamed as it lurched forward.

Jolting from my bed, I sat in panic with my hand across my chest and tears streaming from my eyes. I didn't have the slightest clue what the hell had just happened, but I was glad to know it was all a dream.

Lifting my hand, I brushed the sweat from my forehead and took a moment to catch my breath. At the same time, my bedroom door burst open, and Damian ran in wide eyed with James right behind him. "What happened?"

Taking a moment, I took a deep breath and pushed through my calming panic.

"Nothing, just a bad dream is all. I'm sorry I woke you guys."

Damian and James looked at each other with confused expressions before stepping forward. "Do you want to talk about it?" James asked.

"No, no. It's nothing. Why don't you guys go back to bed? I'm just gonna read for a while. I think all those action movies last night got to me."

With annoyance on his face, Damian turned and walked out of the room, telling me to rest. Things had gotten better with him over the last few months, but he was hard to read.

I knew he loved me, but I don't think he knew how to honestly handle everything going on. I often had to remind myself it isn't just my life that has changed, but all of theirs, as well.

Glancing at James, he leaned down and kissed me softly. "Get some rest, sweetie. Tomorrow we can go shopping for things for the nursery."

"Sounds like a plan," I replied as he made his way from my room and closed the door behind him. My mind slowly drifted back to the flash of images in my mind from my dream.

Never once had a dream frighten me as much as that one did.

Who did the woman call me mother?

And why was there a baby in the middle of darkness with a beast looking to devour it?

Perhaps this was just me and an overbearing imagination as a new mother worried about the world her children were going to come into. I didn't know what to make of it, but the more I thought about it, the higher my anxiety became.

Was I bearing children into a world that did not deserve them?

Was I living a life that was no longer safe?

Granted, humanity wasn't ever safe, but those evils I was aware of, and I could protect my children. Instead, I am in a world of supernatural creatures I barely know anything about.

Creatures that, at any moment, could take everything from me I love and there wouldn't be anything I could do to stop it.

Sliding from the bed, I let my feet gently touch the floor. There was one person who I could go to that would know what to do. I still couldn't believe she was actually their aunt. Why wouldn't have they told me that?

Making my way towards the attic staircase, I turned on the light and ascended the stairs. Priscilla had taken up residence in our converted attic and made it more incredible than I thought possible.

Knocking three times on her door, I waited and slowly Priscilla opened the door with a smile spread across her face letting me know she already knew I was coming. "Come in, dear. I set the kettle."

Stepping through the threshold, I shut the door behind me and glanced around her suite she had created. She had impeccable taste, and even though it was more of the garden variety, I found comfort in it where Damien would not let me decorate the rest of the house in this kind of decor.

"I'm sorry to intrude on you so early in the morning, Priscilla."

She gazed up at me from where she stood near the fireplace and grinned. "I knew you were coming, dear."

Of course she did. "I know, but still..."

"I take it you are having bad dreams again?" she commented as she continued meandering around the room.

"Yes. This one though was much different from the others though."

"Aren't they all?" she cackled softly. "Whatever it is, has you worried?"

Once again, she could read me like a book. I didn't even have to tell her what was going on and she would already be aware, which in the end made things a lot less complicated when I needed to tell somebody something.

"This one is different, though. I feel like it is trying to warn me about something. Like something horrible is going to happen, and I can't stop it."

Lifting two cups, she made her way to where I had taken a seat on a small pillow near her coffee table. "Our dreams are often the reflections of fate we are unprepared for. Don't ignore them, but remember that you can't change them."

"That's not exactly comforting," I groaned while sipping on the tea she had sat in front of me. "I wish I knew what to do."

"Have you spoken to the guys about these dreams?"

Glancing at her quickly, I shook my head. "No, definitely not."

"Why not?" she asked, slightly taken aback. "They are your mates, and can help."

"They are more likely to have a heart attack and board me up in this house forever. You should know this, considering they are your nephews." I said, letting her know I knew who she really was.

Frozen for a moment, a smile crept across her face that met her eyes. "They told you?"

"One of them did. The others just didn't object."

Laughter escaped the two of us as she shook her head, raising her brow. "Hale is very informative."

"He is, but what I want to know is why you didn't tell me. We have been working together for months to get down to what I am and how I can control myself, and you said nothing."

Priscilla hesitated as she played with the spoon in her tea. Her mind seemed to wander for a moment, but then, with her usual glance, she looked at me and smiled.

"Not everything is easy to explain, Ivy. Sometimes things must be discovered on your own." That wasn't the response I wanted, but it was clear it would be the only response I would get from her right now.

"Okay," I said with a little enthusiasm. "What do you suggest I do about these dreams, then? I mean, I can't keep on like this. The lack of sleep is getting to me."

"Perhaps you should talk to the goddess again. She had much to tell you before."

There was a feeling inside me telling me the same thing, but I didn't want to have to stoop to that unless I needed to. Just because I could reach out to them didn't mean I needed to for every minor issue I had.

"Maybe I should talk to the guys and see what they think first."

I hadn't told the guys the details of my dreams simply because I didn't want to worry them, but now I thought that was my best course of action.

"Avoiding the problem will not get you anywhere, Ivy. If you want to tell them, you can, but in the end you don't need to put off talking to the goddess. She came to you for the first time for a reason. You're a Celestial."

Priscilla was right as usual, even though I refused to tell her that. It wasn't because I was too prideful to admit she was right, but simply because if I did, then I would only further be showing I can't do anything without her guidance.

If that actually made any sense.

Conflicted with the possibilities of what the dream had meant, even though I knew it was a warning, the rational side of me just wanted to toss it up as nerves and nothing more.

Was that foolish? Perhaps... but then I felt I was being cautious.

Just because I was told by the 'goddess' I was a celestial and destined for great things, didn't mean that was actually the truth.

How was I sure that they weren't lying to me for their own personal gain, and they weren't the trickster god they had tried to warn me about?

In the end, I had to gain clarity.

But it would be on my own terms when I felt the situation called for it.

CHAPTER THREE

Town Secrets

James

The next morning I knew something was definitely wrong with Ivy. She wasn't acting herself, and when she came downstairs to get breakfast, she was more quiet than usual.

I could feel she was having bad dreams every time she closed her eyes, but she acted as if nothing was wrong. Even though I knew there was.

I just don't think she knew how to confront us about it, or maybe she didn't want to.

Since we completed the mate bond, we could read each other easily. However, the problem was Ivy liked to keep herself cut off from us more than we would have appreciated. At least when she was awake.

She didn't do it because she didn't care. She simply did it because she said she felt it was an invasion of privacy, which was understandable considering she didn't grow up in our world.

"Did you still want to go into town today and look at some stuff for the nursery?" I asked, trying to judge whether she was up for doing anything.

Her eyes met mine for the briefest of moments and, as if she was pushing away an external force clouding her mind, she nodded her head and let the small smile of joy creep across her face.

"Yes, definitely. I'd like to get started on everything. I mean, I know there's a lot that you guys are going to do for me, but I really want to be part of it."

I was happy she was excited about the twins arrival, because from the conversations I and the guys have had, we were concerned she was regretting her decision to be with us and to have our children.

For the past three months, she had done nothing but shrug off the topic of the unborn children or anything that had to do with babies.

Hale and Talon simply explained to me she regretted her decision to be with us. She was young. Her schooling had been changed. Her whole life had been upended and completely rerouted, and now to top it all off, she was pregnant with not just one baby, but two.

She was a new mother, and she was going to need time to get adjusted to it.

"Great. I'm not sure if the twins are still coming—"

"No, Hale and Talon are still on patrol. They did night shift, but unfortunately, Murphy and the other guy that we've got running have both come down with some mysterious cold," Damien said as he entered the kitchen.

"Cold. They're werewolves. How do they have a cold?"

Ivy's question caused Damien and I both to chuckle. "Just because they're wolves doesn't mean they can't get sick. There are certain ailments that trigger us, just like they would any normal human. The difference is we tend to get over it a lot quicker than humans do."

"So, you're telling me you guys have had an actual regular cold before?" Her brows furrowed in confusion, as if she just could not wrap her mind around this.

"Let's get going before you confuse yourself more. I will explain everything in the car on the way there."

Rolling her eyes, she smiled and hugged Damian. The soft interaction with them as he kissed the side of her head made me slightly jealous, but I was going to be spending the day with her, so I couldn't hold it against him.

We were all mates, after all. Even if I didn't like to share.

Leaving his arms, she moved towards me, tucking a strand of hair behind her ear, and grabbing her purse. The sweet smell of her wrapped around me, and with it, I could sense the children growing within her belly.

Children that could have been there because of me.

"Come on, James," she said with an amused glance as she opened the garage door.

Following behind her, she made her way towards the car, and as we climbed in, I couldn't help but stare. "Are you okay?"

Her question pulled me from my thoughts, and chuckling, I nodded. "Yep, I'm good."

"Okay, then," she replied sarcastically with a smile of her own. "Let's get going then."

15 minutes later, Ivy and I were heading down the highway towards the center of town to do a bit of shopping. It had been a while since she had properly been out, but that wasn't because she didn't want to go.

Instead, it was because there were security issues Damian wanted her kept close for.

"So did they ever find the rogues or whatever that were near the north end of the pack?"

"No," I replied. "Damian said that he thinks they were passing by, but the twins think otherwise, so they have been on top of patrol like you wouldn't believe."

"Is it something I need to worry about?" She caused me to glance at her to see her biting her bottom lip with her brow furrowed. "James?"

"Uh–no. Everything is fine, but we always take precautions to protect the pack."

Silence filled the space between us for a moment as we both looked ahead. "You mean to protect me..."

That was what I meant, but I didn't want her to think we would neglect the protection of the pack over her. Even though we would do it if we had to choose. It wasn't because we were heartless... She was our mate.

"It isn't like that, Ivy. Of course, we would do anything to protect you, but protecting the pack is protecting you. People are growing on you being here, whether you choose to see it," I pointed out, giving her a knowing glance that caused her to roll her eyes.

"They don't like me being here, James."

"Of course, they do. You're their Luna, Ivy. They just have to get to know you," I said, trying to reassure her further.

"You know, for as sweet as you are, you really need to learn that you suck at lying."

Gasping, I feigned hurt from her comment, and that expression alone caused her to burst into a small fit of laughter. "I do not," I replied firmly, trying to seem serious.

"Uh, yeah you do." She glanced at her phone. "I haven't heard from Kate in a while... Do you think she is mad at me?"

"Mad at you? Why the hell would she be mad? That woman literally threatened to neuter me at one point if I hurt you."

Thinking about that conversation had my balls aching. It was like it had only happened yesterday, and in reality, it happened two months ago. Two months that not a day went by when I didn't think about it.

"I almost forgot about that," Ivy hummed to herself as we pulled into a parking spot in front of the local shopping complex.

Amongst it were several clothing stores, hardware shops, and baby centers. I had hoped we could get a variety of things on our outing today to keep Ivy preoccupied for the next few weeks while the twins took care of our border issue.

It was honestly the main reason I took her out today.

Damian and the twins were holding a gathering with pack members to go over protocols and other safety measures. I had explained to them Ivy would want to be present, but of course, Damian said no.

He didn't want her to worry in her condition, and I knew very well if she found out later she would be more than pissed about it.

Hopefully, she just wouldn't be pissed at me.

"So, which store do you want to go in first?" I asked as we stepped out of the car into the slowly warming air. "The baby outlet... or maybe the department store..."

Taking a moment, Ivy glanced around, and settled her eyes on a hardware store.

"I want to look at paint swatches," she said with enthusiasm as she made her way towards Harders Tools and Paint.

"Paint?" I replied quickly, catching up to her. "We're painting?"

A softened stare of amusement crossed her face as she laughed. "Yes, James. Painting is something that you typically do."

"You know Damian isn't going to like odd colors, right...."

"Oh, I know," she chimed as she opened the door. "That's why I'm doing it."

Fuck. Of course she was doing it on purpose.

Debating with myself, I watched her look at the swatches going between blues and pinks to shades of green. Should I tell him now and save his wrath for another time?

Or should I say fuck it and let her do it, then watch him explode?

The internal struggle was real, but in the end, I let her have her fun and do what she wanted to do. It would make for a much more entertaining evening.

"So, what are you thinking?" I asked as I stepped closer, looking at the swatches in her hand. "Traditional baby colors?"

Laughter escaped her as she shook her head. "No. I want more earthy tones."

"Oh, my god! Ivy, is that you?!" A voice shrieked from the other side of the store.

I watched Ivy freeze for a moment before turning to look towards the person, and the sensation of dread and irritation flooded her. "Sasha... its been ages."

The brunette girl strode towards Ivy quickly before her eyes went down as she looked down at the growing bump that Ivy carried. "Oh, my god. So it's true... you're pregnant."

"What do you mean, it's true?" Ivy asked, a bit more bitterly than I thought she wanted to sound.

"Oh, well, there was just word going around that you dropped out of school because you got yourself knocked up. I didn't want to believe it, but when Caleb disappeared and then you did, a lot of us wondered—"

"Wait what?" I said, staring at the girl in confusion. "What does Caleb have to do with anything?" The girl was quiet for a moment, as if embarrassed she had even said anything, and with her hesitation, I became more and more enraged.

"Oh, please forgive me," she muttered, flipping her hair over her shoulder. "A couple of students on campus have been gossiping about how close you and the professor were before, and one person saw you guys get in a car together at one point because she lived near him. So she assumed that y'all were together."

A low growl emitted from my throat as Ivy grabbed my upper arm. She stared at me, shaking her head as if to tell me she would handle the situation.

"I don't know who told you that, but you're misinformed. Caleb was a horrible man, and very abusive to other women. Thankfully, I wasn't subjected to that, and I knew when to get away. That's why he left."

Ivy's words caught me off guard. I could tell she was lying a bit, but she was being honest about other things. Staring at Ivy, I watched how rigid her posture was while speaking with the woman, and seeing her uncomfortable didn't please me.

Caleb was dead, as well was the girl who helped him. It was one of the memories I tried so hard to forget and yet, I constantly felt reminded of the past.

"Oh!" She gasped in shock. "I can't believe that no one told me. I'm so sorry to think that the two of you—"

"It's fine," Ivy snapped with a smile. "People don't always get their facts straight before making assumptions."

"That's true," she nodded before glancing between Ivy and I. "So you two are together?"

"Yep. She belongs to me," I claimed before wrapping an arm around Ivy's waist pulling her closer towards me. "My forever, and always."

"If you will excuse us, we really need to look at the paint and move on to the next store," Ivy said with a sickly sweet smile on her face. "I'm sure you understand."

She slowly slid from me before taking my hand and turned towards the sections of paint swatches, ignoring the woman. The mysterious woman stood there for a moment before finally giving up and turning away.

"I can't believe people think that—" I muttered before Ivy quickly cut me off.

"Don't think about it at all. People are going to gossip no matter what we do, and honestly, I don't want to pay it any mind because all it will do is irritate me further."

Oh shit. She was pissed about what Sasha said. Not wanting to see her day ruined by a bunch of gossip, I leaned forward kissing the side of her head.

"Okay, sweetie. What color are you thinking?"

At this point... it was going to be whatever she wanted.

Even if she wanted the entire store.

CHAPTER FOUR

Agree to Disagree

Ivy

After the entire thing with the girl in the store, whose name I couldn't remember, I went on a shopping spree like you wouldn't believe. From paint to furniture and clothing.

Even toys that lord knows the babies wouldn't be able to enjoy for quite some time.

"Holy shit!" Hale said as Talon jumped out of his pickup truck. "Did you buy the entire store?"

Laughter escaped me as I stood at the back of James' car with my arms crossed, staring at the two men who were looking over the large haul I had got today while James and I were in town.

There were so many things I had picked up that halfway through the trip James had to call Talon to bring his truck to help us. The sight of Talon in a baby store was more than amusing, because the man's eyes went wide with the variety of items there were to choose from.

His questions were cute, but at one point, he picked up a breast pump and I had to question whether or not he was all there. The man had placed it in his mouth and asked if it was a breathing machine or a netipot device for the baby's noses.

To say the laughter wasn't in short supply would be an accurate statement, and I was glad I had my phone on me to make sure I caught a photo. I would use it at a later date to show the kids when they were older the things their dad did.

I wasn't exactly into scrapbooking, but my mother did it, so honestly it couldn't be that hard... right?

"Will you guys stop fucking complaining about how much stuff I bought and just take it out of the truck and put it in the living room, please?" I replied with a smile as I rolled my eyes at them.

They were ever so dramatic, and watching them fuss over the stuff they had to move was entertainment on its own.

"Oh, look. Damian has joined us," James said sarcastically as he grabbed a boxes and bags from the car and started making his way towards the front door.

"Put it in the living room!" I yelled at him, not hearing the mumbled comment he made that was undoubtedly sarcastic.

By the time Damian stood beside me with his hands in his pockets, he was almost speechless. "Uh–holy shit, Ivy. When James said that he was taking you shopping, I didn't think you were going to make us go bankrupt."

"Seriously?" I scoffed, crossing my arms over my chest with a smug expression. "Well, Damian. Purchasing things for a baby is expensive, and it's even more expensive when you're purchasing for two."

"Yeah, but you don't even know what they are yet. How do you know that what you bought is going to fit the gender of our children?"

Slowly casting my gaze from the twins unloading to Damian, I raised a brow and smirked. "I already know what they are, Damian."

"No, you don't. The appointment is in two days... how would you know what they are? Did you find out without us?" he asked with a shocked expression that was nothing but humorous.

"Calm your tits, Damian. I would never do something like that. Just call it mother's intuition, okay?"

Letting out a sigh of relief, he stood a little straighter, watching every item go past him. "So, what do you think it is?"

"Oh! So now you want to know... hmm, not sure I should tell you."

"Ivy—" he groaned before a ball hit him in the back of the head, causing him to turn around quickly with his fists clenched and a scowl permanently etched into his brows. "What the fuck, Talon?!"

Looking at Talon, I couldn't stop laughing. He threw his hands up in the air as to say 'what the fuck are you doing' and gestured to the shit that still had to be brought in.

"Stop talking and start fucking helping, mister big bad Alpha."

"Go fuck yourself, Talon," Damian snapped as I gently gripped his upper arm and shook my head no.

"Stop it... help your brothers, please."

He wasn't pleased with the fact Talon did what he did, but letting out a heavy breath of frustration, he moved towards the truck, snatching things off of it as I watched on. "Damian, be careful. Your daughter and son won't appreciate their shit being broken."

Stopping in his tracks, he looked at me for a moment, and the frown he wore slowly became a smile. "You think it's one of each?"

"Yes, now help, and we can talk more about it later."

Every day my stomach grew more and more and as I rubbed my hand over my growing stomach, I couldn't help but imagine how in a few months they would be welcomed into this world of chaos we all lived in.

"Hey, Ivy," Damian said as he came walking back with Hale. "Why are we putting shit into the living room?"

"Because I need to paint the nursery and I also had taken into consideration something that I wanted to speak to you about."

My comments seemed to make him hesitate for a moment before his shoulders sagged in defeat and he pinched the bridge of his nose. "I know that I'm going to regret this. But what is it exactly that you're wanting to do?"

"Well, you know the large bonus room that you have upstairs that you guys use for gaming and guys' nights and all of whatever it is that you guys do...."

"Yes..." he replied as he stared at me. "What about it?"

"Well, since we have two babies coming instead of one, I thought it would be a great idea to turn that specific room into a nursery. After all, it is big enough to support both of them, and it's right next to my room, which means we can put a door between them."

Both Damian and Hale's mouths dropped at my idea. The mixed emotions that crossed their face in that moment were priceless, and as much as I wanted to burst into laughter, I had to hold myself together.

"You can't be serious," Hale replied, speaking for a speechless Damian who didn't seem to know what to say.

"Oh, come on. It isn't that big of a deal, guys. Our family is expanding, and the house needs some renovations. Plus, that is the largest room upstairs near the bedrooms. It will be perfect for the kids."

In the end, I was the one who would push the two of these children out and considering the fact I planned on breastfeeding; I was going to be the one that would have to get up in the middle of the night to feed them unless there was milk stored away for the guys to help.

Regardless of even that, I knew the guy's schedules were hectic. With the Talon and James running patrols and training, and Hale running between patrols and the hospital, I was going to be on my own quite a bit.

Not that I was complaining.

I understood how important everything was and how it worked, and I wouldn't change it for the world. But I wanted a space that could fit me and the children perfectly.

"We all have to make sacrifices, guys. Honestly, this isn't that big of one."

"Hey, Talon!" Hale said over his shoulder as Talon and James came walking towards them. "Ivy wants to take our man cave and turn it into the nursery."

"What?!" Talon all but shouted. "Absolutely no way. Any other room, but not that room."

"Oh, my god..." I groaned in irritation. "Y'all stop being such babies over this. I'm the one pushing out two watermelons from my vajay now, not y'all. Plus, I have a solution to all of that..."

"I'd like the hear it," James replied, walking around to my side and kissing me on the side of my head.

"Of course you do," Talon sneered. "You're so damn pussy-whipped you do anything she says and agree with anything she says."

"No, I don't!" he exclaimed, feigning a hurt expression. "I'm offended you think that?"

The rest of us glanced at James with small smiles as he looked between us all. "James, I love you dearly, but you are the path of least resistance to this lovely relationship we all have."

Rolling his eyes dramatically, he crossed his arms over his chest and sighed. "Well, I still want to hear the idea. Never know, it may be a good one."

It was times like this when I realized how much I loved James. He always stood up for what I wanted, no matter how crazy the idea was. It wasn't because he was a pushover, because I knew firsthand when things got crazy, he would be the one to say no.

"Well, the basement is massive, and I was thinking we can have it done up, so half is the gym, and the other half is your man cave. You can put a bar down there, and anything else you want, and it would be solely yours."

The four of them stood quietly for a moment as they contemplated over the idea, and with a sigh, Damian shook his head. "So you're wanting to do construction?"

"Essentially, yes," I replied sweetly. "It would be beneficial for us all, and with the crazy shifts you're working, you can relax down there without waking the children by being noisy upstairs."

There was a moment of realization that crossed them making me internally chuckle. They opened and closed their mouths, taking the time to look at each other. As if wanting to object, but knowing they had no solid reasoning behind their objection. A converted basement would literally give them twice the room as the current room they were using.

"Fine," Damian sighed, causing Talon to smack him in the arm.

"Seriously?!" he exclaimed as Hale laughed. "I can't believe you gave into her, Damian."

"Look, she has a valid point. Plus, happy wife, happy life, or however that stupid saying fucking goes. Look... I can call my contractor to come look at it tomorrow. We have to get it done soon with the babies coming."

Jumping up and down slightly, I clapped my hands in excitement. "Yay! This is going to be so much fun."

Leaning up, I pressed my lips to Damian's quickly before kissing the rest of them, and pushing past to walk inside. He had given his blessing, and the last thing I wanted was for Damian to run the chance of changing his mind.

Lord knows he did that often.

"Finish bringing the rest in, please!" I called over my shoulder happily. "Looks like rain."

Everything was going according to plan, and I was finally feeling happy about my current situation. For the last few months, I had felt nothing but dread because I was so worried this pregnancy was coming at the worst of times.

Now, though... I wasn't scared about them coming.

Of course, I feared the actual labor, but it was becoming clearer and clearer every day they were going to be with me and support me one hundred percent.

Stepping inside, I skipped merrily towards the living room and searched through the many many bags that littered the area. I seriously had to sort through things and put them into piles so I could wash all the clothes I bought.

Organization was key, and even though I wasn't organized... I had to learn to be.

Thirty minutes into my search for the matching female bear to the male bear, I had the phone in Damian's office ring. Looking out the window, I saw he was struggling with the twins to pull the oddly shaped crib beds out of the truck to put them in the garage and answered the phone myself.

I had never answered Damian's office phone, but I was Luna. So I would assume it would be okay. "Hello?"

"Hello, this is Elder Jenny Harrison. This must be Ivy. How are you?"

"Oh, hello, Miss Harrison. I am doing well. Thank you for asking. Were you looking for Damian? I'm afraid he is preoccupied at the moment." The voice I used was very sweet and Luna-esque. I wasn't entirely Luna material, at least not in my opinion. But they didn't need to know about everything that went on.

"Well, I just wanted to call and check on you all. I'm actually going to be heading down that way for a few days to take care of business in another pack. And I wanted to see if it would be all right with you if I stopped in for a couple of days. I'd love to catch up with you and see how you're doing in your pregnancy."

The idea of having anybody from that Council come to our pack was not something I really wanted to do, especially being pregnant. However, I didn't want to be rude and draw suspicion from an elder counsel that originally wanted to get rid of my mates.

So I did the one thing any good Luna would do. "Of course, that would be fine. We are going to be going through some construction, though. I just want to make you aware of that. We have a lot of renovating before the new arrivals, so I will have the guest house set up for you to stay in."

"Oh, that would be lovely. Thank you so much and please, I completely understand. I remember how it was when I had my first pup. Don't go to too much trouble. I'm just going to be taking care of a few things. And like I said, I just wanted to stop in and check on you."

As pleasant as the woman sounded, I was pretty sure from the conversation there wasn't anything to worry about. She was the new elder everyone had been talking about and perhaps it would be a good way to show the council that we weren't a threat.

"I will see you in a few days, then," I replied quickly, hanging up the phone. The only thing left to do now was break the news to the guys.

We would have a visitor, and it would be one that wasn't wanted.

At least not by Damian.

CHAPTER FIVE

Sexual Tension

"You did what?!" Damian yelled as I informed him and the others of Miss Harrison's impromptu arrival within the next couple of days.

"What exactly did you want me to tell her, Damian? She sounded so pleasant on the phone and I couldn't very well say to the Council... Oh no, you guys are banned from coming to our pack. We have to show them good faith regardless of what has happened. Perhaps we can get her on our side."

Damian pinched the bridge of his nose as he took slow, deep breaths in and out, trying to rein in his anger. I didn't understand why he was making us such a big deal out of this. She was literally going to be here for a few days.

It wasn't like she was just coming here purposely to spy on us, or at least I hoped that wasn't the case. Now that I thought about it, I was suddenly second guessing myself, but it was too late to do anything now.

"Ivy, you always talk to us about stuff like this before you just do whatever you want. You are not in the greatest of conditions right now between the pregnancy and your uncontrollable urges to do whatever the fuck you want. It doesn't really make you the best host," Damien replied, setting my nerves on edge.

Who did he honestly think he was?!

So yes, I might be a little emotional and yes, I may have moments of hunger that range in a variety of ways, but that doesn't mean I can't be a delightful host.

Giving Damian 'the look', I pushed aside the frustration, and let out a heavy sigh. "Damian, for once, will you just trust me. Please get the guest house ready. The elder knows of the construction, and will only be here for like, two days. I will be a proper Luna during that time. I promise."

Turning away from him, I made my way upstairs towards my room, but as soon as I got outside of my bedroom door, I froze in my place, and something inside me told me to go see Priscilla.

I wasn't sure why the sudden urge came over me, but it did so. Groaning in protest, I turned and walked towards the staircase that led to her room. I knew she would expect me, and sure enough, as I got to the top, she opened the door before I could even knock.

"You look absolutely exhausted, dear," she replied with a mischievous glint in her eye.

"I am exhausted. Who knew dealing with these men was going to be so exhausting?"

The sarcastic joke I made caused her to laugh, and as I entered her room, I noticed the two glasses of tea she had sitting on the coffee table waiting for me.

"You always know when I'm coming."

Shrugging her shoulders, she walked forward and took her seat. "Yes, but that isn't important. Why don't you tell me what's on your mind?"

"Where do I even start?" I groaned as I flopped down on the chair, sighing dramatically.

Taking a moment, she watched, "Did you tell them about your dreams?"

Glancing at her, I shook my head no. "I don't know how to, and as much as I want to tell them, I think it'd be best that I speak to those above before I do."

"That choice is yours, dear, but I already gave you my opinion about it. I don't think that you should wait. Especially if it's something of importance."

I knew she was right, but I was in denial.

I had much more important things to think about, and that was the upcoming arrival of our children. They would be here before I knew it, and I wouldn't be able to contemplate the what-ifs of life. I would have to be focused.

"There is something that I wanted to speak to you about. Do you know anything about Elder Harrison?"

"The new elder that was recently put on the board..." she said with slight hesitation in her tone. "Yes, I heard of her. I take it that we are going to be welcoming her here very soon."

"For someone who always knows everything, I figured you would have known that by now," I replied sarcastically as she swatted at me with a smile across her face.

"Behave yourself, Ivy. I may see a lot, but I don't always see everything. So tell me why this woman is coming. What seems to bother you?"

"Well... The guys seemed to think that her being here is not a good thing, that it's the Council spying on us, but honestly, from the conversation I had with her, I don't feel like it is," I replied with a defeated look upon my face as my eyes cast down towards my tea.

"What do you think it is, then?" Priscilla asked, causing my eyes to meet hers again.

"Honestly, I don't know what to think about it. I mean, she's coming and supposedly she'll be here in a few days, but... I just have a feeling that something else is going to happen and I'm not sure what."

Taking a moment, she seemed to think about what I said as she sipped on her tea. "For the first time in a long time, I'm unsure of what to say. I would highly suggest talking to the goddess, otherwise there is a possibility the celestial side of you will take care of it herself."

"You think I'll go on the attack..."

Giving a smug look, she shrugged her shoulders. "Who knows what you may do? All of these hormones can be unpredictable."

"You know I hate it when you give me that look. It's a smug glance that lets me know you know something that I don't, and you know how much I hate being left in the dark."

Patting my knee, she leaned forward with a smile. "I do know, dear. Speaking of which, I spoke to your mother yesterday."

"Why did you speak to my mother?" To know they were secretly talking behind my back was a little weird. I didn't know the women were close like that.

"Ah. Unfortunately, your mother is the one who called me, and if you would like to know what we spoke about, you will have to call her. I will say, though, the conversation was a pleasant one, so no need to worry."

Secrets.

They're always keeping fucking secrets. I hadn't spoken to my mother in almost a week, and that was simply because she had been on vacation with her new mate, the infamous doctor Blake.

He was a man of few words and I had seen him a few times on FaceTime, but he wasn't exactly the kind of man I had ever pictured my mother being with. Then again, I never pictured myself being with four men, either.

"Well, I need to catch up with her. Knowing that she called you means she must be back from her vacation. I hope everything went well."

"That it did, my dear, now. I heard a little rumor that you went shopping today. Did you get everything that you're going to need for the children?" There was excitement in her eyes, and often I was surprised she cared about us at all.

She was an old woman with empty nest syndrome and wanted nothing more than to love on the new babies as soon as they got here.

"I did. James and I went through a few things and I ended up buying a lot more than I expected. Talon had to come and help carry some things with the truck."

"I bet," she laughed. "I'm sure Talon being there was amusing as well."

"It was, but you know, it was nice having them there. Even though I sometimes wonder if they are more terrified than I am at the prospect of these babies coming."

"In time, good things come to us," she smiled. "So just be patient. I'm sure that you will find they will be more supportive than you realize."

Looking down at my watch, I realized what time it was. Dinner would be done soon, and if I wasn't down there to eat James's food, he would be more than unimpressed.

"I have to get going, Priscilla," I said, placing down my cup. "James is cooking tonight, and he will be upset if I'm late."

"Of course, dear." Standing to our feet, she leaned in, giving me a hug and for the first time in a while, I felt the warmth and affection that I dearly needed from my mother.

I hadn't seen my mother since I left for Idaho, and at the moment I missed her dearly.

A few hours later, and much spaghetti was devoured by all the men, I found myself up in my room preparing for a night that hopefully would bring me some type of answers. I wasn't quite sure if the goddesses would hear me, but one could be hopeful.

A knock at my door drew my attention, and as I turned my head, I watched Damian waltz into the room with a look on his face that spoke of the mood he was in.

"I know you are preparing for bed right now, but I hoped that I could join you tonight," he said with a lust filled gaze. "If you want?"

Whereas most would have considered the thought that we would have a massive bed for all of us to share in the end, it was more respectable to do it this way. That way, nobody felt left out and my door was always open to any who wanted to join me.

Not to mention, sometimes we just needed our own space.

It's like four giant children that you have to constantly please and take care of, or else their feelings will be hurt and temper tantrums will be thrown.

"Damian, you never have to ask to spend the night with me. All we have to do is come crawl in bed. I'm your mate..."

He hesitated for a moment as he looked at me. There was something troubling him and I wasn't quite sure what it was. But I felt as if he was holding back, blocking me from reading his thoughts because he didn't want me to know what it was.

"I know, but it's only fair that my brothers and I respect the boundaries that we all decided upon and created."

Staring at him, I let the soft curl of a smile cross my lips as I sauntered his direction with one thought on my mind. This man was mine, and if he felt he couldn't be himself with me, then I would fix that.

Wrapping my arms around his neck, I crashed my lips to his and found myself quickly pressed against his body. The moment between us filled every need that was desired, and as he picked me up, he laid me on the soft blankets of my bed, kissing along my jaw.

"You're so beautiful," he whispered, as he nipped at my ear lobe causing my back to arch slightly in pleasure.

"Mmm... you're such a tease when you want to me."

A soft giggle escaped me as he slid down between my thighs, hiking my nightgown to my waist as he hooked his finger around my panties and pulled them off in one go. The cool air of the room kissed the sensitive bare skin between my legs, and gently his warm breath took its place as his tongue flicked out, causing me to gasp.

Slow circular motions caused moans to slip past my lips, but as my pleasure grew, he became more ravenous and his actions more fevered.

He devoured me until I was spilling over the edge and screaming in pleasure as the rippling orgasm rolled through my body.

One would think that being pregnant, I wouldn't be as horny as I was, but they would be wrong. The farther along I got, the more the need was there, and I was glad I had four men to satisfy me in those ways.

"I need you, Damian," I whined as he stood on his feet.

"On your hands and knees."

The anticipation for what was to come formed a sadistic smirk on my face as I assumed the position. His hands roaming over the bare skin of my ass before giving it a light smack that was hard enough to sting.

I wasn't upset though... oh the contrary... that kind of behavior turned me on like you wouldn't believe.

Slowly, the head of his thick cock slid over the folds of my tight cunt and, with one hand on my firm, plump ass, he pushed his way inside me, allowing me to feel every inch of his erection. The sensation caused a small gasp to leave my lips before I moaned.

"Don't hold back," I groaned in pleasure. "I want it all."

With another slap, the sting sent me into overdrive as his thrusting took off at a rapid pace. Over and over, the sensations of his rigid cock rubbing against the sensitive walls of my pussy put me into a euphoric high that I couldn't get enough of.

"Fuck, yes.."

More. I needed more, and as a wave of change came over me, I watched my nails turn into claws before he gripped my hair in his fist and pulled me back to his chest. His free hand came around to rub against my sensitive clit.

"You like that, don't you?" he growled low in my ear.

Fuck, I didn't like it... I fucking loved it.

"Fuck me like you mean it, asshole," I growled back at him. "Fill me with your cum so every wolf in this pack knows who owns me."

My panted demands were the driving force he needed to ravage me like the primal animal he was. The blissful actions of our union tipped me over the edge until a scream mixed with a carnal roar escaped my throat and he stilled cumming deep within.

These were the moments I cherished with the men I loved.

These were the moments that reminded me I wasn't just a Luna, mother, or someone's mate. I was more than that... I was theirs in every way as they were mine.

Destiny had paired us, and nothing could take that away.

CHAPTER SIX

Hunger Pains

Damian.

Being able to fall asleep next to Ivy is one of the most incredible feelings I had ever been able to be a part of. I wasn't the greatest of men. In fact, I was the type of man that didn't even deserve a girl like Ivy.

I had messed up big time with her.

I had treated her wrong, and I deserved every bit of punishment that had come my way because of my actions. I never intended to hurt her the way I did.

In a sick way, I thought I was saving her.

But we all realized that was not the case in the end.

Soft movements within the bed stirred me awake and, fluttering my eyes open, I looked to see Ivy tossing and turning calmly. Without warning, she suddenly sat upright.

"Ivy, are you OK?" I asked sleepily as I watched her eyes cast towards me and realized the woman sitting before me was slightly different from before.

She said nothing as her celestial orbs stared at me. Instead, what she did was slide from the bed in her white nightgown and moved towards the bedroom door.

"Ivy, where are you going?" I whispered loudly, but still there was no response from her. Instead, she opened the door and moved through it, quickly heading down the hallway towards the stairs.

Jumping from the bed, I moved towards the door in nothing but my boxers. "Ivy!"

Shouting down the hall after her, she continued on whatever mission she was doing without even acknowledging the fact I was speaking to her. The old me would have been angry by the way she was acting, but given the circumstance of everything going on, I knew this was something else.

Popping his head out of his bedroom door, Talon stared at me with confusion. "Damien, what's going on?"

"I don't know. Ivy just jolted from bed, got out, and made her way down the hallway. I'll follow... something is definitely up."

Moving quickly, I took the stairs two at a time until my feet hit the floor—Talon right behind me.

For a woman that was pregnant, she moved fast, and as we made our way through the house towards the open back door. I had to stop and search the grounds in the darkness to see where she went.

After a moment, I spotted her by the treeline, and with haste Talon and I ran across the grassy lawn towards where she was. As soon as I reached her, I grabbed her arm, stopping her in her tracks.

I wasn't sure what she was going to do, but with a quick reaction, she turned to me with those celestial orbs and growled. "Do not interfere."

Her words were a warning and with them, I looked to Talon with utter disbelief as my lips parted and my mouth dropped, trying to understand what had just happened.

"Did she just use her alpha tone on you?" Talon asked, causing me to growl at him in warning he should never bring this up again.

"Shut up. We need to follow her and see where she's going. If she's wandering around like this at night, we have to make sure that nobody is getting hurt."

Watching her, she drifted through the tree lines barefoot, walking as if searching for something. It was magical, in a way, watching her move as she was. It seemed as if she was drifting across the ground in her long nightgown until she stopped in her tracks, her eyes darting to the left.

"Damien, she's hunting," Talon whispered quietly and sure enough, at his words. She took off into a sprint.

Moving through the trees faster than I had ever seen before. She darted in and out in woven patterns until coming to an abrupt stop behind a tree. There, just beyond the tree about a hundred feet in front of her, was a massive stag.

I had seen her act this way once before, but never with this much determination.

Like the violent, deadly predator she was, she stalked closely without the stag, even realizing that she was there. Until, of course, it was too late.

Jumping upon the animal, she ripped into its throat until it laid unmoving. Her claws and teeth dug at its flesh as she gorged herself. There was something beautiful about what was happening.

Perhaps that was just my biased opinion, though, since I was her mate.

With the elder coming, though, there was no way we could allow this behavior to happen. If it did, there was no telling what she would report back to the Council, and there was no reassuring the fact Ivy would remain safe.

Inhaling deeply, she groaned with satisfaction as she ate. Her celestial eyes slowly sliding towards us with a smile spread from ear to ear. "I'm sorry, guys. I was starving, and I had to fill the hunger..."

Ivy wasn't like Talon and Hale. With them, there were two separate entities combined into one permanent thought. She was one celestial individual with the tendency to have a bipolar personality.

Priscilla had assured me the many visits I had had with her to talk in private, that eventually Ivy would be able to control how she acted and, over time, could adapt to situations.

For now, though, we would simply have to deal with everything, because while she was pregnant, she is a little more unpredictable.

She was a creature nobody had ever seen before, carrying twins.

Hormones be damned and all that jazz.

"It's OK," I said as I stepped forward and brushed the hair from her face. "I'm not upset at you, Ivy."

"Damien's right," Talon said quickly as he stepped to my side. "You're pregnant and you have urges, as any primal animal would, to hunt when you're hungry. However, we need to find a better solution to this."

Frowning, she bit her bottom lip as she stood to her feet and nodded her head. She looked guilty for what she had done, and that was not the intention Talon and I had. We didn't want her to think her hunting was a problem because it wasn't.

It was in our nature to do so.

However, unlike her, the four of us went on monthly hunts with the rest of the pack, which was something that we still had not allowed her to do because her uniqueness was quite different from ours.

She didn't shift into a wolf like the rest of us. So for the pack members, it would come as a shock because they wouldn't be used to it. Not to mention we weren't sure if she wouldn't hurt one of them by accident.

In Priscilla's words, Ivy was a gift from the Moon goddess herself, a reincarnation of a mother to walk the earth.

Even though I was pretty sure she was something else entirely.

Taking her hand, we led her back up towards the house just in time to be greeted by James and Hale, who stood at the back door waiting.

"I take it we had an interesting night?" Hale replied with a smirk as James rolled his eyes, wrapping a blanket around Ivy's shoulders.

"Ignore them, sweetie. Let's go get you cleaned up," James said as he ushered her through the house towards the stairs.

Before Ivy, James was never this kind of man. It was like the day the matebond was complete, he became something else entirely. He was sensitive and caring towards her in a way that the rest of us never could be.

Perhaps that was why the goddess gave her four mates.

Each of us holding different aspects of emotions she would need.

When she was finally out of earshot, I turned to my brothers with a pondering expression, trying to find the best way to address this. There was a lot to consider, but protecting her was at the top of the list.

We couldn't let the council see her in this way. They would jump to conclusions for sure.

"We have to figure this out with her. The last thing I would want to happen is for somebody else to get hurt while she's hunting or perhaps her going on a little spree that we can't seem to control, not saying that she would... but you never know what could happen."

"You're acting as if she is a monster," Talon sneered. "She is our mate, and the Luna of this pack. Give her a little more credit."

"I'm not acting like anything, Talon," I growled at him. "I'm merely stating facts. We have to be careful."

With a drink in his hand, Hale sighed, running his other hand through his hair. "Let's stop arguing. She will hear us."

Taking a deep breath, I reined in my anger, and took a moment to compose myself. "You're right. Now, what can we do to help her?"

"I wonder if the need isn't specifically the hunt. But it is the consumption driving her primal nature," Hale replied, looking between Talon and I.

Arching my brow, I considered what he was saying. "Like feed her the meat without her having to hunt."

"Essentially yes. Just like animals in captivity, they are fed every day on a regular schedule and therefore, if put out into the wild, do not know how to instinctively hunt. If we took that into consideration with her, and kept her fed on a regular schedule, it may dim down the primal nature to hunt."

"You do realize that you literally just referred to our mate as a captive animal?" Talon snapped as he crossed his arms over his chest and huffed in displeasure.

"Shut the fuck up, man. That is not what I meant. I was simply using that as an analogy," Hale responded as Talon flipped gave him the middle finger.

At times, they could really be immature, and it was driving me crazy with how they were acting. Sometimes I wasn't sure if they were capable of acting normal.

"Both of you knock it off. This isn't what we need right now," I said as I thought over what Hale had explained. It honestly would make a lot of sense if it worked.

"I'm just saying that if it does work, it could be an excellent solution to this issue. If she does not need to hunt because the fresh meat is being supplied, then perhaps she will be a lot more containable."

I heard the soft patter of feet from the hallway, and as we all turned to look, we saw Ivy standing there freshly showered with a grim expression on her face.

"I'm willing to try it," she whispered as she acted as if nothing at all had happened. "I don't want to hurt anyone."

"Ivy, we're not trying to change. You were just—"

"Damian, stop. I get it and you're right. There are situations where this kind of behavior will not be acceptable, like with the Council member coming. With how uncontrollable these situations happen, I don't want anybody to get hurt because I mistake them when I'm in that mode."

Spoken like a true Luna. I swelled with pride, but I felt incredibly guilty because she accepted us when she first found out. Yet, it felt like we weren't accepting what she was.

"Okay. We will figure something else you," I replied, watching her sip on her water that she pulled from the fridge. "Why don't you try to get some sleep? You need all the rest you can get."

Nodding her head, she cast her glance aside and smiled at the others before pushing past James and walking back upstairs. This was the type of treatment that pissed me off more than anything. She agreed and said that it was okay, but in reality, she was more hurt than anything.

"She's upset with me, isn't she?" I said with a sigh.

"You think? She heard the entire conversation. She does have super hearing, after all, and she knew you were talking about her, so Hale, referring to her as a captive animal, definitely lost you some brownie points."

James looked at each of us, shaking his head before a smile cracked across his face and he turned, heading out of the room. He was right, though. We did mess up and by the look on Hales face; he was absolutely devastated that Ivy misconstrued what he was saying.

It meant that he was going to have to work extra hard to get back in her good graces.

CHAPTER SEVEN

The Elder has come

Ivy

I wasn't sure exactly how I was supposed to feel. Last night, I did the one thing I didn't expect to have done in quite some time. I allowed myself to go too hungry, and in the end, I ended up hunting another animal that was slaughtered without mercy to sustain the hunger burrowed inside of me.

Every time I did it, I felt guilty. Because that was another animal that's life was lost because of what I was. Whereas the werewolves seemed to think it was a natural aspect of life, I did not.

I was a primal creature.

Something the world had never seen before, at least not in my lifetime or that of my forefathers. I was dangerous and unpredictable, or that was the words that the guys kept using repeatedly. As if by some mistake I was placed here and I should have been elsewhere.

They loved me, and I loved them. But I contemplated if what I was doing was even beneficial. Should I really be trying so hard to fit in this pack or should I see if there was a way for me to embark on my own mission and leave?

The thought of leaving left an ache in my chest I couldn't let go.

There was no way I could leave. I had a life with them and I loved them. I just wish I wasn't what I was. Why couldn't I have been normal? Why couldn't they have just allowed me to be a normal werewolf, or even just a fucking human?

Instead, they made me a creature that wasn't normal by any sense.

"Ivy?" Hale called from the bottom of the stairs, causing me to get up from where I was currently sitting in my room looking at paint swatches.

"Yes," I replied as I met him at the stairs.

"The guest room was finished and the contractors are here, so I just wanted to let you know they will need access to your room and that of the den so that they can go ahead and get work underway over the next couple of days."

"Oh okay, that's fine. I will just take all my stuff downstairs into the living room. Perhaps start organizing through a few things."

Sagging my shoulders, I turned with a heavy breath and made my way to my room to gather my belongings. While construction was under way, I would have to sleep with one of the guys, which wasn't a problem in my eyes.

I did feel slightly awkward though because they were acting weird towards me, and I didn't do well with that kind of behavior. It made me feel out-of-place even though I shouldn't have.

Making my way downstairs, I listened to the muffled conversations the guys were having from the kitchen. Once again, my name was being brought up, and knowing they were talking to me behind my back was irritating.

If I was such a problem, I don't understand why they wanted me to be their Luna.

Deciding to ignore it all, I made my way into the living room, and sat upon the sofa with the swatches in my hand. Shades of green, yellow and creams littered across the cushion as I thought over my idea of a nature-based theme for the twins.

I wasn't quite sure how everything would come together yet, but I knew I wanted to keep everything as close to nature as I possibly could.

After all, the twins' lives would revolve around that of wolves, and the darkness of woods.

"Ivy, can you get the door?" I hadn't even realized someone had been knocking as I watched James and Talon carry things from the stairs towards the back of the house.

"Okay."

Standing to my feet, I moved towards the door. To my surprise, when I opened the door, it was Elder Jenny Harrison standing there in front of me. She was two days earlier than I had expected.

"Elder Harrison, I wasn't expecting you for two more days," I exclaimed, pushing away my shock to quickly replace it with a welcoming smile.

"Terribly sorry, I just finished things quite early with the other pack, so I just assumed it would be okay for me to come. If it's not, I'll just go ahead and head back to where I live," she said faking a fake sweet personality that I could tell was anything but sweet.

"No, no, don't be silly. It's perfectly fine. We're just in the middle of having the contractors here to start the process upstairs. Follow me right this way and I can show you where you will be staying." Gesturing with my arm, I opened the door wider for her to pass through.

As she stepped inside, though, I watched Damian make his way to where I was with a scowl on his face. "Elder Harrison, it's a pleasure to see you. I apologize for the construction that is currently taking place."

She looked at him with a curious glance, and a smug expression crossed her face. "Don't worry, I'm sure that the accommodations are more than acceptable. Shall we go, my dear?"

Looking between Elder Harrison and Damian, I slowly nodded my head and gestured for her to continue following me. There was a lot of tension in the room and how the elder had acted wasn't how I was expecting.

She seemed more smug than a woman in her position would have been. As if she thought her authority was much higher than Damian's was.

"So, how much longer do you have?" she asked me as I looked at her, watching how she kept eyeing my stomach.

"A few months," I replied with hesitation. "I should actually find out tomorrow what the genders of the babies are."

"Babies. You mean there's more than one?" she asked with wide eyes.

I suddenly realized the mistake I made by letting that out. I guess it hadn't actually registered that everybody assumed I was having one and not two. It wasn't even something that we'd really made official within the pack.

"Um, yes, we just found out at my last appointment that there were two and not just one." I replied, trying to quickly change the subject into anything else. "Where you'll be staying is just outside of the pack house."

With a frown of disappointment, she stopped at the back door and looked inside the house, and then looked back outside. "So I'm not actually staying in the pack house. You're having me stay outside in the guesthouse?"

Is she seriously going to make a big deal of this?

"Yes, as I told you, we're doing construction inside. So unfortunately, the inside of the pack house doesn't have any availability. Considering that rooms are being redone but the guest house is a one bedroom furnished place and it is absolutely lovely. I actually stayed there when I first came here."

With one raised brow, she stared at me. Her face was void of emotion as she nodded her head, gesturing with her hand for me to lead the way. She wasn't impressed, and perhaps that was because she was expecting to be treated differently.

"Very well. I suppose it will do."

Walking the steps down the path towards the small cottage, I opened the door for her and made way for her to enter. The guys had done a number in fixing the place up from the past few months of dust and cobwebs.

"There are clean linens on the bed right now. Make yourself comfortable. I know you're going to be here for just a couple of days, but there is food and drinks in the fridge. If you should get hungry, we will have dinner tonight, though, in honor of you being here as our guest."

"Of course, that sounds delightful," she replied as the awkwardness between us grew.

"Wonderful. Well, I will just go ahead and leave you to get set in and I will have one of the guys come fetch you when dinner is ready."

Turning quickly, I made my way from the cabin and hastened my pace back up to the main house. Now that she was here, I regret allowing her to come. I should have given the phone to Damian and allowed him to be the one to tell her she couldn't stay here.

Closing the door behind me, I stood there for a moment, lost in thought as to what it was about her I just didn't like. "Are you OK?" A voice said, catching my attention.

Looking up, I met Damien's eyes and watched as he looked at me with concern before casting his glance out the window behind me towards the cottage.

"I'm OK. There is just something about her.... I don't know. I'm just being hormonal. She's getting settled in. She is very lovely, and I told her that one of you guys will go fetch her for dinner."

Without another word, I moved past him quickly and made myself scarce. I had to find something to preoccupy myself with because that woman had gotten me all bent out of shape.

A few hours later, we all prepared to sit down around a long dining table waiting to enjoy the food that had been made. The dining room brought up all sorts of memories I wasn't expecting to relive but pushing them aside, I dealt with it.

With a delicious meal of meats, pastas, fruit and vegetables laid out on display, we all took our seats around the table just as Hale walked in with Elder Harrison. "This looks all delicious."

Smiling sweetly at her, I looked towards the food and looked back. "Thank you. We hope that you enjoy everything."

"I'm sure I will. You honestly didn't have to slave over the stove, Ivy. I would have been perfectly fine with something small."

Her comment shocked me she had actually thought I had cooked this. With a grin spread across my face, I looked around the table, only to land upon James, whose mouth had dropped open and an utter look of disgust crossed him.

"I'm sorry, but I didn't cook this," I said to Elder Harrison, trying to contain my laughter.

"Oh dear. I'm so sorry. You must have an excellent cook then. Nowadays it's hard to hire people who can decently cook." Her comment further caused the snickering around the table and slowly she furrowed her brows in confusion.

"James is the one who cooked dinner. He loves to cook, and typically he is the one that does all the cooking. If the twins don't decide to help him, which I believe tonight, you both took the opportunity to help cook."

Hale nodded his head as Talon sat with his arms crossed and a stone sharp look upon his face. He wasn't pleased with the elder being here, and I didn't blame him. She was a very odd character.

James, however, still had a look of absolute disgust on his face as he scoffed before quietly digging into the food in front of him while mumbling under his breath.

"I'm so terribly sorry I didn't realize that the four of you cooked. It's not typically normal to find men that are in your position that are so willing to cook."

"Well, I'm not sure what alphas you are accustomed to meeting, but here in this pack, things run differently." Damien said, drawing elder Harrison's attention to him.

"Alphas?" She said with confusion and a smug smile upon her face. "There is only one Alpha to a pack, Damien. I'm sure that you, of all people, are aware of this. You are the only alpha. Your brothers are not."

Growls emitted around the room and quickly I snapped my gaze at each of them, telling them to excuse themselves if they cannot control themselves.

This was obviously going to be a conversation I would have to settle because as the Luna of the pack I decided what conversation was acceptable at the dinner table, and I wouldn't tolerate her insulting my mates.

"Elder Harrison, with all due respect, that may be the customs of other packs have, but no pack has ever been faced with something such as we have. So each of them holds a specific title that an alpha normally has, combining one full authoritative entity."

"Of course. My apologies, Luna," she said as she quietly went back to eating.

The apology was fake, of course, but I was glad the conversation was over. The last thing I wanted was to watch Damian or any of the others lose their shit on this woman.

To think... they were fucking worried about me!

I think they gave themselves way too much credit when it came to correcting situations.

"Ivy, I wanted to ask you one question though, if I may?" Elder Harrison said, causing me to internally sigh as I turned to her with a smile as fake as her own.

"Of course. What's on your mind?"

Adjusting herself, the woman sat a little straighter as she placed down her fork, as if preparing for whatever outcome was about to explode upon the room. "Well, now that you're a Luna, I want to talk to you about the customs we have to test gifted wolves."

"Absolutely, fucking not!" Damian said, standing to his feet. "She will not be doing anything of the sort, nor will she be going anywhere outside of this pack. I should have known that was why you were here."

"Damian, it is in your best interest to sit down." The elder growled, showing Damian nothing but disrespect, and that was something I wouldn't tolerate.

"Do not speak to my mate in that tone. You're a guest on my land, and you have done nothing but thrown insults since you arrived," I snapped at her, watching her eyes grow wide.

"Your eyes..." she murmured, placing her hand over her mouth. "I didn't want to believe it..."

Great. Just fucking great. Of course, my eyes would flicker when I'm pissed.

"Yes, my eyes," I growled slowly, standing to my feet. "The council has no jurisdiction on my land, and what I do with my mates, children, and pack members is my business. I will remind you once more that you're a guest. If you don't like it, you're free to leave in the morning."

The fear and surprise on the woman's face brought me delight. Internally, I wanted to bathe in her fear, but I knew how important it was to keep myself together. Slowly, I moved from the dining room and made my way up the stairs towards the closest bedroom I could find.

Which happened to be Talon's. I had to get a hold of myself, because if I couldn't, I'd kill her.

CHAPTER EIGHT

Assuming Information

I hadn't expected dinner to go the way it had. But now that it was over, I was glad considering Damien ended up blowing up into a million different pieces when the elder had conversations in the way she did.

Talk about being completely awkward. I was the center of the awkwardness and it was not a place I wanted to go back to any time soon. If I hadn't lost it slightly in the moment, there was no telling what Damian would have done to her.

Laying on Talon's bed, I got hold of myself, and it didn't take long for Talon and Hale to come find me. Forty minutes of deep breathing and cuddling with both men calmed the internal fire within me and now we were caught up in small talk and sarcastic comments.

"So how pissed off do you think he's really going to continue being?" I asked the boys, who turned to me with nothing but amusement, dancing in their eyes.

"It depends," Talon replied. "One time when we were kids, James stole Damien's favorite T-shirt because he thought it was too small for Damien and completely stained it in one afternoon. When Damian found out, he literally held that grudge for like five years."

"Five years over a fucking T-shirt. That's a bit childish, don't you think?"

"It may have been childish, but then again, we were children. So, to Damian, that was a very big deal," he replied, shrugging his shoulders.

"Talon, if you're gonna tell it, tell the truth," Hale sighed, pinching the bridge of his nose. "The shirt was one that our mother had given him that was our fathers. So, in a sense, it was actually a big deal to him."

"Dude, he had, like, fifty fucking shirts that were our dads and poor James had got none. So I mean, realistically... It wasn't that big of a deal? He could have given that one shirt to James. Lord knows he had asked for it for, like, two freaking weeks," Talon replied in a very dramatic effect.

It made sense now why James and Damian didn't seem as close. Not just because of that, but in general. Damian was the oldest and thought he was entitled because he was the oldest, and James was the youngest... the baby, and he thought he was entitled to.

"I can kind of understand why Damian would be upset, you know, considering it was something sentimental like that. But this is completely different. I mean, the elder was out of line completely and honestly, I don't like whatever she was getting at."

"She literally insulted Damian as an alpha tried to insult us. Lord knows, poor James is probably devastated over her comment on his cooking and in a way she was trying to undermine you as a Luna," Hale replied.

In a way, he was right, and because he was, I couldn't deny the need to get rid of her.

"Okay, I get it. She fucked up. But I mean, maybe that's just her messing up as a new elder. I mean, she hasn't really been in the position long, has she?"

Again, they both shrugged their shoulders.

"I don't know what you're looking to do, Ivy. I mean, she's here for the next couple of days, and you were the one that told her it would be okay for her to stay," Talon rambled on. His comments were not the help I was looking for and picking up a pillow, I quickly chucked it at his head.

"Well, then why don't we find something else to preoccupy our time with?"

Though Damian had tended to me a few nights before, I was equally hungry for the two of them and the fun we had once had in the past. However, upon those words, Hale and Talon both looked at each other and looked at me and shook their heads no.

"Absolutely not," Hale replied quite quickly.

"Are you rejecting me?" I said, feigning a hurt expression across my face. I couldn't believe they didn't want to be intimate with me.

"No. God, no. It's nothing like that," Hale quickly said, trying to redirect the conversation and fix the mess that he had started.

"Then what are you saying?"

"He is afraid," Talon replied with a smirk of his own. "Hale thinks he is going to hurt the baby if his lycan comes out during sex."

With wide eyes, I turned my gaze back to Hale who seemed uncomfortable, and quickly cleared his throat. "I mean it could happen. I don't want to risk it."

"Hale, you won't hurt your children and neither will any other part of you."

"Still, I don't want to risk it," he said firmly as Talon pulled me by the ankle towards him, burying his face in my crotch.

"I want it... god, how I want it."

His response caused me to laugh, but irritation flowed off of Hale from Talon's actions. "No, Talon, this is serious. We only have like two months, and then we can fuck her however we want."

"Hale, I've litterally already had sex with Damian, James and Talon multiple times since I've been pregnant. You don't have to worry... but—" pausing mid-conversation, something he said finally clicked in my head. "Wait... what do you mean two months?"

"You're coming up in four months in your pregnancy. Wolves are only pregnant for six months, so it's like you're entering your third trimester and to do something like that with both of us at the same time, probably not the safest for the babies."

Taking a moment to let what he said soak, I made a face to show my confusion as my mouth dropped open slightly.

"Hale, did you not listen to what you said? I'm literally only almost four months pregnant. I still have, like, what, another five months of my pregnancy. So I'm not anywhere near the third trimester. What are you talking about? Six months."

Both of them sat there in silence, staring at me before Hales' eyes fogged over, linking someone. No words coming from them, and with the silence began the slow increase of panic within my chest.

"Um, Ivy? What have you learned about werewolf pregnancies?"

The question caught me completely off guard, especially since it was Talon asking me the question. When I thought about it, I really knew little. I knew they were rapidly growing and the pregnancies typically were, like, super painful because, you know, the babies were typically stronger and more aggressive.

I guess in the end I didn't know much. Not that I thought to learn or that

"Umm, well, I'm guessing that I don't know as much as I probably should know, considering how you two are acting. So does one of you want to fucking explain to me what exactly is going on? Because you know the way you're making it sound is that I'm about to have this baby in two months and not in five."

The door opened rather quickly, and when it did, I saw a very concerned Damian and James standing in the doorway.

"Ivy, I think we need to have a conversation because I believe you are slightly misinformed from what Hale said."

There it was. The bomb had been dropped.

I had miscalculated how much I knew about werewolf pregnancies. Fuck me.

"Yes, from the sounds of it, I don't know as much as I thought I did, and I don't see how I've literally made it almost four months and nobody has explained to me I'm not pregnant for nine months like normal people," I all but shouted at them in frustration and pure panic.

"Calm down, it's okay. This is our fault because we didn't really take into consideration that you are new to our world. Were-wolves are typically pregnant for about six months. However, it is also known that alpha pregnancies can typically be about five months. It just really depends on the person," James replied with a smile on his face.

Oh, no, he didn't.

"Did you seriously just tell me to calm down?!"

James' eyes went wide at my outburst. I couldn't believe that he really told me to calm down. This wasn't something that was no big deal. It was an enormous deal for me.

Taking slow, deep breaths, I closed my eyes and tried to calm myself.

It will be okay... everything will be okay.

"I'm not angry... I'm just a bit shocked," I said, trying to remain as calm as possible.

"There is no reason for you to be angry," Damian scoffed, shaking his head. "It's not that big of a deal. Just means you won't be pregnant that long."

My eyes flew open at Damian's comment. I couldn't believe how insensitive he was at the moment. It may not have been a big deal to him, but it was to me.

Jumping to my feet, I stormed from the room and made my way towards the private den created for me in the right wing of the house.

It was a small little study with a single loveseat, small tv, and tons of books surrounding the area. It was the one part of the house that was solely mine and even though it was a ten by ten room; I enjoyed every moment of it.

Slamming the door behind me, I sat on the sofa and thought about the situation. How could I honestly forget to ask such questions? I felt completely stupid for never thinking about asking how the pregnancy worked, considering I was raised as a human.

Guess that's what I get for assuming.

At that moment, the only thing I wanted was to speak to the one person who had always comforted me. I had put off calling her for too long, and the time had come where the weight of my issues were too much to bear.

I wanted my mommy.

Pulling my phone from my pocket, I dialed her number and waited as it rang.

"It's so wonderful to hear from you, dear. How are you?"

A sob racked my throat as I tried to speak. "Mama, I don't know how I'm going to do this here."

"Sweetie, what are you talking about? Did something bad happen?"

Taking a moment, I took a deep breath and tried to calm myself.

"No, not exactly, I just have no idea what I'm doing and I was just told by the guys that I'm not even going to be pregnant for nine months, that it's going to be like five or six months. That's literally like a month or two away. How am I supposed to do this?"

"Whoa, whoa, whoa. Are you telling me that nobody informed you of how this works?" she replied in shock.

"No, they didn't. I assumed, and they all didn't think to tell me because it slipped their mind that I knew nothing of their world."

"Oh, honey. I've been away too long. I need to come and visit you. Would you like me to come and visit you?"

As much as I wanted to tell her I could be a big girl and do this on my own, I knew the truth. I couldn't do it on my own. I needed her here with me. I was terrified, and even though I had four strapping mates... they were men, so they didn't understand how I was feeling. Even if they could feel my emotions through the link, they had no fucking clue.

They were trying their best, and I appreciated everything that they had been doing for me. But I needed somebody else to have my back as well.

Someone who understood what I was going through.

"Can you? I mean, I know that you guys have a lot going on and I would hate to take away from anything that you're doing."

"Don't be ridiculous, darling. You are my daughter and I love you. If you need me there, I will be there. Blake will completely understand the situation," she replied, causing me to smile.

"Okay. When do you think you will be here?"

"Tomorrow evening. Now get some rest, and I will see you soon," she replied, making me feel better than I had.

Nodding my head as if she could see me. I wiped the tears from my eyes. "Okay, I'll see you tomorrow. I love you."

"I love you too, sweetheart. Good night."

Hanging up the phone, tears flowed down my face and even though the guys did not knock on the door to check on me, I knew they were standing outside.

They had heard the entire conversation, and I wasn't sure how I was going to make this work, because the elder was here and the only other place I would put my mother would be in the guesthouse.

Which was occupied by the elder herself.

I had to find a way to get her out of here. Especially after everything that had happened with Damian. She wasn't even here for the full time she was supposed to be, and she had already outstayed her welcome.

Let's just hope she wouldn't cause issues for us when we made her go.

CHAPTER NINE

Gender Day

Waking up the next morning, I was surprised to find myself in James's bed. He didn't want to let me sleep in that room even though the other guys had told him to leave me be and let me rest; he refused.

I vaguely remember him coming in, grabbing me and the blanket, lifting me in his arms and carrying me to his bed. He even went as far as changing me out of my clothes and putting me in one of his very large oversized T-shirts before he crawled in behind me.

Out of the four men, he was the sweetest and the most sentimental.

"Good morning, beautiful," he whispered from behind me as he pulled me close to his chest and kissed the side of my cheek.

"Morning. I'm sorry about last night. I didn't mean to lose it on you guys."

"It's okay. Don't even worry about it. Shit happens and honestly, we dropped the ball when we forgot that you're not used to our world." Always apologizing, the ever sweet James slowly slid from behind me and walked towards the ensuite bathroom.

"I take it you heard my mother is coming..." I said with hesitation, knowing how complicated the situation was going to be.

"Yes, we all heard the conversation last night, and I will tell you that Damien and the others were very upset to see you as upset as you were," he replied.

Laughter escaped me, thinking about Damian being upset. "I can understand the twins being slightly upset, but you don't have to lie and throw Damian in there, too. I know he's not that kind of man."

James walked from the bathroom and gave me a knowing look before shaking his head with a grin. "You two are just the oddest couple I've ever met. You love each other one minute and you hate each other the next, both equally irritated with each other. But then you guys can't keep your hands off of each other when the moment calls."

"Well, we have a love-hate relationship. What else do you expect, James?" I asked as I pushed myself further into the blankets of the bed, getting comfortable.

"Very true. Needless to say, yes, we know that your mother's coming and we know the elder needs to go. Damien has already reminded us this morning."

Knowing he recognized the need to get rid of the woman made me feel slightly better, but then again, I was also concerned because I wasn't sure how it would be possible.

"I don't understand why she is like that, James. The woman I spoke to on the phone initially isn't the same woman that's here and if it is, she plays the game very well."

Sitting on the edge of the bed, James sighed, taking a moment. "One thing you will learn is people like her and those in her position can be what they must to get what they want. Just because they are where they are doesn't mean that we trust them. No one trusts them, really."

"So then, why are they even in that position?"

It made little sense to have a council no one cared for. I got it, though. Look at how the humans ran their government. They have had men in office that no one likes but yet year after year they keep electing people.

And year after year those people keep disappointing the nation.

"Maybe Damien can call the council or something and have her call back."

My suggestion made James laugh as he gave me this funny look. "Yeah, right. Like they would actually do something like that. I will tell you, though, she is fucking weird."

"Well, James, we have to get rid of her somehow. So how are we supposed to do that? I mean, I'm pregnant and hormonal and Damian doesn't like her, and she's obsessively interested in knowing everything about me and the babies."

The babies... shit. "That reminds me. My appointment is to-day."

A grin lit up James' face when I mentioned it, and nodding his head, he jumped to his feet. "It sure is. Why do you think I'm already getting up? We are supposed to be leaving soon."

Rolling my eyes, I pulled the blanket over my head, only to have it ripped back down. "It's too early to get up, James."

"I don't care. You're the one who set the appointment," he said as he made his way towards the door. "Get up and meet me downstairs. The faster we go to the appointment, the faster you can take a nap."

A nap sounded good, but the growling in my stomach was louder. "What about food?"

"I'm going to make it," he called from outside the door before closing it behind him.

If I didn't have James, I wasn't sure how I could manage all of this. He was the normalcy I needed to deal with Damian and the twins. Regardless of how sweet Talon and Hale could be... at times, they also irritated me.

Such was the difficulty of relationships. I had never heard of one couple out there that wasn't slightly annoyed by their better half at some point in time.

Just never expected it would happen to me so soon.

Thirty minutes later, I was making my way into the kitchen following the smell of bacon and toast. I was starving, and in an unusually good mood, until my eyes laid upon Elder Harrison and my smile quickly fell.

"Oh, there you are," she said with exaggeration. "I figured you would have been down here earlier to have breakfast with me."

"I'm sorry, what?" I replied, slightly confused.

My comment was not what she was hoping for, and as she raised a brow with her hand on her hip, she pushed away whatever she was feeling and smiled at me. "It's okay. I keep forgetting you know nothing of werewolf culture, and are still learning how to be a proper Luna."

There she went again with the insults. "Look—"

"That's enough!" Damian bellowed, cutting me off. "Elder Harrison, I think it's best that you take your leave. We have been more than hospitable, yet you continually are disrespectful to my mate and my pack. I will not tolerate it any longer."

A gasp left her throat as she placed her hand on her chest in shock. "Excuse me?"

"You heard my brother," Hale added in as he stood next to the kitchen island with his arms crossed over his chest. "As much as the visit has been wonderful, we need you to leave. We still have much work to do on the pack house, and don't have the time for entertaining."

"Never in my life!" she yelled. "I can see what they were talking about now. I didn't want to believe them, but after this... I can't promise to protect you after this."

"What are you talking about?" I asked, stepping forward. "Protect us?"

Once again, that irritating smug smile crossed her lips, and it took everything in me not to smack it off her face. I was tired of the games she was playing, and if she wasn't careful, she would not like the outcome of her actions.

"Yes, I'm to report back things are running smoothly here. I couldn't very well have told you that now, could I? It seems that things are not as they seem. Not to mention you dear..."

'I fucking knew it.' Damian growled through the link. 'I told you, Ivy.'

Glaring at him, I rolled my eyes with disgust and focused my attention back on the elder. "I don't know what you're referring to when it comes to me... can you be a little more enlightening?"

"Oh, please. Stop pretending we know what you are, shifter," she scowled. "You're Sølvmåne, and those kinds are not to be trusted."

Those kinds? She didn't even fucking know me. Not to mention my race is supposedly gone or whatever, and then I'm something else.

Everything was so fucking confusing, and I wanted more than anything to figure it all out, so I knew exactly what I was, but I still had no clue. Perhaps one of these days I would stop putting off speaking to Frigga and finish finding out the details.

Right now, though, I was doing everything in my power not to rip this stupid bitch apart for talking to me like I'm a fucking idiot. "Look, I don't have time to deal with you. I have somewhere to be. My mate asked you to leave, so I expect you gone. Don't make me ask you again."

Snatching the plate of bacon and a piece of toast, I turned on my feet and made my way towards the front door. I wasn't dealing with that woman anymore. I was having a wonderful day, and there was no way I was going to let her ruin it.

"Ivy, wait!" James called from behind me as he came jogging up to where I was.

"Don't you dare tell me I was out of line, James," I grumbled as I stuffed the bacon into my mouth. The last thing I wanted to hear was I was wrong. The only thing that would do would piss me off even further.

"I wasn't going to tell you that," he chuckled as we reached the car. "I was going to tell you that Hale is coming with, but Talon and Damian are going to stay behind to make sure she doesn't try anything stupid."

Stopping in my tracks, I glared at him. "Are you serious?"

"Uh, yeah. I'm sorry, Ivy. We just have to make sure—"

"It's okay," I said, cutting him off. "Let's get going."

Hale made his way to the car as soon as I climbed in, and within minutes we were off towards the pack hospital. The entire time we drove, I kept trying to remind myself that it was okay. Did I want all of my mates there today... yes. But I couldn't have everything I wanted all the time.

As the car came to a stop, I exhaled deeply and climbed out. Hale took my hand, lacing his fingers through mine, causing me to look at him. "It will be okay, Ivy."

"Thanks," I said, happy for the reassurance he was giving me.

Honestly, I needed it because lately I had been at my wit's end with how things had been going. All I wanted to do today was to see my babies and confirm the suspicions of their genders I already had. Knowing that they were okay was going to make everything that much better.

They were my future, and when they got here, it would complete the little family we were growing.

"Good Morning, Ivy," the doctor said with a smile as he opened the ultrasound room door, and gestured for us to enter. "Let's check on the little ones and hopefully see what you're having today."

"Thanks doc, I already have my thoughts on what I'm having," I replied as I climbed up onto the white table. James and Hale at my side as they always were.

"Oh, do you now?" The doctor chuckled. "What do you think you're having?"

"A boy and a girl," I replied. "Just motherly instincts."

Honestly, it was the dream I had that made me think it was going to be a boy and a girl. The pink and blue blanket ran through my mind constantly like the plague, and with Priscilla telling me to trust my instincts, I was.

I had no doubt the baby in the grass was a reference to my unborn children. I was just going to have to wait and see if my assumptions were correct.

Rolling the cool gel and wand over my stomach, the screen lit up, and the doctor took measurements as he had done before. "Your babies are growing wonderfully and actually are putting you closer to your due date."

"Closer? How much closer?" I asked hesitantly.

"Oh, I would say about four to six weeks, tops."

Shit... that meant the guys were right, and I only had a few weeks before the twins would be here. It wasn't much time to prepare, but with my mother on the way, I was sure we would be able to manage.

One thing about my mother I loved was the fact that she was good at getting shit done.

She always had been.

"Alright, are we ready to know what we are having?" The doctor said with a smile as the guy's eyes lit up with excitement.

"Yes, go on with it," James replied, causing me to smack him as everyone broke out into laughter. To be honest, I thought he was the most excited out of us all with the way he acted.

"Well, it seems the Luna was correct in her assumption. There is one boy and one girl."

As happy as I was supposed to be, I felt nothing but dread in that moment.

The dream was real, and it was a warning. The doctor confirmed the worst.

Something dark was coming for my children, and I wasn't going to be able to stop it.

Chapter Ten

Playing with Fire

Talon.

I had always been unsure about Ivy being pregnant, but the moment Hale told us through the link Ivy was having twins, I couldn't be happier. It was a moment I had known was coming, but now that it was here, I was more than nervous.

Was I going to be a good dad? Would they end up liking me?

"It's good news, brother," Damian said, slapping me on the shoulder with a smile.

"Yeah, it is," I replied hesitantly. "Damian, can I ask you something?"

"What's that?" He said as he moved around the nursery, checking everything the contractors were doing.

"Do you remember that old story that mother used to tell us about the great Bjorn?"

Damian stopped in his tracks, looking over his shoulder at me with a smile. "Yeah, what about it? Have old fairy tales been crossing your mind lately?"

"Shut up," I groaned, rolling my eyes. "I'm being serious."

"So was I. I thought James was the sentimental one, and Hale was the nerdy one."

Damian's laughter and comment caught me off guard, but as I narrowed my gaze, he knew I was being serious. I didn't bring things up unless it was important, and right now, I needed him to focus.

"What about it, Talon?" he finally sighed as he went back to what he was doing.

"What if the story was more than a story? What if it was real history?" I asked, trying to remember the details of the story, and how our mother used to tell it.

"Don't be ridiculous, Talon. It's a kids' story. Now focus, we have to get some of this shit done," he replied, completely brushing off what I was telling him.

Go figure that. After all, Damian was a logical man and if there wasn't proof to back something up, he didn't pay it attention. I wouldn't consider that entirely good for an Alpha to think that way, but he had his brothers to help him.

We were stronger because of our unique unity.

"Fair enough. I'll go down and see if the bitch has left yet."

Nodding his head at me, he kept himself preoccupied as I made my way down the stairs only to come face to face with James, Hale and Ivy walking through the front door.

Quickly, I rushed her and swept her off her feet, twirling her around in my arms while she laughed. "A boy and a girl."

"Yes, yes," she laughed. "Put me down Talon or you're going to make me sick."

"Sorry," I said as I placed her on her feet and pulled her in, crashing my lips against hers. "I can't help it. Seeing you pregnant is so damn tempting."

"Yeah, well, that will have to wait, brother," Hale cut in, causing me to look at him.

"Why? Are you still on that kick? I know what you said before, but come on now. Isn't it supposed to help with easing labor or something like that?"

Pinching the bridge of his nose, Hale groaned. "Yes, but she isn't in labor. However, she could have the baby within the next four to six weeks."

"Oh," I knew we had just talked about this, but having the doctor confirm it made it all that much more real. "Well, hopefully one of our problems will be gone soon."

"She is still here?" Ivy snapped. "Why?"

"She said that she had to pack, and then argued with Damian, who told her fine but to hurry and leave."

The look that passed through Ivy's eyes was one of displeasure. She wanted the woman gone now, and she wasn't going to be told that she had to wait. Pushing past us all, she stormed her way towards the back door. And that only meant one thing.

Ivy was going to go into turbo mode on this woman.

"Ivy... Ivy, no," James said, putting himself quickly in between her and the door. "I will go tell her for you. You remember what the doctor said. No stress."

"Move, James," she snarled at him as her eyes changed.

"No. Now, as your mate, I demand you go upstairs and take a nap now."

Never once in my life had I heard James use an almost decent Alpha tone, and the fact he just used it on Ivy was shocking. Hale and I glanced at each other before looking back at them.

Ivy stood with her fists clenched and her brows narrowed, but slowly she relaxed and rolled her eyes. "You'll make sure she is gone by the time I wake up?"

"Yes," he squeaked before quickly clearing his throat. "Yes, I will make sure."

With a sly grin, she leaned forward kissing him, and then turned smiling at Hale and me before she made her way towards the stairs, hopefully to take a nap.

"What the fuck was that?" Hale said as we glanced from where Ivy was back to James.

He looked absolutely pale as can be, but swallowing deeply, he straightened himself and ran his hand through his hair. "We pretend I didn't just about shit myself, and that you watched me manly stand point to her before going to handle a problem."

Turning, he didn't wait for us to comment and exited the back door on a mission. It took a moment for Hale and me to let what happened sink in and as it did, we both burst into laughter.

"I don't think I have ever seen him like that."

Turning to Hale, I shook my head, glancing out the window at James, who was walking towards the cottage, but obviously talking to himself.

"No kidding," Hale replied. "You think he is trying to pump himself up for what he is about to do?"

"Oh, no doubt. Fifty says the old broad doesn't go out easily."

"Hell no, I'm not taking that bet. I have faith in James, but the woman is stubborn as hell. Let's just hope he can get rid of her before Ivy gets back up again. I'd hate to see what would happen if she was still here." Hale was right about one thing.

It wouldn't be good if the woman was still here when Ivy got up.

Then again, part of me would entirely enjoy watching Ivy completely have a go at this woman. It would make for great entertainment.

If this was how things were going to be from now on, I was looking forward to the future for sure.

****

A few hours later, Ivy was refreshed and wide away with a hungry look in her eye. As she made her way into the kitchen, I looked up from the laptop I was working on and watched her search the fridge for something.

"Were you looking for something?" I asked her as she slammed the fridge door, and turned to me with a pout on her lips that I found incredibly sexy.

"I'm hungry, and nothing in there looks good."

"What kind of hungry?" I asked her hesitantly. "Like you want a snack or you're hungry-hungry?"

With a look of disgust, she rolled her eyes dramatically. "Why do you have to say it like that?"

"Say what, like what?" I asked in confusion. "I'm just trying to figure out what kind of hungry you are, so I know what you want to eat."

"I know. I'm sorry." Sitting down on the bar stool, she folded her arms on the counter and rested her chin on it. "I'm grumpy when I'm hungry."

"Oh, I can see that," I replied with soft laughter. "Let's see what I can find for you."

Before I was able to even get up from where I was sitting, commotion from outside drew both of our attention to the front door. The sun was slowly setting off in the distance, and whomever it was did not sound happy.

Jumping to our feet, Ivy and I made our way towards the door, opening it quickly. Out front stood James and the Elder arguing and to top it off, Ivy's mother had arrived with none other than the infamous Kate.

"Who the fuck do you think you are?" Kate yelled at the woman. "Don't you dare fucking speak to him like that? If he told you to go, you need to pack your shit and get one. It shouldn't take this long for you to grasp the understanding of your assignment."

"My assignment?" Elder Harrison scoffed. "What pack are you with—"

"Hey? What the hell is going on?" Ivy yelled, catching everyone's attention. "I thought you were supposed to be gone?"

The elder sneered at Ivy, shaking her head. "And I thought you were supposed to be a Luna. I guess we both thought wrong."

A growl ripped through my throat at the woman's words. However, I didn't have a chance to do anything before Ivy's mother had raised her hand and slapped the woman in her face, stunning us all. "Who the hell do you think you are talking to my daughter like that?!"

Oh, shit. I see where Ivy gets her attitude.

"I will have you arrested by the council for what you just did!" The elder yelled. "This is treason!"

"Treason?" Ivy said, stepping forth, her eyes shifting to their celestial blue. "If you haven't noticed, but I don't answer to the laws of your world."

"Whoa, Ivy... let's calm down just—"

I tried to calm her, but her eyes snapped to me, and I knew what that meant. She was about to lose her shit, and she was hungry. This wasn't going to be good.

'Damian, we have a serious problem, where the fuck are you.' I said through our mind link. The last thing I was aware of was that he had gone to the next town over for a meeting, and he didn't exactly let anyone know when he would be back.

'I'm on my way back. Why?' he replied as I watched the tension grow as the women yelled at each other. All that was but Ivy.

'The elder is about to lose her life because she won't listen.'

'What are you talking about?' he growled. 'She left earlier.'

'Well, I take it she came back, and she has pissed Ivy off.'

Cutting off the link, I grabbed Ivy's arm before she could step closer. The rage of emotions flowing from her through the link was like nothing that I had ever felt before.

"Please just fucking leave, now!" I roared at the elder, who stood quietly for a moment.

"This isn't over. If she can't be controlled, then neither can her children."

That was the wrong thing to say, and as I held Ivy back, I watched the woman climb into her car and leave. Ivy fighting against me was hard to control, but James tried everything he could to calm her.

"Ivy-" her mother said cautiously as my eyes snapped to her.

"Not right now. Kate, take her mother into the house, and we will figure the arrangements out after we calm her down. Go... now."

Kate didn't hesitate to do as I told her. She ushered Ivy's mother into the house, and as she did Ivy slipped from my grasp and tossed James aside like it was nothing.

This was a new side to her that none of us had ever seen, and as her eyes met mine, she growled. "She's mine."

CHAPTER ELEVEN

Understanding Death

Talon

The moment that Ivy glared at me and told me the woman was hers, I knew without a doubt that something terrible was about to happen. Without even a warning, she took off in a full sprint as fast as she could from the property. The car had long sped away down the driveway but knowing Ivy, that wouldn't stop her.

"We have to stop her," James cried out. "She's pregnant and she hurt the babies—"

James had a point. Damien wasn't here yet. Hale was in town until the end of the day. James was a good man and was too able to take care of a lot. But he didn't have the power needed to subdue Ivy like this.

Shifting into my wolf, I took off across pack territory, darting over the lawns down the hills towards the woods where Ivy had disappeared through. I had to find her. I couldn't let her do something she would absolutely regret. Even though she was the same person, she just seemed to have this alter ego that pushed through, making her more dominant when she shifted.

I knew deep down she would feel nothing but guilt if she ended up killing this woman. It would be the first person she had physically killed.

That sort of thing was never easy for anyone.

Catching her scent, I moved faster, pushing myself as hard as I could, her body coming into the distance as I kept trekking over the lands until, abruptly, she stopped. Not wanting her to know I was chasing after her, I halted in my position, hiding behind the shrubbery of the woods, watching her, waiting to see what she was going to do.

She was hunting, seeking this woman as if this woman was an elk that became her prey.

There was no stopping a wolf when it was in mid hunt. They were dangerous, primal and very territorial.

With Ivy not technically being a wolf, but being something else entirely—there was no telling what she could do.

The mind link that linked my brothers and me and even Ivy was going wild. However, Ivy's side was dormant. She had closed herself off in order to focus and I was having to push back mine in order to focus on her.

'Where are you?' Damien pushed through the link, using his alpha tone, catching me by surprise.

'Currently about 5 miles north of the pack. She's hunting.'

'She already ran five miles? There's no way she was able to do that. Are you sure of your location?' Damien snapped.

Did he really, honestly, think I didn't know where I was?

I grew up on these lands. These woods were my gain out of the four of us. I was the more primal hunter. There was no way they would know these woods better than I did.

'Are you seriously going to fucking ask me that question?'

Silence met me, and at the moment I had been dealing with Damian, Ivy bolted without warning, running north, deeper and deeper into the darkness and thicket of the woods. I followed her.

The canopies of leaves above us protected us from the sunlight as where creatures usually blended in with the darkness. Watching and waiting for the right moment to make their move.

However, today they were silent, and it made me wonder if those creatures knew what she was, and they themselves found her terrifying because right now, the shift she had made was nothing like I had ever seen before.

Her figure almost glowed within the darkness, her long hair shimmering in a sea of light that didn't exist from any other source around her.

The way she moved was elegant and as graceful as a fairy. But yet as quick and as dangerous as a wolf. Entranced by who she was and the fact that she was my mate, I didn't dare stop her. I didn't care what the others thought. I couldn't. At least not right now.

There may be a point where I could try to talk sense into her, but the time was not. Now, that was very obvious. After a little while, she came to a slow jog until her feet crept across the floor of the forest.

In the distance, a cabin sat alone within the darkness; the only light in that cabin came from the single pane window near the front door. What shocked me the most, though, was that the car the elder had driven was parked out front.

The woman who supposedly came directly from the council to see us was only 20 miles north of where we actually lived, and that was completely unsettling.

Why was the elder here?

This was not anywhere close to where the Council headquarters was.

I had thought I had concealed myself, tracking her the entire time I had been doing so. But as she stopped in her tracks, her hand upon the trunk of a tree, she looked over her shoulder at me and smiled.

She had known I was there the entire time, and not once did she stop me?

What was she waiting for?

'You joined me, pretty wolf?' her delectable voice said through my mind. It taunted me, egging me on to play with her and I was shocked she had opened the link just enough for me to speak with her, though; it was pretty obvious we were the only two in this conversation.

'Ivy, please turn back now. You're pregnant and cannot be in a fight. Think about our children.'

Turning her attention back to the cabin, I could sense she found nothing but amusement in my words. 'Do you really think that I would do anything that would hurt my children?'

'No,' I replied without hesitation. 'But that doesn't mean that they won't do something that could intentionally hurt them. Please think about this. She is not worth it.'

'That is where you're wrong. My children are hungry.'

Her words were like ice trailing down my spine. Moving forward, faster than I could process, she disappeared from my sight and it wasn't until I heard the shrill screams, growls, and cries from within the cabin I realized what had just happened.

Ivy was tracking at a slower speed so I could keep up with her. This entire time, we had to follow her when she went out on these hunts. It wasn't because she was slow and we were fast enough to keep up with her. It was because she wanted us there and knew we would follow her.

Shifting back into my human form, I ran naked towards the cabin, throwing open the door that was barely cracked, only to find the bloodiest scene I have ever seen before laid out in front of me.

Ivy had killed three people within this cabin. Two of them I knew, one of them I did not.

Blood coated her skin from the top of her head to the tips of her fingers. She was soaked in red and the most peculiar thing of all was she had a satisfied grin on her face as she swallowed down a bit of flesh, closing her eyes and pure satisfaction.

"Did you just eat them?!" I exclaimed in shock, with my eyes wide and an unfamiliar sense of confusion flowed over me I had never felt before.

"Those two?" she replied with a smirk as her eyes glanced towards the elder and another man. "No, I did not eat them."

"Then what did you just swallow? If you didn't just eat them?"

With a small laugh, she lifted her hand and pointed at the other body on the floor. "This one tastes different. The other two are wolves and I have no interest in eating the flesh of my ancestors, but that one. That one is intoxicating, but I don't know what it is."

Her words were almost like riddles. I knew there were other supernatural creatures out there. Everybody was aware of that, but the problem was they rarely come by. So much so, most of the wolves believed them fairy tales.

"What do you mean, they're different?" I asked as I stepped forward, looking down at the body before me. That almost seemed human.

Tilting her head from side to side, she stepped towards the creature and bent to her knees before her hand reached out and grabbed its face, inhaling deeply.

"I don't know what it is, but it tastes delicious. "

Taking a deep breath, I closed my eyes, running my hand over my face as I tried to calm the small, logical part of my personality hidden deep within me. I was primal.

I was considered more of the loose cannon, but yet my beautiful, perfect innocent mate was eating a creature we couldn't identify.

To top it all off, she killed a council member, and Devyn... the son of a neighboring Alpha.

A very particular Alpha that didn't like us whatsoever.

"May I ask why it is Ivy that—Ivy, leave it alone," I said, interrupting myself as I grabbed her hand, pulling it away from the creature. "You have no idea what it is or where it's been."

"Don't be so dramatic," she groaned, rolling her eyes as her senses seemed to rein back in. "What I did was for a reason, and at least one of us did something."

"What are you talking about? You literally killed a council member and the son of an opposing alpha. Not to mention something else entirely that we don't even know. If it was a royalty of its species... look, you can't just go around killing things because you want to."

Raising her brow, she looked me up and down and stepped over the creature, making her way towards the door as she licked her fingers clean. I had no idea where she was going, but wherever it was, she seemed very content with what she did.

"Ivy, will you please stop and talk to me? Tell me what is going on."

Getting out an exaggerated sigh, she stopped in her tracks, closing her eyes for a moment before she turned and opened them, facing me. "There are things I cannot explain because I don't know how to explain them. However, they were a threat to our pack. To my needs and my children, and I took care of it as I will every single time a threat comes about."

"OK, but the problem is you can't just go killing anybody you want to. If you find a problem with someone, you need to let us know so we can handle it properly."

She shook her head, staring at me as if she couldn't believe the words coming out of my mouth. "As I've told you before, I will do what I need to do to protect my children and the laws of your world do not apply to me. Even if I am softer minded at times, this is the side of me that will eventually completely take over."

Hearing her say the side I was looking at now was the side that would eventually take over was not a very comforting thought. The entire conversation, of course, I had opened through the link so that the others could end up hearing it as I was hearing it.

She was making it clear what was going on was going to have to be accepted one way or another. For some odd reason, she considered those people to be a threat, and she executed them appropriately, something my brothers and I were going to have to learn to handle or simply take care of when needed.

"It doesn't have to be this way. You have to let us help you. We're your mates," I finally said, before she turned away from me once more.

"Talon, are you afraid of me?" she asked as she stared at me with an intensity I had never felt before.

"Why are you asking that question, Ivy?"

"Because I want to know the truth. Do you fear me, Talon?" she asked again, waiting for my response.

"No. I don't fear you. I just want to understand you."

Laughter escaped her lips as she walked closer to me. Gently running her finger over my chest, she leaned up and kissed me with the blood of her victims on her lips.

"You should fear me."

CHAPTER TWELVE

Universal Fate of the Twins

Ivy

Stepping out of the shower, I pondered over everything I had done. Yeah, I lost myself a little bit in the commotion of things and I shouldn't have acted the way I did. But the woman was a threat to my family. She was a threat to my children. She was a threat to my mates and a threat to me.

I had given her chance after chance and I do not regret the actions I took when I killed her. Little did the others know she was meeting with two other people who were interested in completely eradicating me and my mates in order to take over territory.

I had overheard their conversations before I burst through the door and slaughtered them. It was only fragments, but it was the only information I needed to dismantle their circle.

I would do it again.

Without hesitation, I would slaughter anybody who posed a threat to my reign, my children and my mates. Even if that meant

I had to slaughter every wolf not part of our pack to ensure we would be protected, I would do it.

Because of my actions, I was well aware of the consequences that were to come.

Was I terrified? Yes, because I didn't want there to be a war brewing on the horizon with the possibility of taking everything from me. But then again, had I not done anything, we would have been at risk.

With a heavy sigh, I took the towel to my hair and gently dried every last bit of it. Staring at my reflection in the mirror, my celestial eyes were almost able to see into my own soul as it glimpsed the darkness that was within. I kept thinking about the dream I had before.

I needed to speak to the goddesses and with the men currently out of the house, I had the perfect opportunity to get the answers I needed.

I couldn't even face my own mother, or Kate until I did. My mind wouldn't allow me solace, and with my mind made up, I prepared to face Frigga.

Placing down the towel, I moved towards my bed, laying upon the soft blankets. It had been a few days since I had used my room properly because of construction, but with them almost done, only small pieces of things stood out of place.

That I was grateful for. The only place I felt comfortable enough to do this was in the seclusion of my own space. Closing my eyes, I let myself fall into a state of REM and, eventually, I was transported once again to the clouds of white that opened up, letting me step forth onto a patch of green where white columns and a podium sat off in the distance.

Frigga stood there, waiting for me alone. Her long hair and white gown blowing gently behind her as she smiled upon seeing me.

"I was wondering when it would be that she would finally show face here," she said with a content grin on her face and her hands clasped in front of her body.

"So are you going to tell me you were expecting me, as Priscilla always is expecting me?"

I said with a sly grin, causing her to chuckle to herself.

"What is it that I can do for you, Ivy? You seem to have a lot of questions and considering your latest actions, it makes me wonder what you've really got on your mind."

Shaking my head, I couldn't hide the exhaustion I felt throughout my entire body. I was a mess, and one that needed to be quickly fixed before I did something else that would be frowned upon. Not that I thought what I did was wrong.

"Where would you like me to start? Should I start with the dreams that I've been having? Or that I just slaughtered three people in a cabin, one of which was a creature I had never encountered before. Even though I am new to this lifestyle, I would have at least thought that the inner me may have recognized it, but not even the inner me knew what the hell it was. Do you have any clue as to what that creature was?"

Staring at me, she took a moment before slowly nodding her head and gesturing for me to follow her over towards a beautiful grassy area that had pillows and blankets thrown upon it.

"The creature that you ingested is considered a Nephilim."

Was she being serious? There was no way.

"I'm sorry... a what? Do you mean like the half human thing?" I asked with complete confusion and utter shock she would even mention that word. I didn't even know those freaking things existed. I thought they were just fairy tales.

"Ivy, you were literally a celestial being and werewolves exist as well as vampires, and you're telling me you have a hard time believing that Nephilims exist?"

She did have a point.

With everything else in the world I kept finding, it shouldn't be hard to believe there is a large index of creatures that probably inhabited the earth I had no clue about.

"OK, so why was an elder wolf, the son of an alpha and a Nephilim in a cabin 20 miles north of where I lived, and why did the Nephilim taste so good?"

"I'm not sure why the creatures were meeting, however they did have dark auras around them. Again, you know we cannot get involved. So we only merely watched, but I knew right away you found the elder to be threatening from the moment she stepped foot inside your home, did you not?" she asked, causing me to think back to the moment the elder stepped inside the home.

I had found her threatening. I had found something about her completely off. It was quite different from the conversation I had originally had on the phone with her. So something about it just didn't add up and when she acted, the way she did out in front of the pack house was when I lost it. She wasn't the person she was supposed to be.

"Something was wrong with her. She wasn't the person she was supposed to be."

"Very good," Frigga replied as she picked up her goblet and sipped from it. "She wasn't the person she was supposed to be because she was corrupted before you received her."

"What do you mean, she was corrupted?"

"Remember when Priscilla and the Valkyrie came to you at the Council members chamber and told you there was one that was divine, that was looking to change the path for those on Earth?" Thinking back to the conversation, I tried to remember exactly what had happened that day was utter chaos, so my mind was a bit fogged over.

"I think so. I don't remember who she said it was, though."

Nodding her head, she placed her cup down and stared at me. "Loki has escaped the Eternal realm, causing mass chaos upon Earth. You are not like the others. As I've told you before, you have a greater purpose. Your purpose, I cannot tell you just yet. But I will tell you it involves your children, and it is very important you protect them at all costs."

"My children. What do you mean it involves my children? Why would anybody be after my children?" I replied with anger in my tone as I narrowed my brows at her.

How could she tell me somebody was after my children and not tell me the reason why?

Or who would want to be?

"You need to calm yourself, Ivy. Getting angry here will do nothing for you," she replied, causing me to take a deep breath in and out to calm my currently racing heart.

"My apologies. But I'm sure you're aware as a mother yourself, learning your children are in trouble is a very painful thing to go through. So, could you please leave me some context as to what you're referring to?"

"Of course. I can give you what I can within the realm of my ability. The rest, you and your mates, will have to figure out for yourself."

Of course, that is her fucking response.

Nodding my head, I sighed. "OK, I will take what I can get."

"Your children are special. They are the children of one ancient and one partially divine. The children you are bearing have, once upon a time, lived in this world a long, long time ago and every few hundred years those children are needed once again to take their place on Earth to fix what man and creature cannot."

So like their fathers, who were once reincarnated to live upon the land again, they were doomed to do so as well. That's just fucking fantastic.

"I take it there is no way to change that?" I asked hopefully, but knowing the answer already.

"No, Ivy. It doesn't work like that."

"Of course not," I frowned, pinching the bridge of my nose.

I knew I should have been acting chaotic and losing my mind, but doing so wouldn't change anything, so why take that course of action? Taking a moment, I thought back to one thing that had been bothering me.

"The dream that I had once before about me standing within the darkness, only to come into the light and see a girl with red hair and sharp teeth. She said she was me, but she called me mother. Was that the future?" I asked hesitantly as I stared at the ground, not wanting to admit there was a part of me that knew eventually one of my twins would die.

"You saw a girl with long red hair and sharp teeth and she had celestial eyes?" With concern in her glance, she leaned forward and lifted my eyes to hers. "Ivy?"

"Yes. Initially, she said that she was me, but then she called me mother. I didn't understand it, but then a baby cried and I turned into the darkness and left, anyway. That was when I came upon a blue and pink blanket on a grassy plain. My feet froze to the floor, and through the shadows, approached a beast. A wolf-like creature dripping with hunger, who then launched itself at my children as I screamed and jolted from my sleep. I did not see how the dream ended."

Quickly standing at her feet, she gestured for me to follow her. I wasn't sure where I was going, but she took me back how we came with haste.

"Listen to me carefully, Ivy. The woman was not who you think she was. The dark wolf-like creature is a foreshadow of the future, but because you woke up, the scream of your pain saved your children and whatever disaster was about to come your way. There's still so much unknown about your future and that of your children. The universe decides what it wants. When the time is appropriate."

"Frigga, you have to tell me why you are concerned? Why are you acting like something terrible is about to happen?" I asked her as she pushed me towards the gate through which I came.

"I need to figure out a few things. Until I can explain who this person is, I can't. I have to be certain, but for now, I need you to stay where you have been. Speak with your mates about the stories they were once told by their mother. It will give you clarity, but until then, you must be strong. Listen to your instincts. The celestial inside you will guide you."

Pushed through the gate, my eyes fluttered open, and I stared at the ceiling above me. Whoever the woman was in my dream, she was bad enough to rattle Frigga, and that was concerning.

I had gained some clarity, but once again, was left with so many questions.

If my children were in danger... I would find a way to protect them.

No matter the cost.

CHAPTER THIRTEEN

Vow of Love

Heading down stairs, I made my way towards where the laughter and conversation was taking place in the living room. Kate and my mother sat with Hale and James on the sofa, looking over the many albums mother brought.

"You didn't bring those with you..."

Her eyes looked up to mine, and as if nothing had happened at all, she smiled and nodded her head. "Of course I did, Ivy. I have been looking forward to the moment of sharing them with your mates forever."

"Of course you have been," I sighed heavily. "I'm glad that you're here, though."

Standing to her feet, she moved towards me with a smile and wrapped her arms around me. The feeling of my mother's hug was definitely what I needed. With everything going on, I had a hard time believing I could do it without her.

"Everything is going to be okay, Ivy. I'm here now, and from what the guys were saying, you need help with the nursery."

Pulling back, I stared at my mother with a smile. "You have no idea. Nothing like learning last minute your babies are due to be here in a few weeks."

"Or sooner..." Kate added, causing my glance to land upon her as she made her way towards me and hugged me as well.

"I didn't even know you were coming," I laughed as I stood back, staring at them both.

"Well, I figured that having us both would help to level the estrogen in this home a bit."

The guys chuckled at each other when I looked at them. They held albums in their hands and were whispering while pointing out different photos.

"You know, that makes the two of you look so sweet and sentimental looking at those."

They both looked up at me with narrowed eyes as Hale lifted his middle finger. "This shits to good to pass up. Wait till Talon sees it."

"Wait till I see what?" Talon said, walking up behind me, kissing me on the cheek. "Hey sweetie. Are you feeling better?"

Were they really going to act like I didn't just slaughter three people?

"Uh–yeah. Where's Damian?" I asked, looking around as Talon moved to where James and Hale were sitting.

"He is in his office.... Oh damn, is that Ivy?" Talon exclaimed with laughter. "Look at the forehead!"

"Go fuck yourselves. I was adorable," I said, crossing my arms over my chest.

Kate and my mother began laughing at the comment as Damian's office door opened, and he moved to stand in its doorway. "Ivy, can we talk?"

There it was. Seriously, Damian. Always looking to conduct business.

"Yeah, sure," I said as I glanced back at my mom. "I'll be right back."

As soon as I entered Damian's office, he pulled me in and pressed his lips to mine. "What the hell were you thinking today, Ivy?"

His actions took me aback, and standing with hesitation, I found myself speechless. "Uh—"

"Uh, what? You could have gotten yourself fucking killed. You're pregnant with the future of this pack, and what you did isn't okay."

"Look, don't preach to me, okay? I know what I did wasn't exactly thought through, but there is a lot more to all of this. To be honest, there is a lot we all need to discuss." Sighing, my shoulders sagged, not even knowing where to begin.

How was I supposed to explain to them everything that had been going on? I honestly didn't even know where to start, because it would leave so many questions unanswered.

"What are you talking about? What's going on?" he asked as he leaned against the wall staring at me.

Deciding against telling him about what Frigga said for now, I went with the information I overheard in the cabin. "Before I killed them, I heard bits and pieces of a conversation. One where the council and others are plotting to get rid of us. We're seen as a threat to a lot of people and they want us gone."

"I kind of figured that when I went to clean up the place. It seems the council is working with some of our enemies."

"We have to be careful, Damian. If they think we are a threat, they will come here, and right now, no one can afford for war to happen," I replied, trying to make him see the point of the conversation.

"Well, that's kind of thrown out the window now. Look what happened at the cabin. They are going to want to know where the elder went. Guess what the last place that she was, was here. So what do you think is going to happen?"

I hadn't entirely thought about that when I had killed them, but thinking on it now, I finally understood what Talon had meant. "Shit."

"Oh, yes. Shit is definitely right. You want to be the Luna this pack needs, you need to think about what you do before you do it. I'm not sure if there is a way for me to talk us out of this one, Ivy. They will be out for blood."

It was clear my actions were not the best. However, I did exactly what Frigga told me I should be doing. I listened to my instincts. That woman had to die, and it led me to two others that needed to be put down as well.

"We will deal with it when it comes to it. For now, we wait and see what happens."

"That isn't how this works!" he snapped at me.

Staring at him, I felt my blood boiling. "It is how this is going to work, Damian. Trust me for once, and just leave it be. When they come looking, we will tell them she left here. We have proof from others that they saw her leaving our pack territory in her car."

He was seething in anger, and honestly had every right to be, but what is done is done.

There was no fixing it, and he shouldn't keep worrying.

We would handle it when the time called for us to handle it.

Taking a deep breath, he nodded. "Fine, but when the time comes, you are going to learn how to fix your own mistakes, Ivy. I may not always be around to do them for you."

Damian.

As soon as Ivy left my office, I felt the rage within me slowly slipping out. I was pissed, of course, because once again she had done something that had made my position as Alpha even harder.

I didn't understand why she couldn't control the urges she had and try to act somewhat normal. With our children on the way, and everything else on our plate, we didn't have time for more problems.

"Everything okay?" Hale said as he entered my office with concern etched in his eyes.

"No, but then again, Ivy doesn't seem to think that anything is an issue anymore. She thinks that doing nothing is the best course of action."

Holding up a bottle of scotch, he shook it in front of me with a smile. "Drink?"

"Yes, make them large," I groaned as I flopped down into my chair. "How is all of this supposed to work if she is constantly taking things into her own hands, Hale? I always feel like I have to be the bad guy in the situation, and I hate it. This isn't what I signed up for."

"No one is telling you to be the bad guy, Damian."

"Oh, no?" I scoffed as he handed me my glass. "Then why am I going to be the one who tells her no, and also has to deal with the cleanup of her killing spree?"

"She saw them as a threat, Damian. She did what any territorial wolf would do."

In a way, Hale was right, but it didn't make things any better. She had killed very important people, and that wasn't going to go over well with the people they were associated with. Instead, it was going to bring people to our doorstep looking for answers.

"We need to prepare for the worst, Hale. Just in case they come for her."

Hale froze in his spot before his eyes slowly slid to me. "No. You're not going to go to that length."

"We have already discussed this, Hale. If they try to put it on Ivy, I'm going to take the blame, and you will take over as Alpha. It has to be that way."

Slamming his glass down onto the table, he glared at me with tight lips. "You're not going to take the blame for anything, because they aren't going to come. She needs you just as much as she needs the rest of us, Damian."

"That's where you're wrong," I laughed softly. "I see the way she is with the three of you. I don't have that connection with her, Hale. All I have ever done was bring her pain and misery. I'm the worst mate to have ever been matched, and I do nothing to make her happy."

"I refuse to listen to this shit, Damian," Hale sneered. "You're needed just as much as the rest of us, and if she loses you, it won't end well for the person who caused it."

Shaking my head, I tried shaking the feeling of my slowly cracking heart. To think I was nothing to her hurt me. However, I wore the pain very well, and I kept my emotions closed off so much I was forgetting what it was like to feel at all.

The night I had spent with Ivy was to help me remember, and even that night I often thought was nothing but a dream, simply because I felt so distant from her.

"Please, Hale. Just promise me if anything goes wrong you will take my place, and protect her as we all vowed to do." I sighed as my eyes met his once more.

As much as I knew, he didn't want to agree. He did. He nodded his head in agreement before standing to his feet and pulling me to mine into his embrace. "You better not do anything fucking stupid, Damian. I mean it."

Hugging my brother wasn't something I had done often, and the weight of the emotions it caused me was almost overbearing. Holding myself together, I pulled from him and gestured to the door. "Go entertain our guests while I finish up here. I'll be out shortly."

Hale's gaze stayed on me for a moment longer before he nodded, and made his way out of my office. As soon as he was out, though, the slow, steady stream of tears flowed down my face.

I had failed so many times before, and I would make sure that this time I didn't.

Even they came for Ivy... I would take the blame and her place.

I would do whatever I had to, to protect my mate and my children.

Even if it meant giving my own life to do so.

I loved her too much to let her go.

CHAPTER FOURTEEN

Baby Shower

Confrontation

Ivy

Two weeks passed with peace, and during that time, I had accomplished getting the nursery put together with the help of the guys, my mother, and Kate. My mother and Kate stayed longer to be with us, and I was more than happy to have them here.

It meant I was able to spend more time with them both, and with the delivery date getting closer, I needed a refreshing change. Something that didn't revolve around what was going to happen and who wanted me dead.

"Hey, do you think we need to add more of the vines to that wall?" Kate asked as she stood staring at the wall above the dresser with her hand on her chin and confusion in her stance.

"I mean, I wouldn't oppose it. I think that would be cute."

She glanced at me for a moment before nodding her head. "You're right. It's way too cute to pass up."

Shaking my head, I continued to fold the baby clothes in the white basket while she had fun. I thought I had bought a lot of things, but after a long shopping trip with those two, these kids had everything they would ever need for the entire first year of their lives.

"Ivy!" my mother called out as she came searching through the rooms until her eyes landed on me. "Ah, there you are. The guests will start arriving soon."

Guests... I had almost forgotten that my mother had thrown a last-minute baby shower for me today. She had invited the entire pack, and made it co-ed so that the guys could be present. I wasn't sure who was going to come, though.

I wasn't exactly liked much.

"Okay, okay," I smirked. "I'm coming down now."

She didn't miss a beat when she stood in front of me with her hands on her hips, staring at me. There was no way she was going downstairs without me, and as much as I wished she would, I knew this battle wasn't one I would win.

"Go, Ivy. I'll finish up here and be down in a minute."

Knowing there was no way to avoid the inevitable, I nodded, and left with my mother to go appear before the non-existent masses she believed were coming. However, when I walked down the stairs, I found myself in shock at how many people were here.

It almost looked like the entire pack had shown up for the celebration. It warmed my heart to be a part of it. To see how many people in this pack came to celebrate the future rulers that would one day inherit this all.

"Congratulations," the voices called out as I walked through the sea of people towards the back door, heading outside to where there was a grand event being held.

"Mom, you really outdid yourself with this. You didn't have to go through all this trouble."

Gazing at my mother, though, I saw the wide smile on her face of pure joy. She was over the moon with the turnout, and would now talk about this day forever.

"I know that I didn't, but you are my only child and you deserve the best. And so the best is what I plan on giving you." The comment warmed my heart, making me even more thankful that she was here.

There were still unsaid things between her and I regarding how this all came about, but I knew that one day eventually we would have that conversation. She was my mother and she would let me know things if it were important, or when the time called upon it.

"Congratulations Luna on the arrival of your children," a woman with dark brown hair and bright green eyes said as she walked up to me, handing me a bouquet of flowers.

"Oh my goodness, these are absolutely beautiful! Thank you so much. What's your name?" I asked, a little unsure of who the woman was. I had remembered seeing her around a few times, but I was still trying to get familiar with everybody.

"My name is Jada. I was actually going to offer you to join the mother's circle that we have down at the park community center. I figured it would be a great way to get to know the other ladies of the pack and when the children are born, a great way for them to play with other children of the pack as well."

The offer was more than generous and I had waited a while to have at least somebody accept me in. So for her to offer such a thing, there was no way that I could refuse. "That sounds wonderful. Please follow up with me later and make sure I get that information because I would really love to be able to join you."

Jada smiled at me, before bowing her head in a show of respect as she continued to walk on to let another come up and speak to me. The procession went on like this for a while until every single woman had said their congratulations to me and delivered whatever gifts they had brought.

I honestly didn't think I needed a baby shower, considering everything was already purchased for the twins, but some gifts that were given were a lot more personal and I loved them.

One gentleman crafted a hand painted glass mobile for the twins' room with glass wolves dancing around a crystal moon. It was one piece that I loved the most out of everything that I had received, because the crystal moon replicated the color of my eyes.

"It looks like you've quite made out today," Hale said as he and Talon came walking up next to me. They were right. I had made out, but seeing them here with me in a coed baby shower was a relief I didn't think I would have.

"Yeah, I sure did. I don't think we're going to need anything for the children for quite some time. Between everything that we got, then what my mother and Kate got, and nowhere at the baby shower, these children literally have things to last a lifetime."

"Ain't that the truth?" Talon chuckled before a loud commotion drew our attention towards the front of the house.

"I want you to stay here," Hale demanded, as I pulled away from him.

"Get out of my way...." I replied as I pushed past him on Talon. Making my way towards the front of the pack house to see what was going on.

It wasn't exactly the greatest of ideas to put myself in the middle of something in my condition, because \ the babies could be here within two weeks. But if there was something going on, it was my responsibility to see what it was.

Coming around to the front of the House, three black cars came into view. All of them carrying security guards from the council's chambers. My heart dropped to the pit of my stomach.

"What in the hell is going on?" I asked as my crystalline eyes showed clear and bright to anyone who was currently in my presence. They had grabbed Damien, who was pushing them off as James was held back from whatever commotion was taking place.

"Luna Ivy, the ancient one. It's a pleasure to see you," replied a dark-haired older man who stepped out from behind the shadows of his security guards.

He didn't look like the type of man that would particularly be a council member, but as he stepped closer, something inside of me snapped. There was something wrong with him, just as there had been once before with the elder Harrison, and I wasn't sure what it was.

But it was something I would not let anywhere near my children.

A deep growl left my throat as I bared my teeth at him. "Do not step any closer to me. I demand that you unhand my mates. For everyone's safety."

"Are you threatening the Council, Luna?" the man asked in a very stern voice, as if he was trying to intimidate me.

"There's no need to threaten you. If I wanted you taken care of, you would have been dead the minute you stepped forward, however... that is not the case. I demand you unhand them and explain to me why you're here ruining my baby shower."

He stared at me for a moment, before laughter quickly left his lips, and he gestured with his hand for the men to allow Damian and James free.

"We are here because two weeks ago, one of our council people disappeared. Later on, they were found completely torn apart, as well as the son of a fellow alpha. Now, the alpha's son, we have no idea why he was where he was, but the elder was last seen here..."

"Yes, I'm aware that the elder was last seen here," I replied, as if it was the most obvious answer there ever had been. "But what do you mean that she's dead? She was literally just here two weeks ago. When she left, she told me she would love to accept the invitation to come to the baby shower. If you check our cameras, you can see that she had taken off. We have security cameras at the guard shacks to monitor who comes in and out. I can assure you she left in her vehicle."

There was a slight pause as his gaze drifted from mine to Damien's and then back to me. "You are a lot more cooperative than your mate is. He wouldn't allow us to obtain anything, but you're telling me you can show proof from footage at your guard shack that Elder Harrison did indeed leave by herself in her vehicle from your property?"

"Why yes, I can. Actually, if you would like, I can have that information sent over to you this afternoon. Of course, I hope you would be considerate of the current events that are going on and would allow us to continue my shower and then have that information sent over afterwards. There's only about two hours left," I replied, smiling sweetly at him.

I knew the footage was there, and it was the only footage I could give him because it was the only footage that didn't implicate us. However, his eyes gazed up at the camera at the corner of the roof of the house and swirling ideas seemed to develop in his mind.

"I'd like the footage from that camera as well. Do you think you might manage that so it shows she got into the car in one piece?"

"As much as I would love to give you that, I can't," I replied with a frown.

"And why can't you? Are you guilty?" he sneered at me as his eyes narrowed.

"No," I laughed. "While Elder Harrison was here, we had construction going on. We were having some remodeling for the new nursery, and the people who were remodeling hit an electrical line, and it fried some of the circuit."

"I see. That sounds very convenient because of the current situation," the gentleman said. "Do you have proof of this?"

"Of course I do. I can actually send you a copy of the invoice from the day that it was called. The situation that had happened, and when they actually came out to fix it, if you would like."

Taking a moment, he thought over everything I said as he ran his tongue crossed his teeth. He quickly glanced back at another man that was with him.

"It seems the Luna and her mates are more than willing to helping us figure out what happened to the elder. Isn't that correct, Luna?" he said before turning back to me. "Just to clear things up, could you tell me where you were that night?"

"Of course I can. My mother and my best friend Kate actually came that very evening. They've been here for the last two weeks. They're from a neighboring pack down in Georgia."

No matter what the elder asked, I had an answer for everything. I was surprised Damian himself didn't speak up. Instead, he stood quietly with a stern glare across his face and his lips tightly met.

"Brilliant. I do apologize for the misunderstanding. I have no problem waiting. As soon as your shower is over, if you could please get that information to me, that would be much appreciated and I hope that you will offer your services. Of course, in order to help us find out exactly who had done this."

Knowing he had nothing else to ask. He was quickly wrapped up in the rest of the conversation, standing unsteadily on his feet as he gestured for the men to get back into their vehicles.

"Of course I will make sure to get everything to you this afternoon."

"Very good." Turning his attention to Damian, I watched the man glare before letting a look of amusement pass over him. "I will see you around, Damian."

Chapter Fifteen

Uncertain Futures

As soon as the party was over and everyone had gone, I helped my mom and Kate move everything I had received up into the nursery. Not twenty minutes into working, Damian found me, and the scowl on his face spoke volumes to the mood he was in.

"Damian, if you have come to yell at me, please don't."

My mother and Kate stopped in their tracks as they glanced towards where Damian stood off to the side. My eyes were concentrating on the beautiful mobile in my hand. The celestial crystal was mesmerizing, and as I looked up towards the cribs, I tried to think of where to hang it.

"Ivy, we need to talk," Damian said, causing a sigh to escape me.

"I figured you would want to." I turned to him. "Kate, can you hang this centered above the twins' cribs please?"

Handing the mobile to Kate I moved towards Damian and exited the nursery making my way towards his room. "Let's talk."

When the door to his room closed behind me, I turned to face him, and the look in his eyes was no longer of anger but extreme remorse. "Why did you interfere today, Ivy?"

"What do you mean, why? You're my mate, Damian. I won't let them take you from me."

Shaking his head, he moved towards me and lowered himself onto the bed. "I don't deserve you, though. I was willing to go with them in order to protect you."

"Protect me? What are you talking about?"

As his eyes met mine, I watched the tears build within him he refused to let fall. "They want to kill you, Ivy. You're a threat to them, and if they take you out, they dismantle our pack."

I hadn't really thought too much about what he was saying before, but honestly, it made a lot of sense. If I was in their position, I would do the same.

"That doesn't mean that you sacrifice yourself for me, Damian. You're needed here and we have two beautiful children on the way that are going to need you. You don't just try and throw that all away."

"I wasn't throwing it away," he scoffed. "Plus, what good am I going to be to them? I'm broken, Ivy."

Never had I once seen Damian in the state he was. He was literally sulking, and something deeper was bothering him. Stepping closer to him, I ran my hand over the side of his face and smiled.

"I can see that you're hiding something from me, and until we talk about it, things are going to remain as they are."

"I'm fine," he sighed, moving his face from my hand.

"No, you're not. Now tell me why you think you're broken."

"It's not something easily explained, Ivy." He stood to his feet. "If I tell you, you're going to look at me differently."

"Don't assume things, Damian. We have been through hell and back since the moment I got here. If I was going to pass judgment like that, I would have done it already."

Staring at him, I could tell whatever it was conflicted him, and I hated it. For him to think he couldn't talk to me because I would think ill of him was ridiculous, but I was patient. I would wait if he wanted me to.

"Ivy, I'm losing my wolf."

The words that came out of his mouth were not the ones I was expecting. It wasn't possible for him to lose his wolf. He was a werewolf. It was who he was.

"How... that doesn't make sense. You're a werewolf, Damian."

"I didn't notice it before, but since the claim... I feel it. It's like part of me is slipping away, and I don't know what's going to happen to me. That's why I was fine with taking your place for judgment," he replied, as if that was logical.

"Damian, why didn't you tell me this before?"

Throwing his hands up in the air, he gave a soft desperate laugh, "I don't know, Ivy. It isn't like we have ever really had the chance to talk about things like this."

Staring at him, I tried to wrap my mind around what he was saying. He wasn't making sense, and for him to think he was losing his wolf was crazy.

"I think you need to talk to Priscilla about this, Damian." I breathed. "I honestly don't know what to say. I mean... what would cause you to lose yourself? Like I said.. You're a werewolf. That's like telling a human they're losing their humanity."

"Maybe you're right," he replied, staring at me. "Priscilla is the right person to talk to."

The sarcasm was heavy in his tone, and that annoyed me more than anything. "Don't act like that. I'm only being honest, Damian. This is serious, and if you really think you are, we need to find out from someone why that would be. She's your aunt... I mean, she should know something, right?"

Turning away from me, he made his way towards the door. "Well, I'll go talk to her then. I'm sorry to have bothered you with this."

"Damian—" I called after him as he walked out of the open doorway, disappearing from my sight. "Are you fucking kidding me, man?" I muttered with aggravation.

"What was that about?" Hale asked in confusion as he glanced at me, and then back down the hallways where Damian had gone. "Don't tell me you guys are fighting again."

"No—" I sighed as I walked towards him. "He just has some shit on his mind, and he thought I could help, but honestly, this is something I wouldn't even know how to deal with."

Pulling me close, he looked down at me with a grin. "Something big bad Ivy can't handle? That's shocking."

"Hey, I never said I could solve the world's issues, Hale. Plus, this is something that needs far more care than I can give him. I don't even know how to fix my own problems. How the hell am I supposed to fix other peoples?"

"You're a goddess, Ivy. You will figure it out."

Rolling my eyes, I groaned. "I'm not a goddess. I don't know why everyone seems to think that I am. I'm far from godly... I'm a murderer."

Gripping my chin, he raised my eyes to his and stared intently. "Don't ever say that. You're not a murderer, Ivy. What you did was to protect your family, and if it had been one of us who had been in your position, we would have done it as well."

"You're just saying that," I sighed.

"No, I'm serious. If I had been in your position, I would have killed them as well."

His words were slightly comforting, but my mind kept drifting back to what Damian had said. I was worried, and I had every right to be. The thought I could possibly lose him wasn't one I wanted to contemplate.

"I guess we can only take things one day at a time."

Hale kissed me gently. Hale kissed me gently.

"Exactly. So for now, don't let it bother you, okay?"

"Okay." I smiled.

"I have to go down to the training field and help James. I will be back later, though. Are you going to be okay?"

Nodding my head, I pulled away from him with a forced smile. "Of course. I'm just going to finish helping my mom and Kate put some things up. I'll be fine."

"Okay then." He whispered as he turned and left me standing in Damian's bedroom doorway by myself. Watching him walk down the hall towards the stairs, I left an exhausted breath escape me.

My life had become one dramatic event after another, and the only thing I wanted was to move past what I was and become accepted as I should be. From everything I had read in the books Priscilla had given me... I wasn't living like a Luna.

Kate's laughing face came into view as she exited the nursery with my mother. I had to find something—anything—to preoccupy my mind. "Hey, wait up."

Stopping, they looked at me with small smiles and questioning glances. "Everything okay?" My mother asked softly.

"Yeah, I'm good. Damian was just going over to safety stuff they are going to be doing."

"That's a good idea," Kate replied. "With how things went today with the council guys, I don't trust it."

Looking at her with confusion, I furrowed my brows. "What do you mean?"

"Ivy..." Kate said with slight hesitation. "The council doesn't act upon anything unless they plan to follow through. You may have deterred them for now, but it won't last."

"So you're saying they will be back?"

The silence from Kate was the only answer I needed, and with a frown, she finally nodded. Of course, they would be back. After all, there was much here they wanted. Me being the primary thing.

Stepping towards me, my mother wrapped her arms around me and pulled me into a hug. "Hey, don't worry about it, okay? Let your mates handle this. The only thing you need to worry about are those two precious babies growing inside you."

As she pulled away, I looked down at my stomach and smiled. "You're right. Goddess knows they are going to be here in a few weeks."

"Ivy, according to the pack doctor, you're measuring at almost full cycle. There is a chance you could have them sooner. So you need to be careful. I don't want there to end up being complications, because you're stressed."

My mother was the most caring woman I knew, and regardless of the past, she was right.

Unknown POV

"Has there been any progress?" I asked, staring at the Alpha in front of me. I was an impatient man, and I had been more patient with this situation than any other I had ever faced. It has been twenty years.

"They have fortified their defenses."

"I take it that is something that you just can't fix, is it?" I sneered with disgust. Pathetic ass wolf was getting on my last damn nerve. He was pissed because his son died, but that was his fault. That boy was still attached to his mother's bosom.

"I will see to it," he growled low, causing me to laugh.

"No, you won't. I will handle it as I always do. Now get out of my face, wolf," I snapped as I crushed the glass I had been holding in my hand. He didn't hesitate to get out of my sight, which was smart, considering I wanted to rip someone apart.

Fucking pathetic—all of them.

Standing to my feet, I quickly let the surge of power wrap around me, and within a matter of seconds, I was walking across the cobbled floor of damp and dark dungeon. There was one person in particular I had toyed with for years dying for the opportunity to fix her mistakes.

"Hello, pet."

Her blue eyes connected with mine from where she sat on the concrete floor. Tattered in dirt and blood, I found the sight before me enjoyable. She was like this because of me, and yet when she looked at me, she still saw hope and love.

"Master... are you here to save me?"

"Perhaps, pet," I replied smoothly as I open the cage she was in and watched her stand to her feet. "Are you ready to be a good girl for me?"

"Yes, master. Please let me show you I can be good."

"Very well. I want you to do one very important thing for me and if you do, I'll reward you heavily. You will once again have your life back, and revenge on the one who hurt you." My teasing comment lit a fire in her eyes as she narrowed her gaze.

"I can kill her?" she asked with a small smile.

"Oh, yes, my dear. You can help me kill them all."

CHAPTER SIXTEEN

Hidden Agenda

Damian

Days seemed to pass since Alokaye, the elder, visited my pack. Things were becoming strange around the surrounding communities, and I couldn't help but wonder if war was upon the horizon.

Ivy had stirred the metaphorical black pot, and with the help of my brothers and her mother, they could keep her fed to prevent her going all out psycho.

The day I told her about my secret, I had expected her to return with more concern than she had, but it was a lot to ask of, I suppose, considering she wasn't as close to me as she was with the others.

Watching her now, I saw how happy and carefree she was with my brothers and some of the other pack members. I had been hesitant about the baby shower when her mother suggested it, but it turned out to be beneficial.

Maybe there was hope for the future of our pack.

Maybe she was the Luna of the future—the Queen of Queens.

"Damian, are you okay?" Kate called from the doorway of my office.

Turning from the window, I set my gaze on her and forced a smile to my lips. "Yeah."

When I had first met Kate, I wasn't sure if she was going to be someone positive I wanted around my mate, but in the end, if it hadn't been for her, Ivy would have died.

The future of our people would have been lost to whatever force was currently lurking within the shadows of my forest. "Did you need something?"

"Actually, yes," she said softly as she stepped into my office, closing the door behind her.

Walking around my desk, I took my place in my seat and waited for her to continue. I had a lot on my plate at the moment and with my upcoming trip, I had little time for idle chitchat.

"I wanted to ask you why you have been spending so much time away from the pack lately. Ivy says nothing about it, but I can tell that it bothers her. Actually, whatever you talked to her about the other day has completely changed her."

Kate was a very perceptive woman, but the last thing I wanted to do was tell her what I had really been up to. "It's complicated, Kate."

"No, that's just a typical Damian personality. I was there when we almost lost her Damian. I saw what losing her did to you, whether you want to admit it. You love her as much as your brothers, if not more, and your actions are driving an invisible wedge between you and the rest of them. Now why?"

Letting a heavy breath escape me, I picked up my glass and took a long sip as I stared silently out the window of my office where she was playing with a group of children.

"If I tell you what's going on, you can't tell her or my brother's, Kate."

"It's that bad?" she said softly as my eyes met hers once more.

"Depends on who's listening, I suppose."

Taking a moment, I watched her fidget in her seat before quickly nodding her head. "Okay, tell me. I won't tell them, but—" she said with a frown. "Only unless they need to know in an emergency."

"Kate, that isn't—"

"No, Damian," she snapped, cutting me off. "If someone is in danger because of this secret, then I have to tell them. I may not be part of your pack, but Ivy is my best friend and I am fiercely loyal to her. So keeping this is betraying her."

Never once had I realized how loyal Kate really was to Ivy until this moment. I didn't understand the connection the two women had, but I couldn't ask Kate to betray her friendship. "If those are your conditions, then so be it.

"When I was younger, my parents were killed, and in the process, I changed. In order to kill what was behind the deaths of my parents, I end up losing the Lycan within me. The ancestral trait that was passed down from my father..."

She listened to me intently, nodding her head as I explained what I remembered about the day my parents died. Of course, there were so many holes in everything, and the only information I knew for certain was what Allison had told me long ago.

"So you became like Hale and Talon in order to save them all."

"Essentially, but it ended up killing the creature inside me. I never thought too much about it because when I was of age, I got my wolf and that was enough for me. However, when the circle with Ivy was completed, I started to feel... off," I replied with a sigh.

"What do you mean, you feel off?" she asked, staring at me with a confused expression.

"I'm losing my wolf."

Silence fell between us for a moment before a soft laugh escaped her, and she shook her head. "That's not possible, Damian. You're a werewolf. You can't just lose who you are."

"I thought the same thing, but every day it's becoming harder and harder for me to shift. Every day, it's becoming harder for me to connect with the side of myself. I have been searching for the last two months for answers, but everything turns up empty."

"You need to see Priscilla..." she said, leaning forward in her seat.

"Kate... I have, months ago. She has known for a while now too, but has been sworn to secrecy."

"Well, then, you need to tell Ivy, Damian. You can't let this go quiet," she replied with a little more anger in her tone than I would have liked.

"Kate, I did tell her. She said the same as you and didn't seem to want to think too much about it. She also told me to speak to Priscilla because there was nothing she could do. I had thought for a moment maybe she could—"

Sagging my shoulders, I shook my head, not finishing my train of thought. I didn't really know what I thought she might be able to do, but it was clear that my situation wasn't as important as Talon's.

She was willing to die for him, but for me... she pushed it off on someone else.

"Damian, you need to speak to her properly. Losing you will destroy her and the circle."

Running my hand through my hair, I sighed. "Why do you think I have been trying to fix it? Honestly, sometimes I wonder if me not being able to solve it is a sign. Maybe it's because I was never meant to be with her."

"That's ridiculous, Damian," Kate snapped, as she stood to her feet. "You need to tell her the truth, and not just part of the truth... the entire fucking thing."

"Why?!" I snapped. "Look at her Kate. Look at her outside right now with the others and her mom. She doesn't seem to care about what I'm doing at all. They are who make her happy... not me."

"Bullshit," she replied, crossing her arms. "You have no idea what's going through her mind. Half the time you're always too busy to take part in anything. You're always pushing everyone away. Maybe they just don't want to bother you."

"Enough, Kate," I groaned, shaking my head as I calmly let my eyes gaze back to her beautiful figure standing outside. Her arm was wrapped around James' arm as she leaned her head against his shoulder. "I can never be what they are for her."

"What about the pack?"

Glancing at her, I frowned, "what about them?"

"Who's going to be their leader, Damian? No one runs this pack like you do."

Chuckling, I let my gaze leave Kate once more as I turned back to Ivy. "Hale."

"Hale? Are you being serious right now?"

It was obvious Kate had the same outlook on Hale being Alpha as he had on himself. He was a smart man and could lead well, whether or not he wanted to believe it. The problem was, he was scared of himself.

He was afraid of the Lycan within him, and because of that, it made him unpredictable.

"Ivy can control him," I replied, as if the answer was obvious.

"Ivy... you mean the same Ivy who can't control herself most of the time? Damian, I honestly don't think that you're thinking this through. You are what holds this family together, whether you think so. Those choices are not good ones and you know it."

Part of me heard her concerns and knew she was right in a way. But with so much chaos consuming our lives over the past few months, I didn't want to think of what would happen if I did and no one was prepared.

"Look... don't get worked up. Nothing is happening yet," I hissed as I clasped my hands together on top of my desk. "I have one more place to go, and it should work."

"Should work?" Kate scoffed. "Where is this place?

"It doesn't matter. What does matter, though, is that the woman I'm going to see can fix me." I explained, hoping that Kate would simmer down.

The anger and frustration rolled off her in waves as she paced around my office, running her hand through her hair while letting out a heavy breath of frustration.

"I can't believe you have been hiding this for months from all of them, Damian."

Coming to a stop, she turned to face me with her golden blue eyes. She was a fearsome sight to behold, and having her here right now made me feel better for Ivy. Kate would help her through anything she had to face.

"The past doesn't matter anymore, Kate. What matters is the future," I replied firmly as I stood to my feet and noted Kate and the others walking up towards the house.

"I need you to do me a favor... if, for some reason, something goes wrong, I need you to look out for Ivy. Help her get over everything."

With parted lips, Kate stared at me wide-eyed and in disbelief. "Are you fucking kidding me right now? How dare you even fucking suggest something will happen? You have two tiny children on the way, don't you fucking dare leave all three of them."

"Kate, for once shut the fuck up and just listen to me. Can you fucking do this or not?"

Closing her mouth, her lips thinly met. She rolled her eyes, sagging her shoulders in defeat as she slowly nodded. "Fine."

"Fine?" I asked in question.

"Yes, damn it. I said fine. I'll do as you say, but if you fucking hurt her. I'll find you in the afterlife and kill you again. So you better figure this shit out, Damian."

Letting a grin spread across my face, I nodded my head in understanding. There was no need for words to go further. We had both made our sentiments known, and knew where we stood.

As Ivy's voice filled the area outside my office, I gestured for Kate to go.

I wasn't sure what was going to happen, but I knew one thing. If I did go, at least Ivy had people to help her get through it.

CHAPTER SEVENTEEN

Dinner and Discussion

Ivy

There was nothing like spending the day with my mates and the rest of the pack. After the warm invitation I had had from a few of the female wolves of the pack to join their play group, I was more than thrilled to entertain the idea.

Kate and my mother had suggested familiarizing myself with other women of the pack would help me be a better Luna.

I was so nervous about the idea of them accepting me. Differing from them, I had spent months watching them gaze at me with wary eyes.

I had thought they perceived me as a monster, but in the end, I was wrong.

There would always be women in the pack who didn't like me. I expected that. It was the same in the real world. Not everyone is going to like you, but I was pleased these women could accept me as I was.

I wanted to be a Luna they respected and wanted around.

After a fun eventful day, I made my way with James, Hale, Talon, and my mother back up to the house to prepare for dinner. The smiles and conversations still on our faces from the fun we all had.

If only Damian had graced us with his presence, then it would have been complete.

"I cannot believe that you spun that little boy around like that, Hale." We made our way through the front door and I laughed. "I thought he was going to puke."

"Hell no, he was having the time of his life. Plus, his mother didn't seem to care, so why ruin mine and the boys' fun?"

He did have a point, but as I looked at him with a small smirk on my lips, I couldn't help but picture him with our children.

"Perhaps that's true, but he was still so tiny, and I cannot believe that he didn't cry. He just laughed and laughed and kept wanting you to do it again."

I had never really seen Hale in his kind of way, but seeing him like this made me excited for the future. He was going to be a good father. I had no doubt about that.

Even James and Talon were more than pleased with being able to spend time with the kids that were there. With things being quiet lately around the borders, the guys had a little more free time, and I was grateful for it.

Passing Damian's office, I watched Kate and Damien come out with expressions of concern across their faces. Something was wrong, and that was obvious.

"Is everything okay with you two?" I asked as I tried not to show I knew something was wrong. Kate's eyes quickly met mine as she forced her frown away.

"Oh yeah, don't be silly. Everything's fine. Just talking about pack stuff back home is all." Kate lying wasn't something she did, and because it wasn't, she was horrible at it.

However, I let it slide. If she wanted to tell me, she would.

Letting my eyes slid from Kate to Damian, I raised a brow staring at him. His dark chocolate eyes gazing at me with a ferocity I had grown accustomed to seeing.

Our conversation hadn't gone the way he had planned previously, and I felt guilty for making it seem like I didn't care about him because I did. I just honestly didn't know what to do.

This was something far beyond me, and with my inexperience, I wasn't sure how to handle it. The only reason I knew how to help James was because of the mate bond healing him. It was clear the bond was hurting Damian instead.

"Everything good?" I asked him as Kate stepped around me, making her way down the hallway towards the kitchen.

"Yes. Why wouldn't it be?" he replied without hesitation.

Shrugging my shoulders, I smiled at him. "Fair enough. I'll go help with dinner then."

There was no point in pressuring him for information he would not give me. Doing that would be pointless, and I wasn't about to make pointless conversations cause arguments. At least not right now.

In the end, we would all need to be honest with each other. We promised no secrets, and yet we all seemed to keep them.

As the night carried on, we all sat down and enjoyed dinner together with light laughter and conversations about what was to come for the rest of the week.

Not to mention baby names.

That was a subject I didn't even want to speak with the guys about.

Through all of it, though, Damian sat quietly watching. He was a mysterious man at times, and even though I loved him dearly, I couldn't help but feel I was missing something extremely important.

There was something I just wasn't getting.

"So, Damian, what are your plans for the rest of the week?"

My calm response seemed to catch his attention, and as he looked up and met my gaze once more, he shrugged his shoulders. "I have some business that I have to attend to, but as soon as that meeting's over, I will be back and more freely able to take part with things around here."

"You mean you're actually going to take a vacation?" James scoffed as laughter quickly flowed from the brothers.

"I suppose if that's what you want to call it, then yes. Ivy is due to have the baby soon, and I want to be here to participate."

A smile grew wider on my face when I heard him. My eyes stared at him in disbelief. Little by little, every day, Damian changed into somebody I could barely recognize.

At times he was cold and distant, but even those days were far and few between. Instead, he was warming up to the idea of our happy family being able to be whole, being able to live in harmony.

He wasn't fighting anything anymore, and it still caught me by surprise every day.

"Well, time to clean up this stuff. I have reruns to catch up on," Talon said quickly, breaking the silence at the table.

"If you're talking about reruns of that stupid romance show, I am absolutely not watching that," Kate responded quickly, causing Talon to look at her in absolute shock.

"There is nothing wrong with that show. I don't know why you're acting like this."

"What do you mean there's nothing wrong with that show?" Hale replied.

"I mean exactly what I said. Why are you guys acting like this?" Talon snapped with disgust on his face. "That show is brilliant."

Talon was not the kind of man you would expect to watch something like that, but in reality, even though he was dangerous at times... he was also a giant teddy bear.

"Talon sweetie, the reason why they find it shocking you enjoyed that show is because of the kind of person who you are. You don't seem like someone who would watch such things," I butted in.

"All right, all right, I get it," he huffed, rolling his eyes as he slid his chair back. "Regardless, that's what I'm watching, so can we get this shit taken care of?"

As everyone stood from the table, my mother remained back with me. A smile on her face as she stretched her hand across the space between us, placing it upon mine.

"Honey, can I just say that I am extremely happy for you being here?"

"You're happy for me being here?" I asked with a small smile.

"I am as much as I hate being you being away. The day that I found out that they were your mates, I knew that you just had to be here. Even when you were a little girl, you showed such potential to be so much more than you were, and I couldn't believe it. That you could be mated like that. I couldn't believe that I could, but then I met Blake."

Tears slowly filled her eyes as she forced them back.

"No, mom, please don't cry. You know I love them and I love you and I wish that we were closer, but I know that you have a life there. Moving here wouldn't be an option for you."

"I know, but perhaps I can convince Blake to want to move." My mother laughed, and as I heard Kate yell from the kitchen, that was not happening.

It turned out that Blake was actually Angel's uncle, and the only remaining family that he had. If Blake left, Angel would try to make it to where Kate had to move as well, and Kate, as much as she enjoyed visiting Idaho, was not excited about having to move here.

With the conversation over, my mother and I stood to help the others. Yet, I could feel Damian staring at me and, as I turned around, I saw him standing there. His eyes were fixated, and a gaze that I found almost unreadable.

Until he gestured for me to follow him.

I wasn't sure what he was going to say, but I was intrigued.

"Are you okay?" I said, as he pulled me into the living room.

"Yeah, everything's fine. I just wanted to apologize for the conversation that we had before. You were right. If I honestly think that something is wrong like this, I need to speak to someone who would know how to handle this. I shouldn't expect you to handle everything just because of who you are."

"Damian, you don't have to apologize—" I whispered before he held up his hand, causing me to stop talking.

"Let me finish, please," he whispered as he took a deep breath. "I found somebody who can help me and I'm going to see them. I spoke with Kate earlier and told her the idea that I had, and she persuaded me to let you know what I was going to do."

"Is that the business meeting that you have to have? Were you going to try and keep this from me?" I asked, shaking my head in disbelief.

Why would he want to hide something like this? It just made little sense.

"Yes, I know. Please don't get upset with me, Ivy. I didn't want to tell you because I didn't want you to get your hopes up. I didn't want to tell you that everything could be ok and in the end, we find out that it's not." He replied, making my heart slowly fall.

"Damian, you're not going to leave me and you're not going to die. I love you too much for that. You are a big part of my life, and even though our relationship started out rocky, that doesn't mean that it has to be that way again."

"I know it doesn't," he said as he reached up with his hand and brushed the hair from my face behind my ear. "That's why I'm telling you, because I don't want there to be secrets."

Stepping forward, I wrapped my arms around him, pulling him close to me. His chin rested upon my head and slowly I inhaled him deeply, relishing in the smell of his cologne. Each one of the guys had their own particular scent.

And Damians was the most unique out of them all.

"When are you leaving?" I asked him, after a moment's silence that had passed between the two of us. If he was going to leave,

I wanted to know when, I wanted to know where, who he was going with, and how long he was going to be gone.

It was just how things worked when you were in a relationship. You let people know this kind of stuff, so they knew where you were and that you were okay. Even if, at one point in time, I didn't actually give him that kind of satisfaction.

Chucking, he lifted my head to look up at him, and slowly he kissed my lips. "I leave bright and early in the morning before you wake up, and I shouldn't be gone more than a day. But I will let you know when I get there, and I will let you know when I'm on my way home."

Hearing his reply, I felt a little satisfied.

Of course, he didn't exactly tell me where he was going, but I knew with him there were some things he couldn't quite explain and he would always have a good reason for why he couldn't.

"You better not forget to tell me when you get there," I said teasingly before he leaned down and kissed me once more.

"I won't. I promise to let you know, and just to show you how serious I am about keeping my promises, I will have words with my brothers about the current situation."

"You promise?" I asked with wide eyes, slightly shocked that he was going to actually go into detail with them about what he thinks is going on.

"Yes, I promise I will actually go do that here in just a moment. In the meantime, why don't you go upstairs, take a nice long bath or hot shower, get yourself relaxed and perhaps you can sleep in my room tonight?"

Biting my bottom lip, I glanced up at him and nodded my head. It wasn't too often I actually got to share a room with Damian simply because he worked crazy hours and I was often gone sleeping with the others.

With him, I didn't honestly get to spend that much time.

Tonight, though, I would change that because there was no telling what tomorrow would hold.

CHAPTER EIGHTEEN

Betrayed & Captured

Damian

I wasn't sure what to expect, but everything Kate had told me in my office kept swirling through my mind. The entire evening I had spent with Ivy and the others, I couldn't help but think how Kate was right.

I needed to be honest with Ivy. I couldn't keep hiding the truth.

I didn't explain everything, because there were some things too hard for me to explain, but I did let her know what I was doing. I told her I was going, and it was to help fix whatever the hell was going on with me.

Ivy deserved to know, just in case something bad happened.

I didn't want her thinking my demise was her fault. I loved her more than I realized.

Before the sun had risen across the horizon, I had slipped from my bed where Ivy laid sleeping and prepared to leave. Walking around the room, my eyes kept darting to her angelic sleeping figure.

She was extraordinarily beautiful in every way possible, and even though she didn't find herself attractive with her massive protruding belly... I did.

In fact, knowing she was pregnant with our children made her that much more desirable. I couldn't get enough of her, and through the evening I showed her as I pleased her like no other.

Expressing my love for her... in case I wasn't able to again.

As I prepared myself to leave, I found it hard to go. The thought of leaving her was excruciating. Especially because I knew there was a chance I may not come back.

Letting out a heavy sigh, I leaned over, kissing the side of her head once more. My lips lingering just a moment longer than they needed to before I pulled away and made my way towards the bedroom door.

Was I actually doing the right thing or was I being selfish by leaving?

I was constantly conflicted and had been for days since I had found the woman who supposedly could help me. It wasn't easy moving forward with what I was doing, but I just kept reminding myself I was doing this for the sake of the pack, for the sake of Ivy, and for the sake of my unborn children.

Leaving my bedroom, I quietly shut the door so as not to disturb her and made my way down the hallway. After my conversation with Ivy last night, I did go talk to my brothers, and I told them exactly what was going on.

They were in shock and disbelief over the situation, saying it wasn't possible, but in the end they knew I wouldn't make something like this up. If I said it was true, then it was. Talon wanted to come with me in the end.

To have my back, protect me if I needed it, but that wasn't possible.

I had sworn to the woman I would come alone.

She was an outcast in hiding. An enemy of the council that would be killed if she was found, and though I had found her, I promised I wouldn't give her up.

She didn't trust me, and she had every right not to.

Could I possibly be walking into a trap? I had asked myself that many times.

However, I refused to break trust with this woman if she was the only one who could help me get answers to whatever was going on.

Climbing into my car, I didn't waste any time as I made my way down the road towards my destination. It was over an hour away and still dark outside, so making pace, I let the wheels of my black sedan push forward with force propelling me down the road and onto the highway.

The entire time I drove, my mind kept playing over everything that had happened since the moment Ivy had walked into my life. Fate had brought her to us, and with fate we would eventually see what our future had in store.

By the time I slowly began to reach my destination, I pulled off onto a dirt road that lead through a heavily wooded area. When she said seclusion, she wasn't wrong, and as I drove forward, I couldn't help but feel uneasy.

The more and more I thought about it... the more it felt like a trap.

Yet, when the road finally gave way to a clearing in the center of the forest, my eyes landed upon a small brick and wood cabin nestled beneath the trees. Smoke billowed from its chimney while candlelight flickered in the windows.

It was a very ominous sight to behold, but considering her life of seclusion, I almost expected more. Perhaps dead carcasses and vines seemingly unhinging the area.

Yet, there were none. It was old, but looked like someone had dropped here it.

Putting the car in park, I stepped onto the dirt drive, closing my car door behind me. With every footstep I took closer to the door, I predicted what my outcome would be. That was, until the door opened, and I was faced with an old crone of sorts whose hair had grayed but eyes looked far younger than the outside appearance.

"Vivian?" I said, clearly with slight hesitation.

"You came," she smiled.

"I did, and I came alone just as you told me to."

"I see that. That was wise of you. I do not take kindly to having people at my home who are not invited. I'm sure you can understand why." Holding the door open for me, she allowed me to step into her home before closing the door behind me. Her body seemed more frail than it should be.

"I do understand," I replied as I watched her make her way towards a chair placed by the fire. "Your gifts are highly sought after, and the council would not have any problem of relieving you of those gifts if they had the chance."

Hesitating for a moment, her eyes met mine as she slowly nodded in agreement. "So you want to figure out why you are losing your wolf?" She gestured for me to take my place in the seat across from her.

"Yes, I can feel that something isn't right. I don't know what it is, but I can feel it and I know I am dying."

A small chuckle left her lips as she stared at me curiously. "That is both correct and incorrect."

"Would you care to elaborate on that?"

After all, I was here for answers, not to be told riddles. If I wanted riddles, I could have stayed there with Priscilla and eventually had hoped I figured everything out.

Not drive an hour away by myself to be made to look like a fool.

"I can, but if I explain to you the truth, you cannot change the fate that is coming for you. I want you to realize you cannot alter your destiny. You must let it take its course."

Taking a moment, I froze in my thoughts, hoping she was simply joking, but after a moment, I quickly realized she was not. "You say once you tell me what you know, even if I wanted to change my fate, I wouldn't be able to."

"Yes. That is correct," she replied. "Your fate is sealed and what I see will come to pass, no matter the way you look at it. It is best that you try not to alter the course and let what is going to happen."

"Very well," I said after a moment of letting that information sink in. There was nothing like being told your future is sealed and no matter what you do, you're not going to be able to change it, which obviously means you are going to die.

I knew this day would come, though. I knew I would not live long enough to see my children grow. And while that may be the truth, I will listen to what this woman had to say, regardless.

They say knowing your future is a privilege, but I find it to be a curse.

Knowing you're going to die, knowing the reason why, knowing the events of what is going to happen and not being able to change it is not a blessing.

It's nothing but a curse, and one you're doomed to fulfill.

"Damian, your wolf is not dying, but... you are going to die. Everyone dies eventually. The issues that you have, though, are far greater. Your Lycan is gone... stripped from you when you protected your brothers from the creature. What you remember of your past isn't true."

"I'm sorry... what? You're saying that my memories are false?" Hearing myself ask this question out loud made me feel crazier than I already was.

All I remembered from that day was my mother's dying and unleashing a power within me that stopped the darkness. Everything else was stuff Allison had told me in bits and pieces.

"That is correct. The information you were fed for all these years was lies, Damien. They were all lies. But I cannot tell you which was true and which were lies. That is something that you will have to figure out yourself."

"I understand, and you said I'm not dying. Then what is wrong with me?" I asked, hoping for clarification.

"You're a very impatient man," she chuckled, her gaze boring into me behind calculating eyes. "I can see your mate has her hands full with you. However, she was accurate when she said that your wolf could not die because you are a werewolf...."

Furrowing my brows in confusion, I stared at her.

How the hell would she know Ivy said that to me?

"Don't look so surprised. I see everything... Well, almost everything anyway. So I know what has happened and what has not. Your wolf is not dying. What happened is the power Ivy possesses was released and currently only slowly because of her certain circumstances, but you and your brothers help her sustain it."

"I see," I replied, pondering over what she was explaining. "How is it we help her sustain this? My brothers are not feeling the same way that I do. They were actually quite shocked at what I was describing."

"That is because they have their Lycan blood and soul. You do not. Yours was stripped from you. So, therefore, you do not have that power to help channel hers. Which is why, in turn, over time, it will end up killing you. The power will be too much."

"So my link to Ivy is going to be what kills me. How much time do I have? Are we talking months, days, weeks, years?" Fear crept through me slowly, like twisting vines.

I wasn't afraid to die, per se. I was afraid of Ivy finding out that she was the reason I was dying. Everything we had done to complete the circle, and everything we had gone through, was what was killing me.

If she knew the truth, she would never forgive herself.

"You misunderstand me. That could allow you to die, but that is not how you died, Damien. Your death is one that changes the world. Unfortunately, I cannot see beyond that day for you." A glimmer of amusement in her eye caught my attention and for a moment, I found a sense of uneasiness wash over me.

"What do you mean?"

"Unfortunately. If I give you that information, then I will meet my own end. What I can tell you is that you go out beautifully and with a purpose." The moment the words left her lips, the front door flew open, and as it did, I jumped to my feet.

However, it was too late.

By the time I could even take a step forward, I was shot with tranquilizer guns, and my vision quickly went blurry as I dropped to my knees.

"What is going on here?! We had a truce, witch!" I growled in fury.

She had betrayed me, and even though I had gotten some information from her, it didn't matter. Black figures moved about the room as one, in particular, walked towards her, handing her a scroll. "Good work, you're free."

"Thank you," she replied before the figure turned towards me with a wicked smile.

I couldn't believe she betrayed me, and as I looked up into the figure's dark eyes, I recognized him immediately. It was Alokaye, the man who had tried to take me before.

"This will not stand," I snarled at him.

However, my display of aggression did nothing. Instead, he dropped into a crouching position next to me and smiled. "I told you I would see you again. I bet you weren't expecting this one, were you?"

CHAPTER NINETEEN

Arrival of New Blood

Ivy

After a wonderful, wonderful evening with Damian, I couldn't help but find myself in a rather pleasant mood when I woke up the next morning. I took extra care getting myself ready and couldn't help but notice how large my protruding belly had become. For the first time in a long time, I was happy. I felt absolute contentment with how my life was.

To think I had my reservations about everything before seemed silly now. After last night with Damian and me talking about everything I knew, without a doubt, things were going to be better. I had even taken it upon myself to open up a little bit about myself.

However, there was still far more to discuss, but I didn't want him worrying about any of that while he was taking care of his problems. Instead, I planned to discuss it with Hale, Talon, and James first.

Then when Damian got back, I would tell him as well.

Today I was a woman on a mission, and with not much time left in my pregnancy, I needed to make haste to make sure that we were all on the same page. Hopefully, they would understand why I have done the things I have done.

As my feet touched the ground from the stairs, I smiled happily, swaying my dress from side to side as I made my way towards the kitchen in search of food. I was ravenous, so ravenous I couldn't contain myself.

However, Talon and Hale had stocked the freezer and fridge with a variety of things, and my hunger was more easily satisfied.

"You seem to be in an absolutely wonderful mood this morning," Kate laughed out as she came walking into the kitchen, dripping with sweat and holding a water bottle in her hand. It was quite obvious she had been working out this morning.

"Did you literally just get done with training?"

"Sure did," she said with a grin. "You know, after you have those babies, you might want to take up training as well."

Now, I wasn't the prissy kind of girl, but I also wasn't the athletic kind of girl either. I did not take interest in anything requiring me to physically exert myself. I was a bookworm; my go to for fun. The idea of running and getting sweaty and working out wasn't anything that piqued my interest.

"Yeah, I don't know about that one. I think I might have to take a rain check."

Kate laughed as the twins walked into the kitchen, staring between the two of us, silence filling the air before Talon furrowed his brows.

"What the hell's wrong with the two of you?"

"Nothing," I replied, shaking my head. "Kate was simply trying to express the fact that she thinks I should start working out after I have the babies."

"I was referring to you doing training. Thank you very much. Everybody needs to know how to defend themselves."

"Oh well, we don't have to worry about that, Kate. You see, Ivy doesn't need to defend herself. She simply eats them," James retorted as he popped his head into the kitchen, grabbing an apple off the counter and a bottle of water from the fridge.

I couldn't believe he had gone there with that comment. "Oh my God, that literally happened one time and you guys are never going to let that go, are you?"

Every single one of them shook their heads no. There was no way they were going to let me forget what I did. It had now become an ongoing joke, even though it was not something to joke about.

With a heavy sigh, I ignored their jokes and attempted to climb upon the stool at the counter. The only problem was, as I tried to lift a foot, a pain ripped through me I had never felt before, and with it, a blood-curdling scream tore from my throat.

This was not labor, no way. My heart raced, and my head felt like it was being split open with every move I tried to make. "Make it stop!"

Kate's eyes were wide, and panic had set into them all. None of them had the slightest clue what was wrong, but as I dropped to the ground, Talon caught me, and looked over at me with nothing but concern.

"What's wrong? Is that the babies?" Talon asked as the others towered over me.

"No!" I screamed in pain, trying to push away whatever was hurting me. "It's burning. My body feels like it's on fire and my head is throbbing. Please make it stop."

Confusion marred their faces. Talon eyes were frantic over my body, worried for a moment before he seemed to have a sign of recognition flicker within his eyes.

A sign that made my heart plummet. Deep down, I knew something was wrong.

However, I ignored it. "It's Damian. Something's wrong with him. He's in trouble."

Talon nodded his head and as he did, another fitful pain ran through me as I slowly tried to get myself up. The problem, though, was that a puddle of liquid was running down from between my knees puddling on the floor.

"Oh, shit!" Kate screamed as my mother stared on in panic. "Her water broke."

"What do you mean her water broke?!" James said in panic. "She still has two more weeks, right?

Two weeks? Right now, the only thing I wanted was for the pain to stop radiating through my body. I was concerned about the twins, but something inside me told me they would be okay.

"I need to get upstairs," I groaned in pain.

"No, you need to get to the hospital," my mother snapped as she looked at the guys, gesturing for them to get me up.

"No!" I growled as my gaze turned towards her. "It's not safe. Get me upstairs now."

My outburst took aback my mother. Never once had I ever spoken to her like that, but right now, something inside me was telling me to be careful. Telling me I had to stay here and not leave.

Something was wrong, and if Damian was in trouble, that meant someone had gotten to him. The last thing I needed to do was put myself at risk my leaving the safety of my home. The goddess told me to listen to my instincts, and that was what I was doing.

"James, go run her a bath," Kate said quickly before turning her gaze to Talon and Hale. "Can you guys carry her up there? I'll grab some towels and herbs."

"Kate you can't be serious?" my mother gasped as everyone around me started moving and preparing to take me upstairs to have these children.

"Yes!" Kate snapped, glaring at my mother. "We aren't human if you haven't noticed. A she-wolf knows what she can handle, and if Ivy wants to have the babies here, then so be it. She knows more about what is going on than we do. So you can help or move."

Kate wasn't wrong about all of this. My mother had no clue, and nodding her head, she turned to me with a frown. "What can I do?"

Another scream of pain, and I groaned out, trying to push it away. "Get me Priscilla."

Time seemed to fly by, and before I knew it, I was naked in the large tub in my bathroom screaming pain once more, but now from the labor I was going through.

My children were coming, and there was no stopping them.

A wave of power seemed to creep through me, and as the pain ran through my veins, I knew what was to come. Like a door that had been locked for so long, it was finally wearing thin. Finally breaking.

"Did you find, Damian?" I gasped as my eyes darted to Talon. "He needs us."

"You need to worry about the labor you're in, Ivy. Damian will be fine."

"No, he won't!" I growled. "Where is he?!"

Screaming again, the crown of the child's head pressed down on me. Gripping James' hand in one, and Hales in the other, I pushed with everything I had.

"That's it!" Priscilla yelled. "Keep pushing, Ivy. I can see the head."

Breathing through it, I pushed harder, and within in a moment the first of my children push free of me. "Oh, my god. It's a boy!" Kate cried out as I panted with exhaustion.

Reaching down, Priscilla held up the cord, allowing James to cut it. The child pulled from the water and wrapped within a blanket as Kate and my mother cleaned him until he cried. He was huge... bigger than I would have expected, and a smile crossed me seeing him.

"That future Alpha of our pack," Talon said proudly as tears slowly fell down his cheeks.

Kate didn't hesitate to hand the child to Talon, and before I could say anything else, I felt the contractions start again.

This was it. One more to go, and with my son now born, I felt a surge of power coursing through me making my heart race. Something was about to happen, and I wasn't sure what it was, but I had to worry about my daughter now. Taking a deep breath, I screamed through it and pushed the small babe from my body until she was free.

My daughter... blood of my blood, laid between my legs.

Without hesitation, I pulled her up to me with the cord in view for Hale to take care of. She was much smaller than her brother, but as she cried, so did I.

I had done it. I had given birth to my children, and even though one of my mates wasn't here, the situation was perfect. "I did it." Everyone was looking at me.

"You did, sweetie," James whispered in my ear as he kissed the side of my head. "You did it, and they are beautiful."

"I can't believe it," I whispered as I kissed the top of my daughter's head.

Talon moved towards me and handed me my son so I could hold them both while Priscilla took care of cleaning me up and draining the water.

"You still have to decide their names, Luna," she hummed with a smile, and I knew she was right.

For a long time I considered the names of our children, and while the guys have been helpful in giving suggestions, none were ones I wanted to stick with. I wanted to wait until my children were born to give them their names.

I never understood how you could pick someone's name before actually laying eyes on them. What if the name you picked no longer matched them?

Staring down at my children, I was quiet as I stared between the two of them. My son was strong already and looked just like his father. Even though they didn't want to know who the father was, I could tell.

Dark hair and a strong unwillingness to cry, it almost brought tears to my eyes to know and not tell them. They didn't want to know.

As for my daughter, she was petite and gentle. Nestled into my chest, she suckled gently while her brother slept.

"Pollux and Castor," I breathed as I stared at them.

Those were the names of my children, and I knew they would live up to them.

CHAPTER TWENTY

Back from the Grave

Damian

Waking on the cold ground, I took in my surroundings. After hours and hours of torture, I couldn't take any more and had quietly slipped into oblivion. It was clear I had been placed in the dungeon of whatever building they had taken me to.

The damp smell of the air filled my senses, causing the sweeping feeling of nausea to flow through my body. Alokaye had tricked me. He had come after me, even though he had seemed satisfied with Ivy's response before.

Deep down I knew for a fact he wasn't done with me, and even though I had known that, I let myself get carried away hoping to save myself. I was a fool, and looking around at my confines, I now understood now how much of a fool I had been.

Placing my hands upon the floor, my wrist shackled with silver, I pushed myself up into a sitting position and groaned at the pain surging through me as I moved. At least the silver reminded me of what I was.

Otherwise, I wouldn't be as affected.

The words of the woman in the woods burned into my brain. I wasn't dying per se, but I wasn't living either. At the end of the day, my relationship to Ivy had been both a blessing and a curse.

The creaking sound of iron doors opening caught my attention in the darkness. Turning my gaze to the left, I looked up towards the long, dark staircase waiting for my tormentor to approach me again.

Alpha Richard was the man who had taken pleasure in tormenting me for hours. He was convinced I was the one who had killed his son. That there was no way a woman had taken down the son of an Alpha.

Especially one who had no prior knowledge of our ways.

Little did he know, though, Ivy was not any ordinary woman, and even though the whispers through the halls of the building said so, he refused to believe it. He refused to believe some girl who didn't even know a thing about our culture could outwit and outsmart him.

As the footsteps approached, I glared at Richard's shadowed figure as it stepped into the light. He didn't seem as pleased now with being here as he had been hours before. Instead, he seemed uncertain, and as he moved towards me, he hesitated.

Furrowing my brows, I heard the shuffling of feet, and spotted Alokaye approaching from where Richard had come. "Ah, good. You're awake."

"Yeah, you could say that," I croaked as I lifted my burning wrists to show the blood still slowly pooling around me. "I don't think I would give these accommodations five stars, though."

Laughter escaped Alokaye as he nodded. "It pains me to see you like this, Damian. You are a great alpha. The problem is, you have a habit of not listening to what I tell you. We all know Ivy was the one who killed those people. She is a threat to us all."

A scoff echoed from Richard's lips as he crossed his arms over his chest.

"What's wrong, Richard? Do you find it hard that even Alokaye believe a woman is capable of something like this?"

"Go fuck yourself, Damian." Richard snapped. "If your mate did it I will kill her."

"My mate didn't kill anyone! Instead of acusing her you should be out there finding the murderer."

Alokaye glanced over his shoulder at Richard and laughed. "You think this idiot wolf is the one who actually killed the three people in that cabin? Do you honestly think that Damian would have been able to kill a Nephilim?"

"A nephilim?" I replied, narrowing my brows.

"Oh, she didn't tell you? I'm sure that she knows, considering she has such a close connection with the gods, they would have told her what she did. Yes, your dear mate ingested Nephilim. Disgusting, isn't it?"

Alokaye seemed absolutely delighted by the notion, even if that was problematic. Those creatures were rare to find, and even when they were found they were typically used for the raw purity they possessed.

"If you know that I'm not the one that killed them, then why am I here?"

Hesitating, he seemed to think over what I asked, and slowly he nodded his head from side to side before shrugging his shoulders.

"I can see where you would be confused, but that actually is a surprise. Patience is an important attribute to have. In time, you will get the answer you seek."

His words sent a chill down my spine I didn't recognize. For hours I had been trying to reach my brothers or even Ivy, but with the silver in place, I was unable to.

I wanted to reach out and warn them to tell Ivy I loved her, that I was sorry for the things that had happened, and I should have listened to her. I wanted more than anything to travel back in time and never leave the pack, but of course, that was not the path I chose.

"Then get on with it, Alokaye, stop playing games, and finally explain what it is you want, because you and I both know that I'm not leaving this place, so what's holding you back?"

Running his tongue over his teeth, he took a moment before his smile grew wide.

"Perhaps you're right. Maybe I should get on with it. Although, if I rushed into what I wanted to do, there was a chance I would fail. I have to wait for the perfect moment to make my move."

Groaning in frustration, I rolled my eyes and looked down at the bloodied floor beneath me. Was it honestly hard to get a straight answer nowadays?

"It's always the same with you people," I muttered, shaking my head.

"What's on your mind?"

Taking a moment, I let laughter escape me as my eyes looked up to meet his again.

"Do you really want to know what's on my mind?"

Alokaye smirked, nodding his head. "Yes, actually. Please enlighten us about what intrigues you."

"Okay..." I chuckled, readjusting the way I was sitting. "I think you're both ridiculous. I don't think either of you knows what's going on, and honestly, I don't think the council knows I'm even here. So instead of the bullshit, take me to someone who knows what the fuck is going on."

Richard growled, taking a step forward as if he wanted to strike. Yet he stopped when Alokaye lifted his hand. "Very well. If you want to know exactly what is going on, then I will give you that much information."

He didn't waste time gesturing for two guards to grab me. Their rough manhandling as they moved me from the dungeon towards the stairs had my jaw clenched in pain.

"Where are you taking me?" I seethed as my eyes met his briefly.

"To get answers, of course. That is what you wanted, isn't it?"

Staring at him for a moment, he turned back in front of me and continue walking. The stairs were longer than I thought, but as soon as we stepped from the dungeon, I was blinded by the light of the halls. The crisp white coating making me flinch back in protest as I was taken down long white corridors straight for a set of double doors.

The same double doors my brothers and I had gone through once before.

"Don't look so shocked, Damian. If you honestly think that the Council has ever been on your kind side, you are sadly mistaken."

Pushing the doors open, I was dragged inside before the elders and dropped onto the marble flooring. The blood dripping from my body slowly pooled on the floor, drawing gasps from the elders I hadn't expected to hear.

"What is the meaning of this?" The Grand Elder said as glared down upon me. "Why is Damian in the state he is in?!"

My current state outraged the Grand Elder, but as Alokaye stepped forward, I had a feeling it wouldn't last very long. "Damian helped in the murders of elder Harrison and the son of Alpha Richard. I brought here him to seek his punishment."

"Lies," I snapped as I let out a low growl.

"You will hold your tongue, Damian. I will speak with you in a moment." The Grand Elder replied as he turned his gaze back to Alokaye. "What proof do you have of this to accuse the Alpha of something this severe and punish him from the looks of it without approval?"

"I have plenty of proof."

"Damian, what do you have to save for yourself?" The Grand Elder asked, turning his attention back to where I kneeled upon the cold ground.

"They are lies, Grand Elder. I had nothing to do with those murders, nor did anyone in my pack. The elder left our pack perfectly healthy, and Alokaye was given proof of that. Richard is simply using this as an opportunity to kill me. He wants my land and my pack."

"Lies," Richard growled, hitting me. The blow caused two guards to hold him back and the Grand Elder looked down on him in disappointment.

"You will refrain from touching him. Do not make me cast you into the same position that he is. Everyone is allowed a fair trial, and I demand to see the proof."

"It's proof you want, your honor. It's proof I have. Not only do I have proof that Damien's mate was the one who had killed those three people in the cabin, but I have somebody who can testify against his nature that he has slowly lost his mind, considering that he is no longer whole."

Alokaye's smooth words seemed to go over well with the council, but my mind blanked, trying to think of who would be a witness. There is nobody outside of my pack that knows of Ivy. Nobody except the elder counsel, of course. Everybody had heard words, but Ivy had met none of the people that were there.

So who in the hell could he possibly have someone who would have known me when I was younger and known Ivy when she got her powers?

With my mind rattled, I waited to see whom it was Alokaye had on his side. His eyes peering towards the side door of the room as a blonde figure I hadn't expected to see waltzed in as if nothing bad had ever happened to her, and smiled.

It was Allison. A woman who I had long thought dead stood there with a wicked grin on her face, staring at me.

"That isn't possible. She was sentenced to death. Why is she still alive?" I growled in anger as I tried to stand to my feet, to have only three guards hold me back to the ground.

"I stopped her sentencing," Alokaye said with a grin across his lips as he looked down at me. "She had a much larger purpose, and it was to prove that you and your pack have committed great sins."

"You cannot believe a thing this woman says," I yelled out, turning my attention to the council. "She has lied and manipulated the system for many years, and she even allowed her own mate to be killed in the process. She is the worst kind of woman and she cannot be trusted."

Silence befell the council, and as they stared at the situation before them, they seem completely confused. "I think we should deliberate and reconvene on this in the morning."

"Of course. That won't be a problem," Alokaye said.

The Grand Elders' words seemed to please Alokaye, but before the Grand Elder left with the others, he stopped, turning back to Alokaye, and frowned. "If I see him in the dungeons again, we will have a problem. He is still an Alpha and should be treated as one before being judged."

"You're giving him a room?" Richard sneered as his angry glance looked upon me. "He is a murderer."

"Enough from you Alpha Richard. We will decide this tomorrow. Until then, he will be treated as I say. This is my choice. Do you challenge my authority?"

Richard hesitated for a moment before shaking his head and stepping back, remaining quiet. There was no reason to say anything else when the elders have made their final say. The best thing to do is to be quiet and accept it.

At least for now.

"Did you miss me?" A soft, wicked voice said in my ear as I realized Allison had slowly made her way towards me while the elders' words distracted me.

"Go fuck yourself," I snapped, watching as she laughed at my comment with nothing but amusement in her eyes. "I will kill you if I get the chance."

"Well, I guess it's a good thing you won't. I told you before, Damian, you won't win."

CHAPTER TWENTY-ONE

Longing Captivity

Ivy

Twelves hours had gone by since I birthed my children, and even though everything was perfect on that front, my mind kept going back to Damian. Talon and Hale went out to his last location only two hours ago, and every moment they were gone, I panicked.

I couldn't feel my connection to Damian anymore, and as my mind tried to make me think the worse, I couldn't allow myself to.

I had to stay strong.

I had to believe he was alive.

The pain I had felt earlier in the day, before I had given birth to my children, was unlike any pain I had ever felt before and it didn't take until the pain subsided for me to realize it wasn't labor pains I was feeling.

Instead, it was the pain being inflicted upon Damian and because I was bonded to him in a way nobody could explain; I could feel every infliction.

I cried and cried for hours after the twins were born. Pleading with Hale, Talon, and James to allow me to go to him.

I could feel the bond weakening, but they just simply said it was in my head.

Something deep inside me, though, told me his life was ending, and I couldn't allow that to happen, not after everything we had fought for since I had arrived.

It was constantly the back-and-forth motion of love and hate and fighting and confliction and secrets and lies and I was done with it. I was done with all of it. The only thing I wanted was to be with my mates and my children and be whole, be normal.

With the protection of the pack, we were a united front.

The only problem was outside forces sought to destroy us because we were different.

No matter what they said, though, I was not a monster. I was a normal person with unique abilities and a large heart able to love more than just one man.

I wanted to be the Luna this pack could be proud of, but I was so devastatingly misunderstood I didn't know if I could ever overcome and be what they wanted me to be.

Pushing away my fears and thoughts, I kept a wary eye out on the horizon, waiting for two of my mates to arrive, praying Talon and Hale would go to this cabin in the woods and find Damien there.

Find him alive... Maybe slightly wounded, but still alive.

Deep down, though, I knew that wouldn't be the case. I knew without a doubt who had him, and I was terrified because the person who had him wanted nothing more than to see his head on a spike.

And, eventually mine, right next to it.

"Ivy, you must eat something," my mother said softly as I looked out the window of the nursery, scouring the horizon for the return of my mates.

"She's right," Priscilla added as she stepped closer. "You may be worried, but your twins need you, and placing all of your concentration on things you can't change doesn't help them."

With a heavy breath, I turned from the window to face the two women who had helped keep me together over the past few weeks. "I know."

Letting my eyes sweep towards the two small bundles freshly cleaned and sleeping in their beds, I couldn't help but find myself at a loss for how I had created something so beautiful. Something so angelic.

"I don't want them to never know him," I whispered, forcing back the tears that threatened to fall. "I have been such a fool lately."

"Ivy, this isn't your fault," my mother replied as her hand fell upon my shoulder. "The gods have things planned for us, and we must accept the fates they choose."

"No," I snapped, shaking my head as I wiped away a loose tear that had escaped my eyes. "I refuse to believe he is dead. He will be back soon."

Silence fell around us as a soft knock on the door drew my attention. "How are we doing?" James asked with a smile spread across his lips.

"I'm okay. Just worried—"

Clearing the space between us, he wrapped his arms around me and kissed the side of my head. "He isn't dead, Ivy. I can still feel the connection as his brother. It's just faint."

Looking up at him, I held back a sob. "What does that mean?"

"Oh, Ivy, don't cry. It means he is alive, but they are using silver to dull his senses."

"See, you have nothing to worry about," my mother added, trying to reassure me. "You need rest."

There was no way I was going to sleep, though. Pulling back from James, I went back to the window and continued to stare out over the horizon. Until my mates were home, I could not feel comfort.

"I need them all back, James. Until they're home, I won't find peace."

Something deep inside me was growing, and every moment my mates were a way, I felt it sending me into a spiral I didn't know if I could come back from. It was just another piece of the puzzle that left me confused.

"We must do whatever it takes to bring him home," I said.

"We will, Ivy," James said firmly. "But we won't be able to do our job if we are worrying about you. So I need you to rest and eat so I know that you're okay."

Nodding my head slowly, I moved from the window and walked towards my bed. After having the twins, I needed something of Damian's to calm my racing mind, and the only thing I found comfort in was the bedding from his room James had brought to me.

Laying upon my bed, I wrapped myself in the blanket, and closed my eyes.

I didn't have to worry about the twins, and them being okay. With my mother, Priscilla, and James here, I would be able to rest. At least for now.

Damian

Dragged down the hallway after I met with the Elder Council, I was tossed into a white room and locked in. The silver shackles upon my wrist had been removed, but then an injection of silver had been placed in my veins.

It didn't matter what I did. They were going to prevent me from reaching out to the others. Realizing I had no form of communication made my heart sink. I would have given anything in that moment to contact them to make sure the pain I had felt from Ivy wasn't because of the pain I had received.

My eyes swept around the room, taking in the all white decor and the blood that was slowly dripping from my body onto the floor.

I was creating a mess, but it was a mess that the elders had caused.

That Alokaye and Richard had caused.

That stupid prick Alpha was going to meet his end if it was the last thing I did. Even in my weakened state, my brothers were not forgiving.

And Allison—I couldn't believe she was still alive.

To know they had spared Allison's life for something so meaningless as an accusation I had murdered somebody, or that someone from my pack had murdered them and I was protecting them, was absolutely ridiculous.

I mean, yes, I was protecting Ivy.

She had killed those people, but that didn't justify the right for Allison to still be alive after everything she had done, after the betrayals and pain she had caused, not to mention trying to kill Talon.

That woman was evil, and no matter how they tried to spin this, I would find a way to break free and kill her. I would rip her to shreds... unless Ivy did it first.

Nothing was what I would be able to do until I got rest.

My energy was absolutely depleted, and I desperately needed a shower. Making my way towards the bathroom, I turned on the hot water of the shower and stood beneath it, letting it wash away the grime and dirt upon me.

Multiple lacerations and cuts marred my body, and I knew without a doubt they would heal, but the pain was mentally inflicted by them would always remain.

I had been careless and had not thought about the consequences of my actions thoroughly before I trekked out on the journey to find that creature.

Now, in the mayhem of everything, Allison was going to get her way of destroying the pack and taking it over for herself.

That was the only thing she had ever wanted: power and authority.

She may have had it for a short while when Zane was alive, but the moment I came of age, everything started becoming a complication. At first she complained about me and after months and months of trying to prove I was unfit to take over, she started coming on to me, wanting me to see things from a different light.

It was disgusting how she acted and I was repulsed by her, but out of respect for the things she had done for my brothers and me, I had allowed her to live back then. If I knew what I knew now, back then I would have done things completely differently. I would have ripped her apart the moment I turned eighteen.

Cleanly dressed, fresh from the shower, I sat on the edge of the bed and waited to see if somebody would come to the door. From prior stays here, I knew it was close to dinnertime, or at least that's what I had assumed by the things I had seen in the hallways on the way to the room.

If it was, it meant they should bring me food soon. I just wasn't entirely sure who that was going to be. I had a chance. A chance to break out of this place, and even in my weakened state, I would fight that, the last breath, to get home to Ivy.

When my waiting seemed to be never ending, the sound of voices floated towards me from the other side of the door.

"Why is he being treated like a guest?" the feminine voice said.

"Because that is what the Council wants and you will do well to listen to them. If this is going to work, we need them to believe us," Alokaye replied with a voice I knew distinctively.

"It isn't fair, though. This isn't what was promised to me."

"It doesn't matter what you think is fair, woman. You will do as you're told. At the end of the day, when the Solstice moon rises, things will be righted," Alokaye replied as if he was seething in anger at the question she was asking.

It took me a moment of processing before I realized the female speaking was Allison. For her to be acting this way, it meant she wasn't at the top of the information pyramid, and that itself was curious.

Whatever they discussed revolved around the moon that was to take place in a week's time. What did the moon have to do with me?

Slowly the voices died down and the echoes of their footsteps drifted away. Left reeling with questions, my brows narrowed in confusion.

Whatever they were planning was directed towards my pack, and the longer I was away, the more unprepared they would be. I had to protect them.

I had to get out.

My pack... my brothers... my mate and children... they all depended on my escape.

Chapter Twenty-Two

A New Alpha

Hale

Three days had passed since Ivy had the children, and Damian was pronounced missing. I wasn't sure what to expect, but I stepped into my role as alpha of the pack to ensure everything ran smoothly.

We had gone to the cabin where the seer was Damian supposedly met. It wasn't hard for us to find the location with the information he had left on his desk. However, as soon as we got there, it was clear the woman had been long gone, which was lucky for her, considering I would have torn her to shreds to find my brother.

The disheartening feeling of coming home empty-handed wasn't something I wanted to do again. The look in Ivy's eyes when she threw open the front door only to find that Damian wasn't with us... it haunted my mind.

"Have there been any recent signs?" I asked Talon, who walked through the door of the office looking grimmer than he had the day before.

"No, but I do have patrols watching the borders expecting the worst if it comes to it. We have to find Damian. Have you seen the state that Ivy is in?"

I had seen the state of her.

Every single day she refused to eat the right amount of food or get the right amount of rest, and every time we tried to force her to do it, she would snap as if she was slowly losing herself.

For the first time in my life, I had questions I didn't have the answers to, and it burned a hole through my heart, knowing there was nothing I could do right now to help Ivy. We knew who had done it. We knew the Council had Damian, but without proof, we couldn't just storm in there and accuse them of something.

"I'm at a loss for what to do to help her. She's spiraling, and the only time I see her smile is when she's with the twins. She is happy and content one minute, and then it's like someone flips the switch as soon as they're asleep. She becomes unstable."

Talon stared at me. His facial expressions were unreadable, but I had no doubt in his mind he saw the same things I did. "What do you want to do, then? We have to find a way to be able to help her."

Talon was right. We had to help her. I was just at a loss for how to do that. It was hard trying to decipher what was wrong with her while trying to also find my brother.

Letting a heavy sigh escape me, I shook my head. "There's been nothing that's been brought to the border, no sort of message or anything."

"It's only been three days, though," Talon replied. "If they were going to come, they would have surely come by now. The only thing I can think of is the Council didn't do it and someone else is behind it."

Talon's reasoning had crossed my mind more than once, but I didn't want to be so hasty as to believe the Council was actually on our side. They weren't pleased by the outburst that had happened the day we were all taken to court before.

I have thought about that situation a million times over. Tried to contemplate what exactly was going to happen, but every single time I searched for answers, I came up empty-handed.

"I can help with that," Kate said from the open doorway as she stared at Talon and I with determination on her face. I hadn't even realized she had gotten back from her trip. The day after the children were born, she had made her way back home in search of answers from her own family.

"Did you just return?"

"Obviously, I'm glad to see that the two of you are happy to see me," she replied in a sarcastic tone as the corner of her lips turned up into a small smile.

"Did you find anything out, anything at all that could be useful?"

With a tight-lipped expression, she glanced down at her feet, rocking back and forth as she shook her head no. "In all honesty, they didn't want to let me come back."

"Yet you're here, anyway. What changed your mind?" I asked, confused why she would come back if her mate and her family had told her not to.

"Nothing changed my mind, Hale. I was planning to come back regardless of what they said. Ivy is my friend and you guys have become like family to me. She needs me here, and she needs my help whether or not she chooses to see it right now."

"Well, do you have a plan in mind? Because being the alpha isn't something I'm particularly good at. I'm a book nerd. Talon deals with patrols, James helps with training. Damien was always the one that ran everything. And yes, I knew some of what he did, but I was nowhere as good as he was. So any kind of help I can get right now would be brilliant," I sighed as I plumped down into the chair behind the desk.

Laughter escaped Kate as she smiled at me. "You do make a very good book nerd, though."

Of course, that would be what her response was.

Standing still for a moment, she stepped forward. "Look, the Council knows I wasn't here when the murders happen. I have an alibi, and I didn't arrive until the day the Council came seeking answers from you..."

"Okay, but what do you suggest doing?"

"I could go there," she replied, shrugging her shoulders.

A scoff left Talon's lips before the laughter erupted from him. "Angel would fucking kill us if he knew we allowed you to go there."

"I guess it's a good thing I came with her then," Angel said as he stepped up behind Kate. A smile spread across Talon's face upon seeing Angel.

Through the time Kate and Angel had been here before, Talon and Angel had formed a wonderful friendship and kept in touch with each other often. I was happy for Talon because he honestly didn't have many friends.

"It's good to see you, my friend," Talon said happily as he pulled away.

"We can take care of the situation," Angel replied. "Kate and I will head to the Council, scope it out and see if we can find anything. It wouldn't be abnormal for us to go there to pay our respects while being in town. Alokaye may turn around and think something's up, but the Council would toss the idea out the window."

Angel had a point. He and Kate could go up there and the Council would have no reason to suspect them of anything. It was times like this I wondered if I could really do this type of job.

I may have been an alpha, but I wasn't the oldest and I wasn't trained for this, and every day Damien was gone reminded me how much I should have paid attention to what he tried to teach me when I was younger.

"All right, then the two of you can leave at dawn. That way, it'll give you enough time to get up there as the morning sun rises, make your way around and get out of there before anybody really notices you."

"How's she doing?" Kate finally said, speaking up softly. "Is she talking much yet?"

Once again, silence enveloped us, the tension high as I cast my gaze towards the window. Ivy had spoken little in the last three days unless she was talking to the twins, and even then it was baby talk and cooing.

I wished more than anything to see the light of joy in her eyes once more. But now, when she gazed out staring out the window as if expecting for Damien to come strolling back up, I saw nothing but pain and sorrow.

"She is great with kids. They are everything to her, but outside of that... she isn't herself. Something inside of her is changing."

I wasn't sure what it was, but Talon knew exactly what I meant. There was something within our bond that it was changing.

"I'll see if I can talk to her. Start the conversation out slowly and see if she opens up to me." Kate's offer made me smile. Perhaps she would have better luck.

As soon as Kate, Angel, and Talon left the office, and the door was closed, I rested my head within my palms, and tried to understand where I had gone wrong.

We had gone from exotic moments of sexual bliss to chaos that consumed us. A battle for her. The loss, the love, the reuniting, almost bringing death and now? It was as if everything we had gone through was for nothing, because everything was shattered once more.

More than anything, I couldn't wait for the day when things would be normal. I didn't understand what evil out there could cause so much complication for our relationship. Never had I ever heard of wolves that went through the things we do.

It was honestly beyond ridiculous.

I wanted my mate back.

I wanted my brother back.

Deciding I would turn in for the night, I stood up from where I sat, turning off the small lamp at the desk and made my way out of my office, closing the door behind me.

I didn't get far, though, before I ran into Priscilla, coming out from the kitchen, a hot cup of tea in her hand and a low, concentrated look upon her face.

"Are you retiring for the evening as well, Priscilla?" I asked her, trying to be polite and keep the conversation.

She stopped in her tracks, taking a moment as she processed my question, her eyes gazing up at me with an intensity. "I'm actually taking this cup of tea up to Ivy. She's currently speaking with Kate."

A sense of understanding washed over me, realizing Kate didn't miss a beat when it came to the opportunity of trying to make Ivy feel more at home, considering our current circumstances.

"That's good. Hopefully she can get answers to the questions that we cannot. Why is it you looked so troubled, though?"

Priscilla was a very mysterious woman, and while my brothers were not as observant as I was, I could tell she was not saying something that may have been important.

Her wrinkled expression creased up as she smiled at me, a clicking of her tongue as she looked off down the hallway and then back at me once more.

"You have always been the most perceptive of children," she said as she let out a small sigh. "I've had visions lately and the visions I've had are not good. There's something brewing on the horizon and unfortunately, I cannot see past that future anymore."

Her words weren't as riddled as usual, and the concern was etched in her eyes. I'd never once heard her say she could not see into the future any more.

"That doesn't make any sense. What do you mean you can't see past what's coming? You're a seer who sees the future."

"Trust me, boy, I know it is my gift. However, things have changed. Fate has changed, and with it, I can no longer see past what is coming." There was a hidden meaning behind her words, and I couldn't understand why her gift would deny her the ability to see the future.

If I wasn't as worried before, I definitely was now. Priscilla was the seer of our family. The secret we hid deep within our own bones. She was the unwanted child of mates who were more complicated than usual and with her life, she had given us great reason to live.

CHAPTER
TWENTY-THREE

Losing Control

Ivy

Burning fires, distant roars, signs of blood, and many more.

These were things that filled my mind every time I closed my eyes, and though I sought comfort and love that I had for my children, I felt incredibly vulnerable.

It had been three days since I'd had the children and three days since I had even touched Damien. He was still not home and my heart broke every moment he was away.

Some might think I was being selfish because I had three more mates here that doted on me endlessly and wanted my attention, but the problem was, it was hard when part of you was missing.

I wasn't trying to be complicated.

I wasn't trying to ruin the relationships that I had. Everybody seemed to think I should just be okay, but nobody knows what it's like to have a piece of you torn away.

To have someone you love taken from you, and not knowing whether they are alive or dead. That feeling was incredibly raw.

One moment you're trying to pretend you're okay, and the next you're sobbing.

"Hey, you," Kate said, knocking on my door. I hadn't seen her since the day the babies were born. She was full of life, but when we found out that Damian was taken, she headed back home in search of answers.

"You're back," I said with a small smile as I stood from where I sat and wrapped my arms around her, embracing her and her hug I feared would end.

"I told you I'd be back now. Where are my little babies at?"

With a small giggle, she strolled over towards the crib and looked down at the two sleeping babies within. They were beautiful in every way, and I was still amazed every day at how lucky I was to have them.

"Castor is the sleeping beauty, as always. But her brother Pollux does not enjoy sleeping for more than three hours."

Kate smiled down at them, but then turned to me, wrinkling her nose. "I still cannot believe that those are the two names that you chose. Castor is such a boy's name and Pollux, are you trying to have the poor kid picked on?"

Laughter erupted from my lips for the first time in days, and as it did, I watched James pop his head around the corner, staring at me with surprise.

"Holy shit, how did you make her laugh? I've literally been trying to do that for the past few days."

Wide-eyed and brows raised, she stared at him, absolutely dumbfounded by his outburst. "I asked her why she picked those baby names."

Realization dawned on him, and as he looked at the children, he shook his head and shrugged his shoulders. "I've literally tried to talk her out of picking those names and sticking with them, but she is adamant that those are the children's names and so, therefore, I will not argue with her."

"They're not that bad. Castor can be shortened to Cassie, which I'm sure that she will go by and Pollux is a strong, sturdy name and if he really wanted to shorten, he could shorten it to Polly, which is unisex."

Kate stared at me in disbelief, absolutely speechless, as James sighed at my response.

"Yes, but that is not the only reason you named them that," Mom called from the other side of the nursery where she was folding baby clothes. "Why don't you tell them the other part of the reason why you name them that?"

Shaking my head, I had breathed out heavily and took a seat back in the small rocking chair I had near their crib. My eyes falling onto my sleeping children.

"It was a dream that I had. They were the first set of twins born in Gemini. Their bloodlines are strong and if you pay close attention, you can feel the power that they have within them…I can't explain it."

"So they're Gemini twins?" Kate muttered, scrunching her brows as in confusion. "That's impossible. There haven't been Gemini twins in what—"

"In the last one hundred years," Priscilla said as she walked through the door with a cup of hot tea. "Sorry it took me so long, my dear Hale had a few questions to ask me."

Taking the teacup from her, I smiled and gave her a silent thank you. The steam from the piping hot liquid filled my nostrils, and I closed my eyes, sighed in satisfaction.

"This smells absolutely delicious."

"Oh, it is, and the herbs infused in the tea will help to loosen you up and clear your minds so that you can sleep."

I knew Priscilla was right, but the problem was every time I closed my eyes, I saw Damian dying. I knew it was my mind tormenting me because I was so concerned, but to picture him on a boulder as a sacrificial lamb being slaughtered, it was a horrible sight to behold.

"I will try to get some sleep. The problem is, is whether Pollux will allow me to get some sleep."

Everybody in the room chuckled and my mother smiled, standing to her feet as she walked towards me. "Did you express milk today like I told you to do with the pump?"

Staring at her for a moment, I nodded my head slowly. I had a breast pump, but being a new mother, it just felt so unnatural to me. Even though it was super convenient, I enjoyed the feeling of having my children nurse from me. Having my body supply them with an ability to live.

"I did. I stocked just like you said. There is enough for tonight, and tomorrow morning."

"Good," she replied with a smile on her face as she glanced at Priscilla. "Priscilla and I will take tonight's feeding shifts with the milk that you've stored. You will sleep and not wake until morning."

"That's easier said than done, mother," I scoffed as I lifted the teacup to my lips.

"It isn't as hard as you think, and instead of trying to deflect the situation, try to accompany it and agree."

There was no winning with this woman. She refused to leave, no matter how many times she had talked to her mate Blake. He was growing impatient, but she told him if he was so concerned, he could come up here.

"Oh, speaking of that, I wanted to let you know that your mate sent me with parting words to give to you," Kate said as she turned to my mother, whose eyes narrowed slightly before she crossed her arms.

"Is that right? And what were those words?"

"He simply said that if you don't come home, he is going to come here and drag you home, regardless. He wants your one-on-one game night fun. Whatever the fuck that means."

A twinkle in my mother's eye caught me off guard, and I knew exactly what that was a reference to. "Kate, you literally just passed a sex message," I said nonchalant, watching as Kate's eyes widened and a look of disgust crossed her face as she glanced between my mother and I.

"OK, that's just absolutely fucking disgusting. I am not your sex correspondent person over here. You two need to learn how to figure out your arrangements."

Laughter filled the space around us as we enjoyed Kate's disgust over what she had just done. Moments like this were the ones I looked forward to.

"I know that you're trying to keep my spirits high, but I have to know... did you find anything okay, Kate?"

The change in conversation seemed to bring silence to the room. Each of them looked at each other before Kate sighed. "I wasn't able to find anything, but we have a solution."

"Solution? What kind of solution?"

"Angel and I are going to the council at dawn," She said, catching me off guard.

"No," I said quickly, shaking my head. "It's dangerous... you can't, Kate."

"Hey, it's going to be okay."

"I said no!" I roared, jumping to my feet. Those in the room jumped back from me in fear. "I will lose no one else to these people."

"Ivy, my love..." James said softly with his hands in front of him as he stalked towards me. "I need you to take deep breaths and calm down, please."

"Don't tell me to calm down."

"Ivy. Look at yourself... like actually look," James said, causing me to flinch at the tone of his voice. Unsure for a moment, I let my eyes cast towards a mirror hanging on the wall. The reflection was one I didn't recognize, and flinching back, I gasped.

My eyes were no longer the celestial blue, but pitch black and my hair a flaming white with tendrils of darkness spreading across my body.

"What's wrong with me?" I whispered, trying to understand what was going on. However soft cries caught my attention and turned my focus towards the crib.

As if a switch and been turned off, all the anger and fear washed away from me, and quickly I made my way towards Pollux picking him up. "It's okay, don't cry."

"Ivy, how long has this been going on?" Priscilla asked from where she was standing.

"I have never seen that before..."

It wasn't a lie. I had never done that before, but it didn't matter. My baby needed me, and the time to visit was over.

"Ivy, this is important. It's clear to everyone that things are not well with you right now. Your emotions are all over the place. You're changing... not eating right—" James replied.

I knew he was right. I didn't understand the feelings I was having, and deep down I felt something inside me growing that was different from before.

"Something's wrong with me, but I'll be fine. We need to find Damian."

Turning my back to them, I was done with the conversation. There was nothing else to say, and even though I knew I needed to take care of myself, I refused to think about be right now.

The only thing I could think about was making our family whole and getting revenge on those who had harmed us. No one could deny what happened to Damian.

I had felt his pain, and as the darkness deep inside me slowly grew, I found a new determination. One that would lead me on a path of war if it must.

I would kill anyone who betrayed me, and I would protect everyone I loved.

CHAPTER
TWENTY-FOUR

Prisoner

The next few days went by slowly, and as they did, I slowly followed further and further into the darkness, unable to bring myself up. I wasn't sure what I was getting myself into with everything going on, but I had without a doubt, the darkest of feelings.

Every day not knowing if Damien was safe was a step putting me one step closer to completely losing myself and the only thing holding me grounded were the twins silently sleeping upstairs in their crib.

I was an utter mess. A complete disaster.

Making my way downstairs, I tried to push away the darkened thoughts evading my mind. Heading toward the kitchen the indistinct murmurs of conversation drew me to a complete stop as I turned and watched the many figures through the cracked open doorway and Damian's office.

What the hell?

"We have to tell her what's going on," James said softly as I watched him gaze towards Hale, whose back was towards me, staring out the window as if in deep thought.

"No," he replied firmly letting out a heavy breath. "We all saw how she's changing and you, James, of all people, saw first hand what Damian not being here is doing to her. Since she had the twins, she's completely different."

Hale's response broke my heart just a little. He was never the one to keep information from me, and hearing him tell James not to include me hurt. I didn't find myself to be completely different, and yet he was acting as if I was turning into some kind of monster.

"This isn't right. It was delivered to the border for her. We need to let her see it." Talon all but growled, stepping forward, his fists clenched at his side. He was obviously angry, and I wanted to know more than anything what he was referring to.

What had been delivered at the border they didn't want me made aware of?

"It may have been delivered for her, but the thing is, I am the acting alpha right now and I do not see it in her best interest to read this shit, Talon. It doesn't matter what they say, we cannot give in to their demands."

Tired of listening to what they were talking about, I pushed back the anger threatening to lash out if they made one more comment about me. Its shadows twisted and rolled through my veins as if seeking an outlet.

Pushing open the doorway, I stood there, watching as their eyes turned to me. Kate's face fell as she seemed to pale. I hadn't even realized she and Angel had made it back from the council land yet, but here she was, standing there with a grim expression on her face that spoke a million words without even saying anything.

"What is going on here?" I asked, narrowing my glance as I stared at each one of them. "We don't hide secrets, so somebody needs to start talking."

"It's nothing, Ivy. Honestly, just some bullshit. Why don't you head back upstairs and get some rest?" Hale replied as he turned to me with a small smile, stuffing whatever paper it was into his back pocket, as if I wouldn't notice.

"Don't talk to me as if I'm a child, Hale. I'm going to ask you one more time to give me whatever you just put into your pocket that was supposedly addressed to me per your conversation. Before things get worse."

My warning was clear. If there was something he was hiding from me, he would face my wrath, mate or not. "Ivy—"

"No," I said firmly, clenching my fists at my side. "Don't you dare act like this towards me after everything we had been through?

Stopping in his tracks, he stood staring at me with a grim expression across his face I had never seen before. "This isn't up for discussion. My word is final."

When the hell did Hale decide he was going to act like this? I knew Damian had made him the acting alpha before he left, but that was no reason for Hale to let this go to his head. "Don't you dare act like that towards me?" I growled.

I watched the tick in his jaw as he gritted his teeth. The beast within him lurked just beneath his skin. "As I said. You have seen certain sides of me, but don't think for one moment I will let you speak to me this way. I'm doing this for a reason."

"Hale, come on, man," Talon said softly as he and James looked at me with soft eyes.

There was clear hesitation in Hale's eyes as he looked around at everyone in the room. I could see he didn't want to involve me, but everybody staring at him was clear enough of an answer that he needed to.

With Hale distracted, I didn't waste another moment as I quickly snatched the paper from his back pocket and took a step back. A low growl came from him as he reached for it, trying to take it back from me, but the cold glare I gave him made him hesitate in his movements.

He didn't want to fuck with me right now, because I was not in the mood.

Slowly opening the letter, my eyes peered down at the information and my heart almost stopped. It was a letter from the Council and they were requesting my presence in order to exonerate Damien from anything that had happened with the elders, stating they knew for a fact I was the one who killed those people.

If I didn't reply or show up in person, then Damian would be sentenced for the crimes committed, even though they had no proof of who had done it.

"What is the punishment for this?" I whispered softly, without looking up at the others.

"Ivy—" James replied as if he didn't want to say it.

Glancing up at them with parted lips, and my eyes filled with tears as I tried to registry what was going on. "What... is... the punishment?"

Hale stared at me for a moment for letting out a heavy sigh staring down at me. "Death."

I looked at Hale, Talon, and James in absolute disgust. They were willing to let Damian die for something I had done, and then hide it from me.

"Are you fucking kidding me? You weren't going to tell me about this? He is basically on death row for something that I did!" The betrayal ran deep.

How could they do this to me? How could they not want to inform me?

"We will not allow you to go in there like the fool and cause yourself to get caught. It's a trap, Ivy. They will not kill him," Hale snapped with anger in his eyes.

"I'm a fool? Are you really going to go down that road with me? I have done nothing but try to make this work. You're my mates and I understand you want to protect me, but if you honestly think I am going to allow Damien, who is also my mate, to die because of something that I did, you are sadly mistaken."

Turning on my heels, I push towards the door, not sure of what I was going to do, but knowing I had to do something. At least give them a reply, and then settle my twins before going there.

They couldn't hold me. I destroy them all.

However, I wasn't quick enough. Talon wrapped his arms around me as I thrashed about, kicking and screaming at him to let me go. I couldn't believe they were actually doing this, that they were going to let him die for me.

"Let me go right now, Talon!" I screamed even louder as Talon tried to help hold me back.

"Ivy, you have to stop. You can't go. You have children to think about. They cannot afford to lose their mother. Are you freaking insane?" James cried out in aggravation.

I didn't want to listen to them, though. It was my fault this had happened, and the council was giving me less than forty-eight hours to respond to their sentencing or else he would be killed.

"We have to save him," I cried repeatedly, my mother standing in the doorway with tears in her eyes. They didn't know what it was like to lose a mate.

None of them did, and it was as if no one understood how much pain I was truly in.

Held back against my will, I watched as Priscilla whispered something in my mother's ear and then watched my mother disappear up the stairs, more than likely towards the children.

Kate disappeared right behind her, as if unable to watch what was about to happen before her. As Priscilla stocked forward, though, she looked to Hale and nodded her head. Some secret untold agreement between them I wasn't privy to.

"Ivy, unfortunately, I understand how hard this is for you. But you cannot be given to them. It is part of the plan, and I need you to trust me when I say they will not kill him. They will not kill him because he is the bait they need to get to you." I didn't want to listen to her. No matter what she was saying, I couldn't listen to her.

"Bait or not, I am not going to let him sacrifice himself for me," I replied as tears streamed down my cheeks. This was the most agonizing thing I was ever having to go through.

Knowing I could save him, but also knowing they would not allow me to do so.

A rush of tingles crossed over my skin, and as I looked out the window, I watched a strange woman I had never seen before walking the perimeter of the house. A blue cloak over her head and sapphire eyes staring back at me.

"Who was that?" I asked, watching as Priscilla's gaze turned towards the window and then back to me with a small smile.

"Unfortunately, that is an insurance policy that we had to make."

Insurance policy? What the fuck did she mean that was an insurance policy?

As James and Talon lost their hold on me, my eyes darkened over as the power and rage ran through my blood. Throwing James aside, I bolted towards the door only to be thrown back five feet when I met an invisible barrier.

"What is this?" I screamed as I stood up, banging against the barrier once more, only to watch the blue-cook-cloaked woman walk towards me, her dark black hair hanging loosely over her shoulders with a sorrowful look upon her face.

"Hello, my queen," she breathed. "My name is Alvandra from the fae realm. We have allied ourselves in a way with your family. I feel for you when it comes to my mate because I to have lost my own, but this isn't about you. It's about your people."

Staring at the woman in disbelief, I smashed my fist into the barrier once more. "Unleash me now or you will see what I think about alliances," I growled as I felt the darkness wash completely over me.

The woman seemed slightly startled by my comment as she glanced towards the men I knew were staring behind. "I'm sorry, m'lady. I can not. This is to protect everyone."

She didn't give me a chance to say anything to her again before nodding her head and vanishing into thin air. "No!" I screamed as my legs collapsed from under me, and I sunk to my knees. "Please let me out."

"Alavandra is from another realm, Ivy. What is going on here is drifting elsewhere, and has become much bigger than you can hope to imagine."

Priscilla's words weren't comforting. Damian's life depended on me, and while I knew the fate of the pack did as well, I couldn't just let things go.

"Ivy–" Hale said softly as he dropped to his knees behind me. "I'm sorry... please forgive me for what I'm doing, but I promised him I would keep you safe no matter the cost."

I was speechless, and with a broken heart and tears flooding down my face, I didn't reply. Instead, I stood to my feet, slowly staring off at the woods that bordered our world from civilization and wept. I wept for the man I loved, and for the fate that was coming.

But most of all, I wept for the future that wouldn't happen.

I knew my mates were trying to protect me, but I would tear apart the realms to get him.

CHAPTER
TWENTY-FIVE

Waking a New Lycan

Damian

For days I stayed locked within that room, food being brought to me occasionally, until at last I was brought back before the Council and staring up at them and utter disbelief to what they were saying.

My heart breaking with every word as I realized there was nothing I could do.

"Damian, we find you guilty. However, judgment has been sent to your pack that, if for some reason, Ivy, your mate, the Luna of your pack, did in fact kill those people, she can take your place during the reckoning."

The Grand Elder seemed almost robotic in nature as I watched him speak with no single sense of emotion; Alokaye smirking in the distance. His eyes trained on the Grand Elder as Allison's eyes were focused on me with utter disgust.

What the hell was actually going on?

There was no way they could punish me for something I didn't do, and even though Ivy had done it, there was no way I would allow them to punish her. She was my mate, and I would protect her with my last dying breath.

All Ivy did was protect her people—her pack and family—from those conspiring to cause them harm. It was what any Luna or Alpha would do in her situation.

"This is absolutely absurd. You are sentencing an innocent man to death while trying to hold that death over an innocent woman who did nothing wrong," I yelled at them, my roar echoing off the walls as the people looked at each other with confliction.

"Elders, I ask upon you to not let this situation go. Even with his death his brothers and mate are a threat to our ways. We must stop them before they try to destroy us all by killing him. We must confront the problem at it's root," Alokaye said as his words flowed off his lips like silk.

"What is it you suggest Alokaye?" another elder questioned as their eyes stared at him with suspicion. "Are you suggesting the council declare war with the largest pack in the country?"

"Yes, actually. I am."

Shocked whispers flooded the entire room, and with them I thought surely this couldn't be the response they would agree upon. War was never the answer, and what happened wouldn't have been basis enough for it anyways.

"What plan of action would you have?" the Grand Elder asked with a curious glint in his eyes as he leaned back within his chair watching Alokaye closely.

"It's very simple, honestly. We hit the pack when they are at their weakest. The summer solstice. They will celebrate as packs always do, and we will strike out against them."

"Are you kidding me?" I yelled once more, jerking against the chains that bound me. "You cannot do this. We are innocent. There are women and children there. They are all innocent and have done nothing wrong!"

"Enough!" the Grand Elder bellowed. "Your pack's fate is not my problem. They followed you and that woman they whisper about, the false god. She is no god, and I will not have her brainwashing the people with such nonsense."

"You're listening to a man who is lying. Alokaye has no real proof!"

A blow to the back of my head had me seeing stars, and as I steadied myself I peered up into the cold glare of Alokaye. "If that is the case then your mate would have replied by now in order to bring herself forward instead of leaving the suffering of the innocent at the hands of the council. Do you think they are fools to be blinded by your arrogance?"

"What I think is foolish is to listen to a man who doesn't even seem like a man, one who is seeking his own retribution and his own salvation," I spat.

"You dare mock this court!" the Grand Elder yelled, standing to his feet as he slammed his hands against the desk in front of him. "Who do you think you are?"

Slowly I stood from my place on the ground where I had been knelt. The power of the chains holding me down were not enough, and though I was weak, I was still strong at heart. "I am Damien, the Alpha of the North, and there's no way I'm going to allow you to kill my mate or take my pack."

Laughter consumed a small voice to the side, and I realized it was Allison who was laughing. Taking small steps towards me, she bowed her head at the Grand Elder and then turned her glance once more in my direction. "Who said about killing her? It's you that's going to die."

"What?" I muttered in confusion not understanding what was going on.

Leaning closer to me she whispered. "When she unleashes her fury on the world, he will be free... it all starts with you dying first. Funny how things work in the end."

"Who will be free?" I asked her, searching for any answers that I could get.

"Oh, that would ruin the surprise," she whispered. "I can't wait to see her face."

Lashing out, I tried to hit her, bite her in anger. However, she moved out of the way laughing. The elders stared at me with disdain in their face at the actions I had taken.

"It seems that you still are hell bent on causing problems," the Grand Elder said clearly as he narrowed his gaze at me before turning his attention to Alokaye. "Do what you must, but do it with grace."

"NO!" I yelled loudly as the guards gripped my arms pulling me back as Alokaye bowed his head to the elders and turned towards me.

"Take him back to his room, and stick him again. We leave in two days."

Ivy

Darkness fell outside, and as it did, I couldn't help but find the sorrow because I was a captive in my own home. Prevented from leaving no matter how much I protested and tried to make them realize we could make this work.

That we could do this without me being put at risk.

It was pointless though. They were all determined to protect me and the children. Making sure that they held me behind a barrier I couldn't break no matter how much I wanted it to be.

After hours of crying, and hot concoction Priscilla gave me, I drifted off to sleep.

It seemed like hours went by where I tossed and turned in the dark dreams I had. Dreams of watching Damian die before me, and being unable to save him. Unable to do anything to try and get to him.

"No!" I cried out softly as I jolted from my sleep dripping in sweat as I peered into the darkness realizing it was just another dream. I was speechless, and with the eerie darkness in the room and the silence within the house, I cast my glance towards the nursery and saw the twins silently sleeping.

Their bodies laid peacefully next to each other, and not far away was my mother fast asleep. She had made it known she would help with the children whether I wanted it and I tried to protest, but now I was grateful.

As much as I wanted to be the perfect mother, I was a mess.

How was I supposed to be the mother I wanted to be for the twins when all I could do was think about things I couldn't actually change?

Sliding from the bed, I considered going to get a drink. Though when I made my way outside of my bedroom door, I felt a wave of heat rush through me that took my breath away. "The hell..." I muttered softly, placing my hand upon my chest.

Something inside me was pulling me down the hall away from the stairs. I hesitated, but when I did, I felt the heat grow higher inside me. With reluctance I let my body follow the draw leading me down and around the corner until I came to a halt in front of a bedroom door.

It was James' room.

Like a tether binding me to his room, I opened the door and stepped inside. A rush of uneasiness washed over me giving way to a clarity I had never felt before. Closing the door and locking it, moving towards his bed slowly.

With every step I took, I felt the power growing with in me. The desire to prey on him was like a force I had never felt before. *Captive.*

It was the only word that rolled through my mind. I was a captive in my own home, and while they thought they were protecting me, they weren't. It was I who had to protect them, and I would in whatever way I had too.

Tantalizing desires coursed through my veins, and as I stepped closer, I pulled the blanket from him, slowly letting the sight before me of his naked body spur a fire in my core that had to be quenched. It was a thirst, a primal hunger that pushed me forward.

James didn't know what was to await him.

He laid peacefully, sleeping, unaware of the monster lurking within his room. Unaware of the danger he was in, because the darkness inside me was clawing to escape. A sweeping wave of wind blew around me as I let the nightgown I was wearing slowly slide from my body onto the floor.

"James," I whispered softly watching him stir in his sleep. My hands ran across his bare skin until his eyes opened slowly.

"Ivy—" he murmured as I climbed onto the bed, straddling his waist. My hips rocking in circles as I ground myself against him feeling his thick erection spurring to life.

"I need you, James," I said in a seductive tone that seemed to float within the air.

As his eyes finally focused on me they widened in shock. "Ivy, what are you doing—"

"Can't I claim my mate as he once claimed me?"

"Ivy—" he muttered as my lips brushed against his. "Your eyes... you're not you."

"Oh, but I am," I grinned as I bit playfully at his lip.

A moan of satisfaction left him as I slid my wet, tight cunt over his thick erection, letting him penetrate me in such a slow movement by the time his entire length was buried inside me, it felt deeper than it ever had. The sensation caused me to gasp, and as I did something inside me came to life.

Reaching out I gripped his throat. My claws extended and my teeth bared as I rode him hard and fast. "Ivy—oh fuck. God you're fucking amazing."

He grabbed at my hand as I continued on. "It's time for you to awaken, James."

"What?!" he gasped out as I felt us both coming closer and closer to our peak. "Ivy, you have to stop... what's—"

Moaning loudly, he came, and as he did, I opened my mouth and bit down into the side of his neck, feeling the spark of something deep inside him awaken as our connection strengthened even more.

His cock twitched inside me as a low growl left his lips, and darkness swirled within his eyes. "Ivy—"

"Shhh..." I whispered. "It will be over soon."

Slowly a roar left his lips as he shifted beneath me into the lycan he was meant to be. My claws were no longer enough to contain the power within him as he pushed me back sitting up with a carnal hunger in his gaze. "Mate."

Small laughter escaped me as I kissed him. "Welcome, Adnan. The last of my champions. It's time to join your brothers."

With them, I would take back what was mine and leave a wake of destruction in my path. The council wouldn't stand a chance.

Nor would the evil hiding behind them.

CHAPTER TWENTY-SIX

Freaking out James

James

Sitting at the kitchen counter the next morning, I stared off into the abyss, thinking about everything that had happened last night. Ivy had come into my room and rocked my world as she usually did, but she called forth something that I couldn't explain.

A feeling that overwhelmed me, and like a passenger in a car, I was forced to take a back seat while something else moved forward. Thinking of it now, how whatever it was moved with Ivy in sexual pleasure all night long, slightly haunted me.

My Lycan was brought forth, awoken from its slumber and I wasn't sure how it had worked for my brothers, but for me... it was completely done in a sexual nature.

And now that it was awake, I could feel it underneath my skin.

Waiting to break free.

Cackling in the back of my mind.

"Hey, James," Talon exclaimed happily, causing me to jump six inches off my chair as I spun around, staring at him with wide eyes.

"Don't do that."

Laughter escaped him as he stared at me with an odd smirk, furrowing his brows. "What the fuck is wrong with you?"

"I don't want to talk about it," I replied quickly as I tried to divert my attention back to the cereal now soggy in the bowl in front of me.

How was I supposed to explain to my brothers what had happened? How Ivy was acting was completely unnatural.

It was like she was her, but also not.

As Talon stared at me, I tried to ignore his gaze, but then Hale came bounding into the kitchen with a smile upon his face and an empty bottle in his hand. He had taken shifts this morning with Ivy to feed the twins. We kind of rotated it just to make it fair, seeing as I spent most of my time with her and them, and they didn't get to that often.

I was grateful, though, for the rotation this morning because honestly, I didn't think I could face her. After what she had done with me last night... I was in shock.

Whatever was inside me, she put it back to sleeping and just left, and I laid there in the dark, staring at the ceiling, trying to wrap my head around what the fuck had just happened.

"What the hell is the matter with him?" Hale replied, causing me to glance up as he and Talon exchanged curious looks.

"That's what I'm trying to figure out. I came in here and said hey and he jumped out of his seat as if the boogeyman was after him."

As their eyes both turned back towards me, Hale stepped forward, raising a brow, and placed the bottle down on the counter. "What's wrong?"

"Nothing's wrong. Why would you think something's wrong? I'm perfectly fine."

"Cut the shit. I can tell something's wrong with you. I haven't seen you this fucking nervous since the day you lost your virginity," Hale replied, causing Talon to snort with laughter as he crossed his arms over his chest, giving me an amusing look.

"Fuck you. Tracy Ann was a complete fucking psycho bitch, and you, Talon, were the one that set me up with her," I snapped at him, narrowing my gaze as I crossed my own arms over my chest, trying to show him he couldn't get underneath my skin.

Not that he'd be able to.

There was something else lurking beneath there now. Something that laughed in the back of my mind at the entire situation currently going on.

"Oh, stop it," Hale snorted. "I can tell that something is wrong with you, so either you tell us now, or else Ivy will worry when I explain to her you're not yourself."

Mentioning her name, I froze and both of them stared at me and then looked at each other, seeing how I reacted upon saying her name. "There's no need to tell her."

"Did something happen between the two of you?"

Shaking my head rather quickly, I was doing a horrible job and trying to show them I was perfectly fine. So, deciding to avoid the conversation, I quickly stood from the chair, taking my bowl to the sink and rinsing it out. "No. Why would you think that? I just had a bad dream, that's all."

"A bad dream?" Hale replied. I could feel his eyes boring into the back of my head, but I refused to look at him.

"Oh look, here she comes. Now why don't we ask her?" Talon said, making my heart lurched as I spun around, only to see an empty doorway and Talon and Hale, looking at each other with smirks upon their faces.

Fuck, they caught me.

"OK, now that we got that out of the air, we definitely know that it has to do with Ivy. But what I don't understand is why. You were perfectly fine with her yesterday, and now all of the sudden you're acting as if you've seen a ghost. So you can either tell us what's been going on or we can go ask her."

Hale had a point. I couldn't keep it from them forever. I had to tell him what she did, not that I didn't enjoy it. I did enjoy it. I enjoyed it very much.

But she pulled the Lycan from me, awoke it, or whatever she did.

Glancing around, I stepped forward, looking down the hall, and then looked back to my brothers before gesturing to them with my hand to follow me out back. The last thing I wanted was for Ivy to hear the conversation I was about to have with them.

Opening the door, I stepped out into the cool air, and looked over my shoulder at them, waiting. They looked at each other and back at me, letting out a scoff that was almost the sound of laughter as they stepped outside.

But even being out here just on the other side of the door, it wasn't good enough. So instead I started walking towards the guest house. Towards the woods that laid on the other side of it.

I had to get far enough away from the house so Ivy would not hear me tell them what I was about to, or anyone else for that matter. The last thing I needed was somebody else laughing at me.

"Dude, where the fuck are you taking us? We don't have time for this shit today," Talon said as he rolled his eyes, following behind me.

"Will you just shut the fuck up and follow me? Jesus," I whispered harshly as I glared at him.

By the time we made it to the tree line, I looked around at the house, making sure she wasn't looking at any of the windows or anything like that and when the coast felt clear enough, I finally let out the breath I had been holding.

"Well..." Hale said with irritation. "Speak, now that you have us all the way out here."

Glaring at him, I hesitated a moment before rolling my eyes. "Okay, so... last night I was sleeping. We all went to bed, remember?" I said, starting off the conversation.

"Yeah. You were one of the first people that went to bed and said you were tired and had a headache," Hale replied, giving me a scrutinizing gaze.

"Okay, well, I know that's true. I hadn't been feeling well all day yesterday. But that's besides the point, because I woke up in the middle of the night to Ivy standing in my bedroom naked... and not just that, she was calling my name like some weird... ritual or something. Then she straddled me! We, you know...."

Gesturing with my hands, I tried to get them to understand what I meant without actually saying it. The two of them smirked at me again, crossing their arms with laughter.

"No, we don't know. Can you be specific about what you did?" Talon asked, causing me to groan with frustration.

"We fucked okay?" I snapped at him, running my hand over the front of my face before it reached up to rub the back of my neck as I thought about what had happened.

"Okay, so why are you acting like that's a bad thing? You've had sex with her many times."

Hale's statement was true, but none of those times were quite exactly like they were last night. "Trust me, I know. The problem being though, is that she was like different and not just regular different, like she was really different. Eyes black, wing whipping... you know that kind of difference. To top it all off.... she did something..."

"She did something?" Talon said with annoyance. "Well, you just fucking tell us exactly what it is she did and stop beating around the bush... I have shit to do today."

"Fuck my life," I sighed. I just had to say it. It was going to be like ripping off a Band-Aid. I just had to take a deep breath and do it. "I think she awakened my Lycan."

Both of my brothers stood there stunned in silence with dead panned expressions on their faces as their arms that were once crossed over their chest fell loosely at their sides.

"Dude, did you hear me? I think she awakened—"

"I fucking heard you," Hale said, cutting me off and mid-sentence. "What exactly... in detail... not the sex detail, but that situation detail..." he sighed. "What exactly happened?"

Now they want fucking details on that shit!

Like it was something I really wanted to explain. I mean, being a werewolf is one thing I had years to adapt to. The fact that I shifted into a wolf, that is.

This, though, was not natural to me at all.

"She was... you know..." I shrugged. "Riding me and then she kind of like, I don't know, said this name. It's a name I don't want to say because I don't want to accidentally wake myself up again... but it was like I was pushed into the back of my mind and was watching as a passenger. As she and the animal, whatever thing I was kind of like, continued to fornicate."

My explanations were exaggerated as I used my hands to kind of show the motions of fornication. All of which made Talon burst into laughter, as if it was the funniest shit he had ever seen in his life, slapping his hand against his knees, clutching his stomach kind of laughter.

Hale, however, didn't laugh.

He stared at me with that scrutinizing gaze once more, as if he was unsure to believe what I was telling him. But I was being honest. I wouldn't have been freaked out if it was all a fucking joke.

I mean, come on, it's not every day your girl comes in and wakes you up playing with your Johnson and then decides she's just going to awaken the beast like a tickle me fucking Elmo.

"I think we may have a problem," Hale replied before he reached over to Talon and shoved him to get him to shut up.

"Hey man, why did you do that?" Talon yelled at him. "You can't say this shit ain't funny. I mean, we all knew it was going to happen one day. She just did it a lot sooner."

"The problem is though, Talon, she shouldn't have been able to do that until he had already shifted, and he hasn't. The Lycan awakens in battle. That is the story. That is what we've been told, even what Father wrote down in his journals. The Lycan always awakened in battle."

Never once had I heard that, and perhaps that was something Hale and Talon should have shared with Damien and I a long time ago when he did the research about it. However, I was also always too busy with the different women, so I can see where that lesson would have been lost in translation, so to speak.

"Can I read the journals?" I asked, watching as Hale turned to me with a curious glint in his eyes.

"You know, I did try to get you to read them and learn about it years ago, but instead, at the time, you're only thinking with your dick. So now that your dick has gotten you in trouble, you finally want to take heed of the warning that I gave you."

Nodding slowly, I bit on my bottom lip until a voice called through the air that made me freeze on the spot. It was Ivy, and as I glanced towards the house, she was standing at the backdoor calling for me and my brothers.

"James, where are you?"

Fuck.

What the fuck was I supposed to do now? I couldn't confront her. What if she was gonna, like, make me change again? I was panicking and my brothers must have been able to tell because they each laid a hand on my shoulder and smiled at me.

"Hey man, you need to calm down," Talon said softly before Hale spoke up.

"Talon is right? You need to get your shit together, because right now, Ivy is herself, and if she feels like she's done something to upset you, there is a good chance that she will fucking snap at you. So unless you want to have an argument with her, pull yourself together. You're acting like she just gave you the fucking plague."

As my brothers turned and walked towards her, clearing the massive grassy space in between where we were standing at the back of the house, I could see the smile on her face light up as they drew near.

The same smile that drew me from my panic and urged me forward.

They were right. I did need to get my shit together, but I could not believe the crap that happened last night.

I wasn't sure what exactly she was, but she was my mate and I had to trust her.

Maybe this was for the best... or maybe I was delusional and she was up to something.

CHAPTER
TWENTY-SEVEN

Teasing James

Ivy

Standing at the back door, looking at the guys by the clubhouse, I found confusion in what was going on. It wasn't like them to ignore me the first time I called, but again, I knew I wasn't the center of their world.

At least I didn't think I was.

However, though, what caught my attention the most was how uncomfortable James looked. I had watched them before I came outside, and I saw how James dramatically flailed his arms around as if he was telling them a story. A story I fully knew already.

I could tell what happened last night had been on his mind this morning. The link we shared going crazy as he tried to push his thoughts aside and think of baseball, of all things, as I was trying to read him.

It was all too obvious though, and chuckling internally, I found amusement in how the great 'playboy' James was acting right now.

Power surged through me like nothing I had ever felt before and for once I was content, determined to get Damian back instead of feeling depressed.

I missed him, but instead of whining and crying about something I couldn't change, I was taking the initiative. I was going to fix this.

I was going to get him back one way or another.

"What's going on? Is everything okay?" Hale said with a soft smile as he looked at me.

I could sense the beast lurking beneath his skin. It called out to me. Purring in a sense, but he held him back quite well. The Lycan respected him and chose to stay held back, not that it couldn't break free if it wanted to.

Hale and Talon had years of experience, though. Years of practice at control.

James was new to it, and the more he freaked out, the more out of control he would be.

I could almost see the electrifying aura that flowed over their skin. After awakening James last night, something in me changed, and I awoke this morning with a whole new outlook on life. I could see things I had never seen before.

"Yes, of course. Everything's okay," I smiled. "Is James okay? He looks absolutely flustered."

The boys turned back to see James walking up towards us. A forced smile upon his face before he stopped, rubbing the back of his neck as he stared at me with a lopsided grin. "Hey Ivy, everything okay?"

Taking a moment, I stared at him as the corners of my lips turned up into a small smirk. "I'm great. A better question would be, are you okay?"

The amusement in my tone and the seduction of the way I asked him seemed to startle him. Both Talon and Hale looked between James and I before Talon burst out laughing once more, shaking his head as he walked past me back into the house.

My suspicions had been correct. Then James had told them what had happened last night and as I gave Hale a side glance, he hesitated for a moment before nodding and walking inside as well. He knew I needed a moment with James.

Yet, as James realized this, his face went pale.

"James, you a little out of sorts after last night? I can see that something's bothering you, and nothing else has happened to you since then that I know of, and considering the fact Talon was just laughing, I can only assume—"

Tilting my head from side to side with a smile, I waited for him to finish the conversation I had started. If he was honestly that worked up about what happened last night, then of course I would apologize.

I didn't mean for it to happen—it just did.

"Ivy, about last night. I wasn't going to say anything," he said, trailing off as he swallowed deeply my eyes, watching his Adam's apple move up and down with his hesitation. "I honestly don't even know what to say."

Stepping forward, I kissed his lips, gently running a finger over the side of his face. "There's no need for you to be afraid, James. I'm sorry that things happened the way they did last night. I didn't mean for that to happen, but it was like something else inside me came alive. A name that was there... to fix all our problems."

"My name?" he whispered, staring at me.

"Your true name... yes."

Letting the information slowly sink in, he nodded his head before wrapping his arms around my waist, pulling me closely. "I'm sorry that I acted a little weird."

"A little weird?" I teased playfully, letting a small giggle escape my lips.

"OK, maybe I was acting a little weird, but Ivy, you scared the shit out of me. I was literally a passenger in my own mind. You can't do stuff like that." There was a seriousness in what James said, and I felt guilty. At the same time, though, I didn't feel guilty.

It was a complicated feeling I didn't understand, but knew eventually I would.

"I know, and I'm sorry that I upset you. Did you really not enjoy the moments we had last night?" Looking up at him, batting my eyelashes, I sought forgiveness and, of course, the puppy dog look I gave him made him instantly melt as he pulled me closer, kissing me gently.

"You know, I can't be upset with you and last night was absolutely amazing. I mean, we've had a lot of amazing sex, but last night it was almost electrifying."

That was not a word I had thought to describe what had happened, but I guess with the rush of sexual tension and power that was flowing around his room last night, one could almost assume that I had been electrifying.

"Hmm... I never really thought about it, calling it electrifying. But perhaps the next time we have fun, it could be a lot more intense." Placing my lips against his once more, I bit playfully before turning round and sashaying my happy ass back inside the house.

James was a complicated man. Once upon a time he had been a complete ladies' man looking to take whatever woman looked appeasing to him. That was until he met me, and in a way, I turned his life upside down.

I turned him from the town playboy into a gentle family man who only thought of others, and what he could do for them. I knew without a doubt he was going to be the perfect father as the years went on, and honestly, I couldn't wait to have more children with him.

He was perfect in every way... even if he got spooked easily.

James just wasn't expecting things to turn out the way they have with us, I suppose, which does honestly make a lot of sense because I don't think anybody normally would have been able to comprehend what the fuck we had going on.

Making my way inside, I passed through the kitchen towards the living room, where Hale and Talon sat talking with Kate. I had gone off the day before on them when they had done what they did and I felt guilty because I could have handled it better.

I could see now they were trying to protect me and bless their hearts for thinking that putting a binding spell on the house would keep me locked in it.

Now that my warriors were awakened, it was going to be a lot easier to break from this place. I simply needed a few more things.

And to fulfill what I needed, of course—I needed Damian.

But getting Damien was the problem. Once I broke the barrier, I would have to find a way to surpass everything the Council was doing and the darkness, of course, that was hiding behind them.

"Hey guys. What are you up to?" I asked as I stood by the opening to the living room, watching. Their eyes turned to me with curiosity.

"Not much," Kate sighed as she gave me a small smile of reassurance. "Angel went back out past the border to see if he could make his way to getting another audience with the council, but they turned him away, saying that they had business elsewhere and that they wouldn't be available for a few weeks."

Business elsewhere? I thought to myself as I tried to comprehend what she was saying. What kind of business could the Council have that they would refuse an audience? There were always elder members there, so it didn't make any sense.

Deep inside me, though, had that answer, and as much as I wanted to ignore it, I had learned from the goddesses and also Priscilla, to listen to the voices and to take my gut instincts seriously. Because at the end of the day, they would give me the answers I needed.

"You don't think that they're possibly coming here, do you?"

I watched as both Hale, Talon and Kate sat quietly, glancing between each other before looking back at me. "Honestly, Ivy, there's no point in lying. I was just trying to protect you before, and I do apologize for the things that we have done. However, that doesn't mean that I'm going to let the barrier down, because keeping you protected is the most important thing to me right now. You and the children."

I wanted to argue with him, to tell him he was incorrect in his statement, but I chose a different path. "I understand, and even though I'm not happy with it, I'll accept it for now."

Lies. It was all lies. I wasn't going to sit idly by.

"Good," he replied before he stood to his feet. "I have a feeling that they might come here, Ivy, to get you, and that is another reason why the barrier was put up. Because we can protect the house, but not if you try to run out and give yourself up in order to protect one of us."

He knew me too well, and as a small smile tried to force its way onto my lips, I held it back. I didn't want him to see I knew very well what he would do if they came for me. Each of those men would turn around and lay their lives on the line to protect me and the children from whatever forces tried to take me. But what they didn't realize was I was prepared for that game should the Council come seeking to take me.

It would honestly make things one hundred times easier if they came here because it meant I had fewer miles to travel. I needed to seek the guidance of the Goddesses to speak to Frigga and make sure what was coming was what I had thought I had seen before.

"Well, I'm feeling a little tired after everything from last night, so I'm just gonna go take a nap. Is that okay with you guys?"

Talon snorted at my comment as he laughed, knowing full well what I was referring to. James pushed past me though entering the living room and did not find amusement in what I said. "It's not funny."

"Of course, it's not James. Nobody's laughing. Talon simply seems to have lost his mind this morning," I replied as a twinkling glint of amusement loomed within my eyes as I glanced over at Talon.

"Am I missing something?" Kate asked as she looked between all of us.

"No, nothing too serious, but I'm sure the guys can fill you in. Anyway, I'm going to go take a nap. You guys try not to get into too much trouble and wake me up if anything happens?"

My hanging question in the air caused them all to nod in agreement. But as I made my way up the stairs, I sent a tantalizing vibe directly towards Talon. He had been a very naughty boy, laughing at his brother in his stressed out situation.

Perhaps it was time he had his fill of me.

Or was it I'd have my fill of him?

CHAPTER TWENTY-EIGHT

Preparing for War

They say when you are with someone long enough, you can almost feel their intentions before they even move. With the guys and I, it was just like that. Heading up the stairs slowly, I knew, without a doubt, Talon was following behind closely.

He had felt the taunting pull I had sent him, and as soon as I hit the top steps of the second floor, he grabbed me, spun me around, and pushed me up against the doorway.

"What are you doing, little wolf?" he whispered huskily into my ear, my lips parting as my tongue brushed against my bottom lip just in time for me to bite down upon it with a smirk.

"Little Wolf? I think you know I'm way more than just a wolf."

My taunting reply was just what he wanted before he dragged me into his bedroom and threw me down onto the bed. "I could feel you pulling me. Calling me to you. Is that what you want, Ivy? Do you want my hard, throbbing cock shoved down your pretty little throat?"

God, the way he spoke to me with his stern glare did nothing but make my cunt tighten with the desire to have him fill me.

I wanted him more than anything. My mouth watering at the thought of tasting him again. "Yes."

Walking towards me, I slowly gazed up at him under dark lashes, just to feel the powerful tug on my hair as he yanked my head back with a sinister gaze.

"Do you wanna taste?"

"Yes," I said breathlessly, licking my lips as I watched him use his free hand to undo his pants, releasing the monster he kept hidden away. The curve ridges of his cock were hard and waiting. The shimmering glint of pre-cum across the head called my name.

I wanted it, and from the hungry look in his eyes, I could tell he saw my desire.

I slid from the bed and onto my knees on the floor; my mouth quickly wrapped around the length of his cock as I moaned in pleasure, closing my eyes, relishing in how good he tasted.

Over and over again, he used my hair to guide my head along the length of his throbbing erection, the soft moans coming from his lips as my eyes cast up to his face, watching his eyes close and his head tilt back in pleasure. He was enjoying this, and so was I.

Wet with arousal, my core ached as I clenched, wanting him to fill me and do terrible things to me.

I honestly couldn't wait for it, and also, I wanted Hale to join.

I knew I had to be patient, though. Hale wasn't in the mood for something like this, but eventually, I would get to lie with him again, and he would share my body with his brothers. Each of them taking a piece of me.

All of their Lycans claiming me—especially now that Adnan, James' Lycan—was awake.

With a small pop of my mouth, I slid his erection from my throat, slowly standing to my feet. He didn't waste time grabbing me by the throat as he pulled me close.

"You are an amusing creature, aren't you?" his Lycan side said with a twisted grin. "Pulling me forward, taunting me. Do you want me to ravage you, girl?"

Out of the three of them, Talon's Lycan was the one who got my body on fire the most because he was more primal, whereas the others were analytical and cautious, more likely to surprise their prey before ravaging them.

"Yes," I whispered as I slowly slid the dress over my head, revealing my naked body beneath it. "Want this?"

His eyes flickered over my body, taking in every curve, every inch of naked flesh until a growl of pleasure bellowed from his chest.

Not wasting time, he crashed his lips to mine and lifted me up to wrap my legs around his waist. My dress was gone, and his clothing soon followed. He thrust inside me, ravaging me as a cry of pleasure escaped my lips.

But I couldn't wait for the day when the four of them would take me at once.

He was relentless in his venture, taking me over and over again before pulling out and tossing me down on the bed. He flipped me over, grabbed my hair, arched my back, and slid into me from behind.

The way he possessed my body was addicting.

"You're a good girl," he whispered in my ear. The sensations of our shared pleasure brought me closer and closer to the edge until I couldn't take anymore.

"You're a good girl," he whispered in my ear. The sensations of our pleasure brought me closer and closer to the edge until I couldn't take anymore.

With a loud roar, he pulled out, spilling himself all over me. As I came undone with him, I had to admit I was a little disappointed he didn't come inside me, but then again, I just had children I didn't need anymore right now.

Laughter escaped me as I stood to my feet, sticky from his release, and walked towards the bathroom, turning on the shower. Talon was a caring man when the deed was done, and he didn't waste a moment joining me.

His hands slowly cleaned away the mess from my skin as he kissed the side of my face.

"Can I ask you something?" he said softly, causing me to smile.

"Of course, you can."

"Why did you awaken James' Lycan?"

The last thing I expected was for him to bring this up right now, but now that he did, I couldn't help but feel slightly amused. "Because he will be needed."

"What do you mean, needed?"

With a sigh, I turned to face him, raising my brow before reaching over and shutting off the water. "Not really a topic for the shower, is it?"

"Ivy—"

Stepping from the shower, I grabbed a towel, wrapped it around my body, and went out into the bedroom. I knew very well he was following right behind me, and the conversation was far from over.

"Will you stop?" He grabbed my arm gently as he turned me around to face him. "What's going on?"

Taking a moment, I stared at him with curiosity. "War is coming, Talon. You, of all people, should be able to feel that."

"War?" He laughed, shaking his head. "We're the strongest pack in North America."

"That's missing its leader."

Shaking my head, I grabbed my dress and pulled it back over my head, ensuring it was in place. Talon didn't understand right now what I was talking about, but in time he would. He would see what was coming.

"You have changed, Ivy." The whispered response stopped me in my tracks as I made my way toward the door. Deep down, I knew what he said was true, but I wanted to pretend it wasn't.

I wanted to pretend I was the same person, but I couldn't keep lying to myself.

I was changing.

"I'm fine, Talon," I replied softly as I glanced over my shoulder at him. "And soon... we all will be in a much better position. Our family will be whole again."

Talon

As soon as Ivy left the room, I stood clueless in the center, staring at the closed door she exited from. She was acting more bizarre than I had remembered her being, and the way she pulled me from the conversation downstairs still confused me.

I had felt the pull. Felt a swirl of calm and longing tugging at the beast inside me. As soon as I cleared the room, he came forward, pushing me to the back of my mind as he took over and went after Ivy.

Taking her this time was completely different from before.

She was different.

Power coursed through her, and the moment I touched her, I became drunk on the feeling she created. Then when I acted in.... that way... fuck me.

Running a hand over my face, I groaned before grabbing a pair of shorts from my dresser and pulling them on. Ivy's words echoed through my mind, and as my eyes glanced out the window, I couldn't help but wonder if she was right.

Deep down, I felt like something was coming, but I didn't want to admit it.

"Talon!" Hale said, coming through my bedroom door. "We need to talk."

Turning, I watched Hale stop in his tracks as his eyes slid around the room, taking in a long whiff of the air. "Ivy was just here—"

"Yes, and we fucked. Now, what do you want?" I snapped.

He opened and closed his clenched fists before sneering in my direction, pressing his lips into a fine line. "Lose the attitude."

"Well, don't waste my time."

"Waste your time?" Hales scoffed. "Anyway... Derek from the Blue Wolf pack just called and said his scouts got a whiff of council warriors near his land."

"What?" I sneered as I felt the shift burning beneath my skin. "When?"

"This morning. He said they didn't see the rest of them, but guessed two, maybe three. It looks like they are heading this way, but I don't want us to jump to conclusions. Perhaps they are simply heading somewhere."

"Without notifying packs?!" I growled. "I doubt that. They're on their way here."

Hale stared at me for a moment before laughter escaped his lips. "Why would they be on their way here? To get Ivy?"

"Are you insane?" I asked him with disgust. "Do you not remember the letter?"

He was quiet for a moment and then sighed. "I know, but come on... do you really think so?"

"Yeah. I do."

Pacing back and forth, I pushed past him into the hallway and stormed down the stairs with Hale on my heel. There was no telling what was going to happen, and if, for some reason, they were on their way here, we needed to be prepared.

'All warriors meet at the pack house.'

I called out through the mind link. We didn't need to procrastinate any longer. Perhaps they weren't on their way here, but we needed to be ready either way. I would not risk the pack being hurt because of my lack of protection.

"Talon, what are you doing?" James called out as he and Hale stood behind me with confusion. "Why are you assembling the warriors?"

"Because..." I said, looking over at him. "We need to be prepared if something is coming. Damian would expect this, and I will not let us be blindsided."

The look on my brother's faces was one of shock but determination. They knew how dangerous our world could be, and the woman and children inside were what we had to protect.

Our pack was something we had to protect, and if we didn't, we would lose everything.

CHAPTER
TWENTY-NINE

Chaos at the Border

Damian

It didn't take long for them to decide they were going to move forward with the plan, and before I knew it, I was dragged from the room, cuffed and blindfolded, and thrown into a vehicle. I knew deep down the destination they had planned. It was going to be my pack; it was going to be my family.

Everything I had worked so hard to protect was going to fall.

Call me a pessimist if you will, but what was I supposed to think?

I wasn't there to protect my family.

I was an alpha, not able to protect his pack. What kind of alpha did that make me? Weak... pathetic.

I couldn't allow myself to go ahead with this frame of mind. I was better than this, better than them, and I spent my entire life trying to show I could be more than just damaged.

Plans started formulating in my mind.

I had to find a way to divert the attention.

If I could cause a distraction, perhaps I could find a way to escape. Find a way to make it back to my pack before it was too late.

From what I could tell, the Council had sent scouts ahead to assess the situation from the whispers and murmurs of the guards surrounding me. They were going to try for a surprise attack.

They were going to take down my pack little by little, with no warning.

There were defenseless women and children in my pack. I didn't make my women fight unless they wanted to. They had that freedom, so those who could not protect themselves, even though they had gained strength when Ivy completed the connection with the pack, would still be defenseless.

A sense of hopelessness washed over me, and before I knew it, the chitter chatter around began once again.

"I still can't believe that we're actually going to go in there and do this." A man with a gruff voice to my left proclaimed. "If she's anything like they said she is, she'll kill us before we get there."

I couldn't help but chuckle internally. He had a point. If Ivy could escape, pregnant or not, she would kill them all.

She was fearless when she wanted to be, and looking at her, you would never think such a thing because she was such a delicate woman, so petite, so thin and beautiful. She didn't seem like she'd be the type of person to hurt a fly, yet she was the most deadly out of all of us.

"Man, stop being such a little bitch. That stupid whore won't stand a chance if I get my hands on her."

A low growl echoed from me, and I moved to jolt forward and hit the man at my right, who said what he did. However, I was restricted and unable to move, and because of it, I found myself even angrier.

I couldn't even defend her honor. No matter how much I tried.

"Oh, look, the Alphas decided to try to be brave. What, you don't want me messing with your little whore? Maybe I'll try her out myself before I kill her."

"Fucking touch her, and I will rip you apart and then kill everyone you love dearly," I threatened in a low and menacing tone as I gritted my teeth together, wanting nothing more than to tear this man apart at my side.

No one would touch my mate, no matter the circumstances.

If they laid one fucking finger on that pretty little head of hers, I would kill them all. I had worked too hard to ensure her happiness, to ensure she had a life with my brothers, a life that she deserved, and for the Council to unhinge that...

Well, it made me more lethal than I ever had been before.

"I'd like to see you try," the guard sneered.

"Yeah, you keep talking, big boy, but if I weren't tied down right now, you wouldn't have a mouth to talk from."

Laughter consumed the surrounding air, and as much as I wanted to rip them apart, I couldn't. I was drained, weakened by the silver in my veins and the silver on my wrists. There was nothing I could honestly do, and that upset me because I wanted to get revenge for my mate.

I wanted to be the strength she needed.

"You talk a lot of shit about a man who's unable to do anything," the man to my left said with amusement in his voice.

If only I could see them. I had their scent, but I wanted to see what they looked like. Remember their faces so I could watch the fear drain from their eyes when I hunted them down.

"Yeah, and you guys talk a lot of shit for two men who have me downed with silver and afraid of a tiny, petite woman as if she could end your life at any moment."

My retort earned me a blow to the back of my head. I could tell the man to the left of me was not pleased with what I had said because I was pointed out a fact. They were terrified of her, of what was to come, because they knew we were not normal.

They ripped the blindfold from my head, and as it was, my eyes had to focus in order to see what was around me.

The two men, both burly and grim, stared back at me. The one to my left was fat and balding, while the man to my right had a large jagged scar down the left side of his face. Both of them tried to be intimidating and sinister, but it wasn't working.

"There's no point in having him blindfolded. He can't communicate with them anyway; plus, it'll be a lot more fun having him watch us prepare to destroy his pack."

The sadistic comment from the man to my right, the burly one with the scar, and he stared at me with hatred. I wasn't afraid of him, though. Only one thing could scare me, and it wasn't anywhere near me—right now.

If I got free, he would be the first one I ripped apart simply for thinking he could fuck my mate as if she would actually allow it.

"You really must compensate for that tiny dick you have. Sitting there talking and thinking about raping a woman," I spat. "Not to mention you have a death grip on the knife like you think you will actually use it on me. He'd kill you for that."

His eyes widened as his jaw clenched, his knuckles turning white against the blade's hilt. Before he could even say a word, though, the other man quickly hit me again, and eventually, black spots invaded my vision, causing me to slip into darkness.

"Fucking let him watch. It'll be more fun seeing the terrified expression in his eyes when he realizes he's going to die." One of the men said, his voice getting shallower and shallower until they tossed me into absolutely nothing.

I wasn't sure how long I was out, but as I slowly came to, I realized one thing.

We had stopped moving, and I was not alone in the van.

Fear crept through me, wondering if we had made it to my back yet. If we were here, and my people were dying.

However, approaching footsteps caused my mind to calm a little as the door opened, showing Alokaye and Allison standing before me. His eyes trained on me with a smirk.

"Good, you're awake. It's time to prepare for the final event."

"What are you doing? This is absolutely ridiculous. There are innocent people behind those borders," I snapped at him, rage showing on my face as the effects of the silver slowly dissipated in my veins.

However, not enough for me to be able to fight back properly.

"That is their problem. They chose their side," Allison sneered as she placed her hands on her hips. "Plus, they're not the goal that we want. It's that stupid little bitch you call a mate I want."

Chuckling to myself, I shook my head. "You have no idea what you're messing with regarding her. She will kill you all."

I was warning them, hoping they would heed that warning and turn back and realize how foolish they have been, but that was not the case. Instead, they were going to continue pressing forward and learn how unforgiving my brothers could be.

"She can try. She is nothing compared to me."

Alokaye turned to her with a narrowed gaze and shook his head. "You're foolish to underestimate her, Allison. She will kill you."

He knew it to be true, and thinking about her now, a pit of guilt formed in my stomach.

All I wanted was one more kiss, one more night with her, one more chance to tell Ivy how sorry I was and how much I loved her. Instead, I was dragged from the van, put on my feet, and forced to walk. I knew what was coming as if the fates had sent out a calling song to take me home.

Walking and walking, my feet crunched against the dirt and gravel on the ground. The men of the Council were both dressed and, in their wolf forms, and slowly maneuvered through the woods towards my border.

I knew by now my brothers would have had the guards on full alert, and I would have prayed they heeded my warnings and taken serious precautions.

Goddess knows, though, I had given them plenty of guidance on what we would do in case of an attack, and Talon being the man that he was... knew what to do.

Talon wasn't like the rest of us. He was murderous, and his Lycan had a taste for blood far surpassing anything I had ever seen. He would fight to protect what was his until his last dying breath.

"We're closing in on the border," one warrior said softly as he approached Alokaye and Allison, who stood with smiles on their faces.

Casting his gaze up towards the sky, Alokaye smiled brightly. "It's almost time."

"What is?" I snapped with worry.

He turned to me with a wicked grin and laughed. "We cannot proceed properly until she is present." Turning from me, he smiled at the warrior. "Let them know that we're here. Let them know that I have arrived."

Shock filled me, realizing just how serious this was and exactly what would happen. They were going to be awoken in the middle of the night;, unprepared, unaware, and Ivy, my children, they all were going to suffer because of this because I allowed the Council to get me.

This was all my fault.

"No!" I cried out, trying to break free. Trying to get word to them to be prepared.

There was not much fight left in me, and now with every piece to the puzzle fitting together, I could have a little more clarity. I was the bait to get to Ivy. I was the sacrifice they were going to make.

I wasn't sure why I was being sacrificed... but nothing was done under this moon unless ritual. Something big was brewing, and with me being incapable of doing anything, my people and my pack's fate were literally in the hands of my brothers and my mate.

Goddess, protect them.

Chapter Thirty

Sound of Battle

Hale

After Talon had called upon the pack and explained everything going on, the three of us stood as a united front, letting our warriors know the battle was coming—the war was coming–and with it, death, but we had to fight for what we loved.

All the warriors agreed, and they knew what was expected of them. They had been trained for this their entire life, and now that it was here, they would not back down.

We separated the women and the children who were not part of the battle and prepared them for the underground bunkers that would keep them safe while war raged above them.

We knew what was expected. We knew exactly what we needed to do.

The only thing was actually executing the plan.

So, after hours of preparing for the worst and hoping for the best, the bunkers were ready, and those who would use them knew if the howl was sounded, to go straight there. Hopefully, we wouldn't need them, but that was wishful thinking on my part.

As the sun sank below the sky, we sat waiting at the borders, all three of us, with our warriors, ready for whatever was to come.

If it was actually coming.

Part of me still thought Talon was over-exaggerating, but the other part of me, deep down, had a feeling he wasn't. I felt he was right, and because of that, I stood waiting.

The only problem was when we faced the roars of hundreds of wolves approaching our borders, we realized that though we had the power and equal numbers... the council wasn't alone.

Richard's pack and two other small leaders had joined them.

This was a battle we weren't prepared for after all, and as I watched the vicious snarls of ravaging wolves approach us closer, we shifted, preparing for battle. I didn't understand why my Lycan refused to come forth at the moment.

But in the back of my head, he whispered, "not yet..."

The clashing of bodies and the scent of blood filled the air as their wolves clashed with our own. Somewhere in the mix of things, I was separated from my brothers. Their bodies were lost in the wave of wolves that battled around me.

One by one, I tore through the wolves who came at me. Breaking one wolf's neck and then tore through the throat of another. There was no way I would allow this pack to fall at the hands of our enemies, and from what I could tell, everyone from my pack felt the same way.

'Hale!' James cried through the mind link. 'Wolves just headed towards the house!'

I could sense his panic through our link, and looking towards the house, I saw the enemy wolves running there. Dread filled me, and before I could move toward them, I was surrounded by three more wolves and unable to run to their aid.

'We have to protect them!' I called out to anyone who was able to hear me. 'We have to protect the Luna.'

However, it didn't seem like anyone could do anything, and instead, I prayed she had made it to the panic room safely with the children.

"She has awakened," the Lycan inside me said. "The time is coming."

Ivy

I felt a pit of sorrow within the darkness that told me to wake up.

It was a feeling I couldn't shake, but the screams and howls of despair came through into the darkness. The sounds shook me from my slumber and laying on the bed, I took a deep breath, trying to calm my currently racing mine.

That was until I heard it again. The screams of everybody around me. Screams that made blood run cold. Jolting from where I had laid within the comforts of my bed, I sat up, my eyes wide as the door to my room burst open.

Kara, the Valkyrie who had once visited me before in the sanctum of elders, stood before me with her mighty sword strapped to her back and her wings folded behind her. "You need to get up now. We have to get the children, and we have to protect them."

I was shocked to see her. I hadn't seen her in months, and yet here she was, just in time for chaos to consume the outside world. Jumping from the bed, I ran to the window. The fires outside the lands of our pack and the howls of wolves surrounded us.

The scene before me was unlike anything I had ever seen, yet it felt so familiar.

The elders were attacking, and I was left in the center. "I have to help them."

"No," Kara said firmly as she took two steps forward, striding closer as she grabbed me by my arm. "You cannot help them."

My mother and Priscilla quickly entered the door behind, stopping to look at Kara. My mother's eyes widened, never having seen a creature like that before, a soft gasp leaving her lips as the twins began to cry. Their cry was different, though. It was almost ear-piercing, and as I strode towards them, I picked them up to soothe them.

And as I did, the crying stopped.

It was odd... I had never seen them act the way they did, but looking down at them now, I knew their safety came first. No matter how much I wanted to go out there to help my mates.

"Please, you must tell me what is going on out there."

"Ivy, you already know who is here. They are here for you, and they are here for your children. The panic room that you created, where is it?" Kara's question caught me off guard. She had never been inside this house that I knew of, so how would she know I had a panic room?

"How was it that you knew about this?"

She hesitated for a moment, staring at me with thinly met lips before crossing her arms over her chest, shaking her head. "I am your guardian, Ivy. I am your Valkyrie. It is my job to know these things. I would have assumed that you had already realized this."

Staring at her for about a second, I took a heavy breath. With my children in my arms, I made my way from the nursery to my room and pushed the button that moved a shelf from the wall sideways, revealing a large ten-foot by twelve-foot panic room.

The panic room had never been used before, but as soon as the children came and their fathers knew these troubles were coming, they made sure to have everything stocked. So that way, if anything happened, the twins would be safe. It was Talon's idea at first, and the brothers quickly agreed.

Talon was very paranoid. Very... paranoid.

However, we can see now that he had every reason to be.

Looking over at my mother, I gestured with my head for her to enter, and she did not say a single word as she nodded and moved with Priscilla into the panic room.

"I cannot stay in this room. You know that."

My eyes cast over to Kara, whom I had been talking to, and as the stern gaze upon her face slowly started to melt, she looked around, rolling her eyes as if she didn't want to allow me to do whatever it is that I felt that I had to.

"I have my orders to protect you. Now get in, and I will stand guard."

I didn't want to do as she said. I didn't want to get in, but as my eyes gazed down at my children... I knew I had no other choice. Quietly, I walked forward and stepped inside, and as I did, she nodded her head at me, and I hit the red button.

The door to the panic room closed, and within it, the cameras that had been scattered throughout the house revealed the scene before me.

The chaos that would slowly consume us.

"You're doing the right thing," my mother said softly as she took Pollux from my arms.

"Am I, though? My mates are out there, and I'm stuck in a panic room with my children, my mother and a Seer, instead of out there fighting for my pack. No offense, Priscilla."

"None taken," she replied with a wicked smile as she brushed off the jab I made.

My mother couldn't say anything. What was she to say? She wasn't one of us.

I didn't want to think the way I was, but I couldn't help it.

What kind of Luna did that make me? What kind of goddess did that make me?

The guilt that swirled and filled me was unlike anything I had ever felt before. I stood there watching the cameras, and as I did, I watched the front doors blow open. The cracking of wood splinters shot across my foyer as a gasp left my lips.

"They just broke my fucking door," I snarled, watching two wolves enter my home downstairs. Their massive forms caused more damage than I would have liked. It was not long-lasting, though, as Kara appeared into view, slashing her sword through one of the wolves as if it was nothing and then stabbing the other.

Their mangled bodies dropped to the floor as I heard her snicker, shaking her head before stepping in front of the doorway. She was staying true to her word. Guarding the house and protecting us was top priority, but I couldn't allow her to do this alone.

It wasn't right, and she was only one person. From the looks of it, hundreds of wolves were out there, and my mates were somewhere in the mix. "I have to get out there."

I could feel their pain and anger through our bond. It was fueling a fire deep inside me that wanted to escape. A fire that wanted to destroy everything I held dear.

"You can't do anything for them," my mother said as she laid her hand on my arm. "You're safer here with us."

Turning to face her once more, I shook my head in disbelief. "How can you say that?"

She seemed shocked and a little taken aback but pushing through it, she opened her mouth and surprised me. "They are fighting to protect you. You're not built for this kind of thing, Ivy. You're safer here, just like the rest of the women and children are in the bunker."

I wasn't built for this?

I was the fucking Luna of this pack!

"This is my birthright, mother. You may not understand that, but fate proclaimed me their leader. Fate proclaimed me to be what brings forth peace."

"What are you talking about?" she asked as her brows furrowed in confusion.

"It doesn't matter," I muttered, turning back to glance at the cameras. "There is more to this than you realize."

"Don't tell me it doesn't matter, Ivy. I am your mother."

I cringed at her words. Not because she said she was my mother, but because of the tone she was using. I loved her dearly, but her ignorance of how this world worked killed me. She had no idea what she was in, but she sure liked to think she did.

Just as I was about to say something, I watched three figures on the screen come into view, and as they did, my blood ran cold.

The elder Alokaye stood side by side with Allison. A woman who was supposed to be dead, and at her feet, kneeled a man I knew all too well.

It was Damian, and he was their prisoner.

CHAPTER THIRTY-ONE

Sweet Sweet Destiny

Shock filled me.

He was here... but he was at the mercy of that cold-hearted bitch!

No one ever tells you what it feels like to watch the person you love to be tormented. To be held captive and forced into the will of another. No one tells you how much your heart can shatter from just one look.

He was out there... at their mercy, and here I was behind cold walls.

It wasn't fair to think he was going through this alone out there, and I was stuck here. For weeks I had been worried about it. Wondering where he was and if he was okay.

Shit, if he was even alive.

He even was forced to miss the birth of his children because of them.

As if a damn broke, I lost all clarity for a moment. Priscilla's mumbled words went unheard as I slowly turned to them and held out a sleeping Castor, who was still in my arms. "Take her."

Priscilla didn't hesitate to take the child, and as she did, she nodded at me in understanding. She knew already what I was going to do, and she also knew there was no stopping me.

I had promised to tear them apart if they hurt Damian, and that offer still stood. Killing Allison, though... well, was going to be for pure pleasure.

I couldn't wait to watch her blood run from my lips as I tore out her throat.

I could feel the purring satisfaction of the darkness under my skin as I thought of the various ways to make that woman suffer. To make her blood run upon the pack's ground as a river with no end.

I would kill anyone who hurt my mates, and there would be no way to stop me.

"Ivy, what are you doing?" Mother cried with a panicked look in her eyes as she watched me step closer to the door.

I didn't bother to answer her, though.

There was no point when she already told me what she thought.

With my children taken care of, I glanced towards the cameras once more to see Kara taking care of another set of wolves who had surrounded her. They wouldn't get off easy. None of them would.

Pushing the button on the wall, the door opened, and a panicked cry from my mother escaped her lips. "Ivy! What are you doing?! Get back in here. Have you lost your mind?"

"I'm going to do what I was created for."

"You can't do anything!"

"You would do well to remember who I am," I said with a snarl as I glanced briefly over my shoulder at her. "You will stay with Priscilla to protect the children. Do you understand?"

She stared at me in shock as I turned to face her. There was nothing else to say, and deciding not to give her a chance to find a reason to argue, I hit the trigger outside the panic room and watched the door close with my children and mother inside.

They would be safe, and that was what was important. Even if the wolves found out they were inside, there was no way to get into the room. Priscilla knew what was at stake, and she would lock the door from the other side to ensure that no one could open in from where I stood.

My heart ached to know that anything could happen, and this might be the last time I saw them, but I wasn't going to let that stop me. My people needed me, my mates needed me, and there was no way that I was going to let them down.

There was no way I would allow my children to grow up in a world where they were subjected to punishment by a council who sought to control us all. We deserved to be free, and we would be when I was done with them.

With a heavy breath, I put my feelings aside and walked towards my bedroom door and out into the hallway. The only thing on my mind now was my mates.

And Damian, to be more specific.

It was the only thought on my mind as I moved down the hallway in my pajamas, my feet hitting the top of the stairs as I stared at the scene below me. The wolves were massive. More massive than I had ever remembered them being, and as Kara fought with them, her eyes met mine.

"What are you doing?!" she yelled as she tossed a wolf over her shoulder and thrust her sword within it. "Get back now!"

"No," I replied firmly. "I'm needed out there, and I will not sit idly by. The children are safe."

She didn't have time to argue with me, and as one wolf slipped by her and bounded right for me, she seemed concerned. However, that concern was slowly drained away when she watched me grab the wolf by its head, prying its jaws apart as I slowly ripped him into two pieces. His blood sprayed over me and the surrounding walls.

It didn't bother me, though; from the look in her eyes, she could see that.

Kara had misjudged me and my capabilities.

"Protect my children," I told her sternly. "Don't worry about me... I can handle myself."

She didn't seem to know what to do, but with the wolves dead at her feet, she simply nodded her head and allowed me to pass. Nothing was up for discussion.

I would get back what belonged to me, even if it meant everyone died.

My mind seemed on overdrive as I moved from the front door out onto the yard in the front of the house. I wasn't quite sure what I had expected, but it definitely wasn't this.

Blood ran upon the grass, and mixed within it was fur. But that wasn't the most shocking thing. The most shocking thing was the dead wolves that littered the area shredded into pieces. Kara had taken her blade to them. She had ruthlessly executed anyone who tried to get near the home.

Those who were weak had gone first; from the connection, I could tell we hadn't lost many. I was glad to have Kara. I knew, without a doubt, that she would keep my mother, Priscilla, and the children safe. She would ensure they would never be harmed while I ventured out into the war to protect what belonged to me.

Stepping over the mess, I made my way towards the top of the hill to see the war beneath me, and the sight I got wasn't one I expected. Our wolves were fighting for everything they had, but off in the distance was Alokaye, and most importantly, there was Allison at his side.

The devil stood on the rock overlooking chaos, and every now and again, she would reach down to stroke Damian's hair. Seeing her make such an intimate gesture towards my mate disgusted me.

He was mine... not hers. Yet, she still seemed to think she could win this.

She still thought she had a chance to come out on top.

With every step that I took, I found myself moving closer and closer to him, as if a shield was around my body, protecting me. The wolves diverted their attention to other means of the area, tearing apart each other as fur, blood, and howls of pain echoed and scattered around me. Like leaves blowing through the wind.

Alokaye had no idea what he had done coming here. He had no idea who he was honestly facing, but after everything they had done, I was happy to show him. I was happy to give a demonstration.

I would simply need a volunteer... like Allison.

They may have had numbers, but the wolves of my pack had my energy, my essence running through their veins and, with it, a power that could not be matched.

Talon and Hale's voices sounded off in the distance, but I did not pay them mind as I looked straight ahead, walking closer and closer to what it is I wanted. I knew what they would do if they got to me.

They would try to protect me. Try to save me... but that wasn't what I needed.

I needed to end this war, and doing so meant dealing with two people in front of me who had no reason to live after everything they had done to my family.

"Enough!" I bellowed, like a tidal wave of sound echoing far across the battlefield. Wolves near me whimpered, bowing their heads, looking at each other with confusion as I stared up at Alokaye. "You will leave my home now."

"You came," Alokaye said as he stared at me with a Cheshire smile that spoke of nothing evil running through his veins. He was excited to see me. This is exactly what they wanted. For me to be brought out into the open so they could try to kill me.

A sinister fit of laughter inside my mind echoed through the blackened abyss as I stared at Alokaye, shaking my head. "What is it you want?"

His brows lifted as he rubbed his hand over his chin with a smile. "You're so impatient. Do you not enjoy the gift that I brought for you? A little favor to show you how pleased I am with everything that you've been doing."

He had to be joking if he thought I would buy that. I didn't think for a second he wouldn't hesitate to kill me and then kill everybody else just to see some type of satisfaction.

I wouldn't be a fool, though. I wouldn't allow him to use me.

I wouldn't allow him to provoke me in the way he wanted. My eyes cast towards Damian, who refused to look at me. He was but a broken version of his former self, and while the beast inside me wanted to run to him. Wanted to kill them all—I couldn't.

Not yet, at least.

"It isn't that I'm impatient, but I have better things to do with my time." My reply made Allison scowl, but once again, Alokaye showed nothing but a smile.

"Time is an interesting thing, isn't it?" he chuckled. "I remember having all the time I needed once upon a time, but then things changed. You... caused a lot of change."

I had no idea what he was talking about, but Allison looked up at the sky and grabbed Alokaye's arm before I could. "It's happening."

I wasn't sure what was happening, but panic started to set in as Alokaye shifted, pulling a blade from beneath his attire, and walked towards Damian. Everything seemed to happen in slow motion. His movements, my movements.

I couldn't process the scene before me, but when Damian's eyes met mine, it all suddenly rushed in. "I love you, Ivy," he mouthed as Alokaye brought the blade across Damian's throat, a rush of blood spraying out as something inside me completely broke.

I wasn't sure what was louder at that moment. The screams ripped from my throat watching him or the roars of three terrifying monsters ripped from their wolf forms at the brother that was just taken from them.

CHAPTER
THIRTY-TWO
Vengeance is Best Served Cold

James

When Damian was killed, I felt like a piece of me had been ripped away. I wasn't sure how it had been possible, but my brother had been taken from me and I let out a howl of despair into the air.

Ivy's scream shook all of us and not just the wolves of her pack but those of our enemies as well. I never heard anything like it before, but watching her drop to her knees next to Damian, crying, nearly killed me.

'They will all die for this.' Talon said through our link.

'Kill them all.' Hale replied with a snarl.

War had come for us, and regardless of the situation, we weren't going to let them get away with killing Damian. We weren't going to let them get away with anything.

Before I could step forward, a force surrounded me, holding me in place. I tried with all my might to move, but I could not. And suddenly, a shift was forced over me, turning me back into the human body I usually held.

'What's going on?!' I yelled through the link. 'Something made me shift back.'

'Me too.' Talon growled.

'It seems it has for all of us. Something is happening.' Hale replied.

He wasn't wrong. Something was happening.

A buzzing under my skin started to burn like fire, and a voice deep inside me spoke with it. 'It's almost time.'

What was almost time? Was this the beast Ivy freed?'

I tried to fight against what was happening but was unable. A force pushed against me, and the beast came forward snarling. Watching, I saw the wolves of our enemies stepping backward. Their ears lay back as they seemed to look at each other with confusion and uncertainty.

It was obvious I was something to fear. Something they shouldn't get involved with, and I would tear them apart with my new form.

My eyes cast towards where Ivy was, and watching, I saw the power building within her. She was magnificent, and though I couldn't hear what she was saying, the moment a roar sounded and the wolves started the battle once more, she shot a source of power toward the man in front of her with fury.

"Kill them all."

My beast growled before he threw himself at our enemies, slowly tearing them apart. His hunger for blood was a feeling I would never be able to forget.

Ivy

When Damien died, chaos consumed my soul like nothing I had ever felt before. A scream ripped through me I wasn't sure belonged to me. As the tears streamed down my face, I fell to my knees before him.

The light from his eyes had slipped away, and with it, my heart.

"Why?" I cried out softly, trying to understand why someone would want to kill him. Trying to understand why they hated us so much. Just because we were different. "What have you done?"

The echoed howls of mourning from our pack members and Damian's brothers resonated through the air. The moment his heart stopped beating, we felt the snap of his bond, and with it, the snap of my mind.

"You had to be controlled, and with him gone, the circle is no longer complete."

The circle... that was what this was about?

My mate was killed because they thought it would cut the circle and diminish everything. They were fucking idiots. As my eyes snapped to him with hatred and anger in my gaze, I contemplated his words. "What do you mean, the circle is gone?"

"With his death, the portal shall forever be closed, and nothing you can do will open it." His words were riddles, and I was honestly over listening to riddles.

I had no idea what portal he was talking about or why this man would act the way he did, but as I tried to calm my racing mind, I attempted to push back the power, craving to break free. "What portal?"

With a sly grin, the haze washed over him like a waterfall washing away debris. He changed before my eyes, and as he came back into view, the man standing before me was not Alokaye.

Onyx eyes as black as night with midnight blue hair hung loosely down over his shoulders were the first things that caught my attention. The man before me stood with pale skin covered in black and green intricate tattoos.

Something about him was familiar, and the mischievous grin on his face let me know that he had expected this reaction. "The portal that I came from."

"Who are you, exactly? Because nothing about you is familiar."

"Well, that's a shame," he replied with a smirk.

This was enjoyable for him. While I was here falling apart at the loss of my mate in front of me, he was relishing the destruction he caused. Standing to my feet slowly, I let the power within me build up. My heart raced, and my fists clenched so tight that my knuckles turned white.

I was going to kill him. "You have no idea who I am, do you?"

Cocking an eyebrow, the corner of his lip twitched at my response. "You're the goddess of Earth... or so they have proclaimed. But now the circle is broken, you will never reach that potential. The portal will never open, and I will rule over this realm. Everyone you love will die at my hands."

With his words, a roar sounded, and the battle commenced again. Some of my warriors were caught off guard as more wolves pushed from the treeline. Richard included.

"That's what you think," I snarled as my eyes washed over black, releasing the power inside me. A power that had been slowly growing over time. Slowly leaking out and infecting the people around me.

Perhaps I was darkness... perhaps I was light.

At this moment, I didn't care. The only thing I wanted was revenge for my fallen mate. Revenge for the man I lost and the men I loved.

With a swish of my hands, I thrust my hands in front of me and directed my power at him. It caught him off guard, and as it did, he tried to shield himself and failed. Step by step, I moved closer, watching him struggle under me before a hit from my side sent me spiraling through the air, hitting the ground with an intensity I hadn't expected.

It was Allison. The stupid cunt had stopped me, and as I turned, I growled at her, watching as she stared at me, baring her teeth. Her golden wolf was ready to rip me apart, yet I welcomed it. "Oh, you fucked up."

She charged at me, and as she did, I slid past her, twisting and turning with every snap of her jaw. I wasn't going to let her get me, and movement after movement, I pushed forward.

Bursting through the masses with her hot on my tail. I wasn't sure where the man had gone, but after I dealt with her, he was going to die as well.

Another hit to my side sent me flying to the ground, but as I turned on my knees, I stared at the salivating wolf with golden eyes. "Are you ready to die?"

She let out something close to a snort, and as she did, she lunged, which was her biggest mistake. Grabbing her, I jumped onto her back, wrapping my arms around her neck, slowly crushing her windpipe as she tried desperately to throw me off her.

She fell to the ground with a pop and a yelp, and I stood staring down at her slowly shifting body. She lay there, eyes wide, gasping for air as she clawed at her throat.

"I told you I would kill you," I muttered with venom. "You have caused far too much damage to my family for me to allow you to go free. This time, I will make sure that you have no way to come back."

Thrusting my claws down towards her chest, I plunged my hand in deep, grabbing her heart. As I stared down at her, the look in her eyes fed the primal animal inside me. Blood lust filled me, and her fear made a sadistic smile cross my lips right before I ripped her heart from her chest.

Allison was dead, and killing her caused a loud roar of anger to fill the air.

It was the man, and his glaring gaze stared at me with hatred.

"What did you do!" he yelled furiously as he jumped down from the rock he was standing on, stalking me. "She was my favorite."

"And Damian was one of mine," I snapped. "He was my mate, and you took him."

"I am Loki, one of the gods of Asgard, and you will pay for your crimes."

So that was who he was. The Loki of Asgard, God of mischief.

Running at me, a staff appeared in his hand that he swung at me, causing me to jump back, avoiding getting hit. The man was powerful, but one thing he didn't realize was I was never alone.

Hit after hit, we went toe to toe until Hale and Talon grabbed him long enough for me. A hand of dark swirling matter grabbed him by the throat, pushing him to his knees.

"Frigga has been searching for you," The coldness of my voice caused him to narrow his eyes in response to what I said.

"That bitch can kiss my ass," he gasped as I held him in place.

A deafening crack of lightning sounded through the air, and as it did, a swirling mass of wind let through a glimpse of shimmering light in the air. Hale, Talon, and James howled in response to it, and as he did, the enemy wolves moved nervously before they retreated to where they had come from.

The battle was over for now, but the damage wasn't done.

Through the light, I watched the hazed figures of two people step forth, and with them, my breath was almost taken away. I wasn't sure what was going on, but looking at my mates, they knew. Even Loki seemed to know as fear radiated from him.

"Ivy," A soft voice said as I spotted Frigga stepping onto the grassy clearing.

"Frigga?" I replied with confusion. "What's going on?"

"We have come to bring Loki home," she smiled. "Your pain unleashed the power that was needed to drop the veil and open the portal. It allowed us to come through to take Loki."

My pain... my pain dropped the veil.

As if someone turned on the faucet, my eyes filled with tears, slowly slipping down my face. "He's gone."

She shook her head with a sad smile. "Maybe not."

"What do you mean?" I asked quickly. "He's dead. You can't come back from death."

As I stared at Frigga, another large burly form stepped through the portal, and as he did, my mates dropped to their knees, bowing their heads before him as if a force made them submit. I wasn't sure who the man was, but I felt safe as I looked into his blue eyes.

"There is a way," he said as he stepped toward me.

"What—" I gasped, "who are you?"

"Forgive my manners, sweet child. I just have been so looking forward to meeting you. My name is Odin, and I am your father, Ivy."

Holy fucking shit.

CHAPTER THIRTY-THREE

Bring Him Back

Staring up at the eyes of the man who stepped through the portal, my ears almost went deaf from what he had said. Not only did he say he was Odin... as in the freaking God of Gods... but he was also my fucking dad.

"What are you talking about?" I was a chaotic mess and as the tears flowed freely down my face, I tried to wrap my mind around what had happened. The war might have been over, but the problem was Damian was gone.

With him gone, it had all been for nothing.

My heart was absolutely broken.

"I mean exactly what I said, my daughter. I am your actual father, though the circumstances behind that are not as you would expect."

"So you're telling me that my father is actually a God and the man Zane, who had proclaimed to be my father, wasn't?" I asked, with confusion. There was no way this was possible, that I was the daughter of Odin.

He stared at me for a moment before Frigga nudged him, catching his attention. No words came from her mouth, but instead she nodded to Damian and cocked an expectant brow.

"Of course, dear," he replied under his breath, before turning and making his way towards Damian.

I wasn't quite sure what they were planning on doing, but Odin wasted no time in kneeling down at Damian's side, his eyes gazing over the wound on Damian's neck with concern. "Please, don't take him from me."

My words caused him to turn his gaze towards me with furrowed brows. "Your mate has not passed over into the land of the dead yet. His spirit still lingers here with us now. I can heal his wounds, but it is up to you and his brothers to bring him back."

"Bring him back? We can do that?" James's voice said in shock.

Turning my gaze behind me, I looked at my three mates, who had all shifted back. They stared with tears in their eyes, and hope on their faces. Never had I seen them this upset before, but Damian was their brother.

He was the person they had always looked up to.

"Yes, my children, you can bring your brother back. But it is also down to him if he wishes to return. He may be here in spirit among us, but his will is what will drive him to stay with you."

Nothing but riddles floated in the air between us all. I wasn't quite sure whether we could make it happen, but if we had to, I would do whatever it took to bring him back to me.

"Heal him then. I will bring him back. Even if it takes every ounce of me, I will do it."

A small smile crossed Odin's face as he nodded his head, bending down towards Damien's lifeless body. He waved his hand over the wound on Damien's neck and instantly had healed. I was still in shock over how these gods and goddesses could work magic, but as soon as he was done, he turned his gaze back towards me.

"Loki will be taken care of for everything that he has done here. If it had not been for the strength of you and your mates, none of this would have been possible, but I do ask one thing of you."

"What is it? I will do anything to make sure that I have my mate back," I replied with desperation.

"We will need to close this gate once more. That way, no one can come back through who isn't supposed to be here. It was done before, but it will need to be done again," he replied as he looked at frigga. "As much as we would love to be able to come and go... we cannot. It isn't safe for the human realm to mingle with our kind."

I realized what he's saying. There was too much power in the realm of where they lived for the mortal realm to be able to withstand it. We had our own issues here and while the Council members who had come here were now dead—we weren't safe.

There were now packs without Alpha's and wolves without mates.

Retaliation would more than likely come one day, and when it did, we would have to be ready. We would have to realize that standing together would be our only way to survive.

"I understand. As soon as you leave, I will close the portal and seal it from our world."

Nodding his head, he turned back to the portal that stood shimmering in the air. Loki had been cast back and was now their problem to bear. I, however, was left with nothing but kind words from Frigga before her and Odin, and those who had come with them disappeared from our sight.

Closing my eyes, I let my celestial orbs take in the shimmering portal and with a wave of my hand, I closed and sealed it forever. Never again would their realm walk amongst ours. At least, not while I was alive.

Turning my eyes back toward Damian, a sob escaped my throat as I came closer and brushed the hair from his face. "My love, I know that you can hear me. Odin said that you were here with me in spirit and I want you to know that I need you. We all do. It doesn't matter to me you think that you're incomplete, because in my eyes you're not. You are everything to me."

"Ivy, if we're going to do this, we need to do it soon," Hale said softly as he knelt down at my side, staring at his brother, who lay lifeless on the ground.

I wasn't sure how I was supposed to bring him back, but somewhere deep inside me, I felt like there was an answer.

I felt like there was something that I could use to give him life.

"I'm not sure what's going to happen to us, but it could be painful. I just need you to bear with me... this is for Damian."

Each of them nodded in agreement. They were well aware of what was being asked of them. "To give life, I must take life. I must replace the mortality of four for the life of one."

Closing my eyes, I searched deep within myself. The darkness that had once been laying under my skin floated freely and within that darkness, I found a speck of light.

Pulling the images of what our family had been before Damian had gone missing, I used it to pull the light towards me. How I felt about him, the love that I had for him and his brothers, I pulled every ounce of it forward and pushed it into Damien.

As my eyes flew open, I saw the swirling mass of blue and white auras coming from my mates and I. The essence of our being. The life force for which we were celestial.

The only life that we had to give Damian to bring him back was that of our immortality.

Our Celestial connections would save him... and bind him to use once more.

"I love you, Damian."

The more I pushed, the louder my screams of pain echoed from my throat. The pain was unlike anything I had ever felt before and with one final, death-stricken scream, I shove the last of what I had straight at Damian watching his body glow with a light I had never seen before.

As the light brightened, darkness swirled around me. I wasn't sure if I was dying or if this was simply something else, but slowly I slipped into the darkness. Watching Damian's body fade from my sight like the closing of a movie.

"Please Damian... come back to me. I can't do this without you."

Hale

Never once had I seen such immense power as I did from Ivy. She had poured everything she had and pulled every ounce of power we had out of us and into her before pushing it, projecting it into Damian. It was like the life had been almost sucked out of me and in a way, it had been.

Our Lycan's had been stripped of us, and we were left as simple shifters.

Our wolves were now free in our minds, no longer hiding from the Lycan beasts that had always sat in the forefront. "What the fuck?"

As soon as Ivy collapsed, I watched Damien's eyes flutter open. A glimmer of hope radiating through me and through the link that I had with my brothers.

She had done it. Ivy had brought him back, but not without her own cost.

She laid on the ground, her hair no longer its white coloring, but had returned to the reddish brown she had before. I couldn't help but wonder if this meant she was human again or perhaps was she something else?

"Damian?" I stammered quickly as I rushed to him. Talon and James right by my side as he coughed and sputtered trying to understand what was going on.

"What happened?" He croaked out.

"Dude." James choked out with a laugh. "You fucking died, man. Can we try not to do that again?"

The three of us laughed at James's comment and though Damian had a hard time moving, he still laughed, which ended up causing him to wince in pain. "Perhaps you should relax, man," I said to him, shaking my head.

"Where's Ivy?" he said through a strained voice as he looked around searching for her. My eyes lifted from his and turned toward where she was laying.

"It took everything out of her, but she isn't dead."

"I need her—" he said, trying to move, but Talon and James held him back.

"No, we need to get both of you back to the pack house. The wounded are being treated at the hospital."

"Wounded. Did I miss the battle?" Damian smirked. "I was really hoping to kill someone for fucking up my hair."

Talon laughed and reached over, messing Damian's hair up further. "Yeah man, you missed the fucking battle, that's for sure. You should have seen Ivy. She kicked some serious ass out there."

As James picked up Ivy in his arms, Talon and I helped Damien to his feet as we attempted to make our way back towards the pack house. It wasn't as easy as it looked, but I will take on any difficulty life had to throw at me to make sure I had my brothers and Ivy by my side.

"Did she have the babies?" Damian asked softly. His eyes reached mine with guilt.

"She did, and wait till you see them. You have a lot to make up for."

It would take a while for things to get back to normal, and I knew more than anything, but if that meant I still had to stay as alpha for the time being, then I was fine with that. I did not have a problem helping my brother out.

The only thing that mattered to me was that he was alive and Ivy was alive and the twins were safe, which meant that our family could be whole again.

Our family could move past what had happened and try to rebuild the home that we had.

CHAPTER THIRTY-FOUR

Sleeping Beauty

Damian

I never really thought about what it would be like to die. However, the moment I faced it, the only thing I could think of was Ivy. Her beautiful blue eyes. Her long, enchanting hair. Not to mention how she trembled beneath my fingers when I took her, kissed her and loved her.

The way she deserved to be loved.

That moment ran through my mind often. Plagued my dreams with nightmares as I tried to forget what had happened. I was alive now.

But, even though I was, it didn't stop the nightmares from coming.

Two days ago, I opened my eyes. Two days ago, I breathed life into my lungs once more. Now that I was awake though, it forced me to face everything that happened, and the one thing that upset me the most was Ivy... my beautiful mate was unconscious.

From the looks of it, she didn't seem like she would wake up soon.

I felt bad that she was injured, but my brothers reassured me time and time again she knew what she was doing. That she wasn't dead, so that we simply had to give her time to wake back up.

I couldn't help but worry, though. What if she didn't wake up? What if we lost her again because of me... because she saved me?

Slowly, they had filled me in with all the details of things I had missed. Chaos that had happened. Things that happened to Ivy, and even the day she gave birth to our children. They helped me pick up all the missing pieces, so nothing was left out.

I was still broken, though.

To know I had missed out on the birth of my children killed me.

I would use this second chance at life to fix things that had happened to me previously. I would learn to forgive and forget and to love with unconditional devotion.

Because that was what a person with a second chance did.

Standing in the nursery, looking down at Pollux and Castor sleeping, I couldn't help but wonder what a future would have been like had I not been part of it. What they would have gone through had I not been here.

I knew they would have been taken care of and had my brothers, but still I couldn't help but wonder what they would have missed out on without me here.

Ivy had made me whole again, and for that, I would be forever indebted to her.

Turning my gaze away from the crib, I looked over to Ivy's bed, where she lay, sleeping peacefully. The soft pinks of her lips were so plump, so delicious. I wanted more than anything to kiss her, but in the end, all I wanted was for her to be awake.

For me, to hear her reprimanding me for some stupid shit I had done.

For her to tell me I'm being an asshole.

For her to put me in my place, that was all that I wanted.

I just wanted to have her back.

To know that she was OK.

My brothers and I hadn't always been good to her, especially me. Yet, time and time again, she forgave us though and tried to make our family whole. Time and time again, she put her life on the line to save us. But this would be the last time she needed to do that.

This would be the last time she ever had to put herself on the line for one of us, because it was our turn to protect her and to keep her safe.

"How are they doing?" Talon said, causing me to look over my shoulder at him. He walked from the open doorway of Ivy's room, through the passageway to the nursery, and smiled down at the twins.

"I still can't get over the fact that I've missed out on so much already."

"Dude, it's been like two weeks. You have plenty of time with them. Trust me, Pollux is one who likes to get up multiple times in the middle of the night. So you can have all of those shifts." Talon replied as he clasped a hand on my shoulder.

"I would take that a million times over if it meant being able to have my family whole."

He knew what I meant, and without having to say another word, he nodded his head in agreement before he, too, turned his glance over towards Ivy and slowly made his way to her bedside.

"I wish she would wake up and let us know she was okay," he said softly as he brushed his hand through her hair, rubbing his thumb against her cheek.

"She just needs time to heal."

Talon didn't waste a moment of time before looking over at me and shaking his head once more, laughing. "You're sounding like Hale. The only difference is he sounds like a broken record and you just sound like an echo."

"The only difference is I'm better looking," I replied, causing us both to laugh.

As much as I used to hate the comments Talon made, I was glad for them. I had missed this between us, and I was ready to make amends with it. I was ready to be the brother they needed.

~Six Months Later~

I still wasn't sure what was going on. She still hadn't woken up, and it had been six months since the day of the war. Even though the world outside kept turning without her there, she laid upstairs in the bed, still fast asleep.

I was losing hope.

I was feeling like we werould never t her back.

"She isn't dead," Priscilla said as she finished helping the doctor take Ivy's vitals. They two were just as concerned about her not having woken up, but Priscilla was ever the optimist in this.

"I don't understand why she's not waking up."

My comment caused her to glance over at where my brothers and I were standing. A small smile littered her face as she slowly stood. "It will be okay."

"Will it though?" I snapped in frustration. It had been six months and though we had been taking care of the twins, she had missed out on so much.

From their first time crawling to them eating solid foods. There was so much she had missed out on, and it killed me every day knowing she had.

We needed her back desperately.

We needed her to be here with us, because without her here, nothing in this world made sense.

"Just give her time and she will wake up. Things like this can't be rushed. She used a lot of energy to bring you back, Damien.

She exerted herself to limits we didn't think were possible. If she were dead, we would know, but her heart still beats very strong. It is her mind that is weak and her mind can take a long time to heal."

Priscilla was right, as usual, and as we all nodded in agreement, she stood and left with the doctor. "I suppose for now we continue what we were doing."

Hale's comment caused me to turn and glare at him. I knew he was right, but it didn't mean that he had to point out the obvious. A lot of things had changed around the back since I had last been here before the war.

One of them being that, I left Hale in charge.

When I came back, he tried to get me to take back over being Alpha, but in the end I declined. He had done a far better job that I and honestly, I never wanted it.

I wanted none of it.

The only reason I took the position was because I was the oldest, and looking back, I shouldn't have. I should have given it to Hale back then because he was the only one out of the four of us who could do it with a level head.

And I was proud of him.

"You have a meeting today with our allies, correct?" I asked him as I turned from the room with my brothers and headed downstairs.

"You know, Damien, if you're going to constantly keep reminding me of the things that I need to do, you should have just stayed alpha."

"Look, you are the alpha. I was no good at it, and you have done wonderfully accept your position," I replied as I plopped down onto the sofa with a smirk on my lips.

"I have accepted my position, yet you keep trying to interfere in all of it. Why don't you find yourself a hobby then? I mean, you've never had free time in your life. Spend more time with the children. Go find something to do."

Something to do like that was even fucking possible. I hadn't actually had fun since I had been in school, and even then, I still had responsibilities.

"When Ivy is awake, I will then take free time. Until then, I will continue to help the three of you run this pack properly and I will spend more time with the children as I have been since the day I woke up." They knew I was serious, as I always was.

Yet, deep down in their bond, I could tell that they were unsure if I was actually okay. How was I supposed to show them I was okay, considering everything that we had been through?

"Just give it time, Damien. Everything is going to work out." James's words were comforting in a way. I knew he was right. In time, Ivy would wake up and everything would go back to normal.

But until that happened, I would simply have to patiently wait.

A knock at the front door drew all of our attention, and narrowing my brows, I looked at my brothers with confusion. We weren't expecting anybody, and the doctor and Priscilla had left a while ago.

Standing to my feet, I walked towards the doors with my brothers behind me and as I opened it, my eyes went wide with surprise. Standing before me was none other than the Valkyrie that had once aided Ivy.

"Kara, isn't it?" I asked with slight confusion, hoping that I had gotten her name right.

"I am glad that you still remember me," she said with a hint of amusement in her voice as she pushed past me and my brothers and entered the house.

"What are you doing here? Ivy isn't awake yet."

"Oh, I know she is, and I have waited six months patiently for her to do so. However, it seems that things are slightly in limbo for the time being, so unfortunately there's something that I'm going to have to discuss with you guys and you will not be happy about it."

Fuck, why does she always come with bad news?

CHAPTER THIRTY-FIVE

Odin's Order

Damien

The moment I saw Kara, I had an inkling suspicion she wasn't here for pleasure. However, despite my uncertainties, I tried to remain positive. Perhaps she was simply down here from the realm to check in on Ivy, considering as far as I was told, she is Odin's daughter.

How that is even possible I still can't comprehend, but then again, with as many crazy things that currently go down regularly, I try not to comprehend much.

Trying to understand how this all worked did nothing but give me migraines.

So the moment she walked in, and informed us we would not be happy about the news she had to share, my mind almost snapped.

Were we not able to have one moment where we weren't stressed out or trying not to die?

"I don't understand," Hale replied, staring at Kara with confusion. "What could you possibly have to tell us that would make us unhappy?"

"A lot actually," she hummed.

"Will you just tell us what the fuck you want?" Talon snapped.

"Calm yourself. I'm far older than you are. You stand no chance against me."

"What are you talking about?" James asked, looking completely confused. I felt the same as he did. How was just going to come in here, and act like this and not tell us what it is she wanted?

"Why don't we go into the living room and sit down and take a seat? Because what I have to tell you will not go over well." Kara finally sighed, gesturing towards the living room.

Why is it anytime anybody came to give you bad news, they typically started the conversation off like that?

I didn't understand these people and though I have been a dick most of my life, I still tried the hardest I could to be more forthcoming when I was giving information.

Unlike people, obviously like Kara, who beat around the bush and then drop everything at all at once. Always riddles with these people.

As the five of us moved into the living room, taking our seats, Kara stayed standing in the doorway. Her wings folded back behind her, with a concerned gaze within her eyes as she stared at the four of us.

"Are you going to leave us in suspense, or are you going to get on with it?" I asked her, watching as her eyes finally landed on me.

"It's about your children."

"What about my children?" I replied, feeling the bond between my brothers and I perk with attention. We would protect our children with our lives.

So when someone came talking about our pups, we were ready to go to battle no matter the situation. We would protect them with our lives.

"Well, right to the point, of course," she sighed. "The day your children were born, a new prophecy was born, and with it a future that only they can paint. It has made the gods consider the terms of the agreements we once had about keeping the portal closed."

"You can't be serious," Talon laughed. "The portal is to remain sealed so nothing can pass. Ivy made sure of that, before giving her immortality, along with ours, to bring Damian back."

I couldn't help but notice how Talon talked about what they did for me. He hadn't been himself since that day, and I was fairly sure it had something to do with his Lycan being taken away from him. Something he never wanted to talk about.

"We understand the situation between the five of you, but unfortunately, that doesn't matter," Kara replied. "Things have changed."

"Changed?!" Talon growled, standing to his feet. "She has been out since the day it happened six months ago, Kara!"

Her eyes narrowed at Talon, and as they did, I watched Hale stand and walk towards his brother, who all but relaxed at what he said. It only took a moment, and Talon stormed from the room, disappearing from sight. The sound of the back door slamming shut echoed through the house, to which Kara rolled her eyes.

"You mortals are all so temperamental."

"Again, Kara, please get to the point," I replied, pinching the bridge of my nose in annoyance.

"As I was saying," she sighed heavily. "Your children aren't normal. They belong to the realm of the gods with the powers they possess and will grow into one day. This is the concern Odin has about his grandchildren."

I was too stunned at what she was saying to speak, but Hale was not.

Turning to face her, I watched him cock a brow with his jaw clenched in anger. "No. I don't care what Odin wants, but that will not happen."

As Kara's eyes turned towards him, she raised her own brow and laughed. "You have no say in that, Hale. It's what is being demanded."

I had no clue what the hell they were talking about, but the more they talked in code, the more I felt aggravated by it all. "Do either of you care to explain what the fuck is going on? Because I'm tired of this bullshit."

Both Hale and Kara turned their attention toward me. Kara's face seemed to look disgusted because I wasn't keeping up with the current conversation, whereas Hale simply sighed in a frustrated manner, and started pacing around the room.

"What she's trying to say in not so many words is that she feels the twins would do better in an environment where they could travel back and forth between our realms."

Taking a moment to let what Hale said sink in, I contemplated the idea of them traveling back and forth between realms as they got older. It honestly wouldn't be the worst thing for them and if they had the abilities their mother did, then there was a lot that they could learn.

"I don't see what's wrong with them traveling back and forth. Oden's their grandfather, after all, and they have a family there with Frigga and Kara. It would be beneficial if they have these powers to learn from people who can help. Of course, when they're older, that is."

My reply seemed to shock Hale, but the look on Kara's face spoke of something else. She was amused by what was going on, but said nothing to voice this.

"You both seem to miss exactly what I'm talking about. Your initial assumption was close to being accurate however, I wasn't talking about them traveling back and forth."

"Well, do you care to explain, then?" I asked, gesturing for her to continue, considering she had wasted the last thirty minutes of our time standing here, speaking in riddles and beating around the bush.

"She wants to take them," James's voice piped up from the silence that consumed where he had been sitting the entire time. He had remained quiet, watching the three of us go back and forth, observing what exactly was going on.

But the moment he said that, my heart all stopped.

"At least one of you is perceptive," Kara muttered as she crossed her arms over her chest and leaned against the wall.

"Take them? You're not taking the twins. That is absolutely ridiculous and completely out of the question."

"Hale, you don't really have a say in this. Odin has demanded that they be brought to us. They don't belong in this world. They are celestials... you all are not. Even Ivy isn't considered part of our world anymore. She may have the blood of a celestial running through her veins, but that is it," Kara replied.

I couldn't wrap my hand around it. Kara actually thought she could come in here and take my children... and Odin... he was willing to do this to his daughter?

What kind of father would do that regardless if the children were special?

I couldn't let it happen. I had to stop her from destroying us.

"I don't give a fuck what Odin says. We are not allowing you to take our children. They're babies and their mother is unconscious upstairs. How would you feel if you woke up to see that your children were gone?" I snapped at her.

I couldn't believe she had actually come here under the assumption we were just going to hand over our children and let her take them from us, never able to see them again.

"It isn't up to you. I don't understand what you're not getting. I'm here to collect your children, and the four of you cannot stop me from doing so."

Kara was issuing a challenge.

One that I will face head on if I had to.

I may have only just woken up, but there was no way I was going to allow this woman to come in here and tell me she was taking my children away.

Children I had only gotten a few months to spend time with. Children who Ivy, my mate, hadn't even properly been able to spend time with because of her current situation.

God knows what will happen when she wakes up and sees that so much time has passed.

"Look, there has to be something, some type of agreement that we can come up with. Something that Odin will make an exception for. Give us time. At least let us spend the first eighteen years of their life with them, and then by that point, when they're adults, if they need to go there, then so be it."

My response made her hesitate, her fingers running over her jawline as she seemed to ponder over what I had said. "That might possibly work. From what the prophecy says, the children won't come into their powers properly until they turn eighteen."

"Talk to him then. See what he says. See if he would make this deal with us. Give us until they turn eighteen." I was all but begging her to agree, and after a moment of silence, she nodded.

"Very well. I will be back in a few days with my answer. Until then, you may continue to have your brief family reunion, and hopefully Ivy will join you soon."

I felt a sense of relief was over me the moment Kara turned and made her way from our home. We were safe for now, and hopefully Odin would agree to what I asked. Give us time... that was all that I wanted.

"Was she fucking serious?" Hale said softly as he stared out the window.

"It doesn't matter right now. At least she's gone."

Turning my attention to my brothers, they stood staring at me.

"What the fuck did you just do?" James whispered.

"What? I just made sure she didn't take our kids."

"Yeah for now!" he screamed at me, jumping to his feet with his fists clenched at his sides. "How the fuck could you offer that and without Ivy even being awake!"

"We don't even know if she will ever wake up!" I snapped back as I moved from where I was sitting towards the stairs. I had nothing else to say to them. In the end, I was doing what I had to, to make sure that I didn't lose my children.

If he agreed, it would give us eighteen years to try to find a way out of the deal. To try to change their minds so that our children didn't have to go.

Kara hadn't been lying when she said we couldn't stop her.

If she had really wanted to take them, she wouldn't have come to speak with us in the first place. She would have taken them when we were sleeping, and we wouldn't have been able to stop it.

Deep down, I think her coming to speak with us was her way of saying she didn't agree with Odin. She hoped we could give her something Odin would end up agreeing to. It was just a shame she couldn't come out and say that to begin with.

Yet, knowing this, I couldn't stop thinking about what James said.

I had made the offer while Ivy wasn't even present, and I could only hope she wouldn't hate me when she woke up. I didn't want to start things off wrong again.

CHAPTER THIRTY-SIX

Leaving the Void

Ivy

A swirling light wrapped around me. A feeling that made me feel as if I was floating. All of the pain I had once felt completely slipped away from me and I was left unsure of where I was, but I knew I had a purpose, and that purpose was to get back to wherever I was supposed to be.

If only I knew exactly where that was.

Looking around through the white space around me, I searched for anything that could help me remember exactly what had happened. I knew I had to get back to somebody very important. The only problem was I didn't know how I was supposed to do that.

Glancing around, I freed myself from the weightlessness of my situation. My feet hit the floor of the white void with ease. There was no telling in which direction I was to go in order to get out of this place, but I knew I had to go somewhere.

A figure walked toward me from the distance. A woman with long brown hair that seemed to fall down her back in waves. Her blue eyes stared at me with amusement before she stopped mere feet from where I stood.

There was no way she was from the same time as me considering that instead of normal clothing she wore furs and linen, her appearance almost medieval causing my confusion to fold in even more.

"Who are you?" I asked slowly, hoping she could understand me.

"I'm not stupid, if that's what you think," she chuckled as she crossed her arms over her chest. "My names is Anna."

Now I felt completely stupid. Of course she wasn't... nevermind.

"Do you know where I am?"

"You don't know where you are?" she replied, cracking a smile. "That isn't good, is it?"

Rolling my eyes, I groaned. "Look, if you're here to piss me off, please don't. I have had a long day... or well. God, I don't even know. Regardless, I have to get out of here."

"I know you do. That's why I'm here."

Was she being serious? She was here to help me, and instead she was doing nothing but confusing me. "Well, what are you waiting for, then?"

"For you to decide to be polite for one," she laughed. "Never did I think I would get this honor, but circumstances aren't always what we expect them to be now, are they?"

I didn't have the slightest clue what she was referring to, but with annoyance filling me, I pushed it aside, praying she would attempt to help me other than how she was currently acting. "Look, I'm sorry. We started off wrong."

"Fair enough, Ivy." She smirked as she walked past me, heading into the white void, as if she had a destination in mind.

"Wait! Where are you going?!" I called out as I ran along after her.

"It isn't easy getting back, but it is definitely something that you need to do."

She was talking was as if she knew where I came from. As if she knew me. "How did you know my name?" I asked, hoping she would give me a real answer.

Instead of answering right away, she stopped in the middle of the void and turned to me, raising a brow. "Because you gave birth to me. Don't you think I would know my own mother?"

Mother?!

This woman must be on something. I wasn't her mother.

"I think you have me mixed up with someone else," I laughed, shaking my head. "It's obvious that you can't help me. I do hope you're searching—"

"He was right when he said you talked a lot," she chuckled. "Regardless, you are my mother. Just not in this form of me."

"What do you mean, not this form of you—"

It suddenly dawned on me the possibility of what she was saying. Stranger things had happened to me every day, and one thing I knew for sure is that if it was weird, it was probably true.

"Castor?" I whispered, watching as Anna's eyes lit up.

"Yes, sweet darling Castor is the new version of me."

This couldn't possibly be happening. There was no way my child was to have a nearly identical fate to me. There was no way... wait. How can I suddenly remember them and just a little while ago I couldn't fucking remember anything?!

"My memories—"

"Yeah, they are coming back, aren't they? It happens sometimes. You really got hurt in that battle, and though Castor doesn't understand everything because she is a baby. I do." Her words caught me by surprise. How was it she knew?

With so many questions, my head hurt as I tried to grasp what she was saying.

What was I honestly going to do in my current situation?

She knew a way out, and I needed her help. There was no way I was going to do this on my own, and the last thing I wanted to do was stay here longer.

"OK, show me what you need to show me..."

The woman who called herself Anna stared at me, her blue eyes twinkling with nothing but amusement because of my current situation. It often reminded me of how James or even Hale would look at me, as if they knew I was being silly and I would end up finding out the results of my actions later on.

"Before you go, there are some things that we need to discuss." She caught me completely off guard as I was preparing for her to just magically wave her hands or something and shimmer me back to where I was supposed to be.

But no, of course, that wouldn't be the fucking case.

"Okay then," I said in a very dramatic tone as I waited patiently for her to explain. "What else it is that I needed to know?"

Hesitating for a moment as if she didn't like my response, she seemed to ponder over what I said. "You're irritated by me."

I groaned. "Now I am."

You would think she would listen to her mother. Maybe I can make her.

"You can't," she replied, crossing her arms over her chest with a smug smile. "I'm far older than you, regardless if you are the mother to the person who I belong inside."

Holy shit, had she just read my mind?

Like... she can actually read my mind! What the fuck is going on?

"Yes, I can read your mind now. Will you please stop swearing so much? It's not ladylike." Anna complained as she rolled her eyes, walking another twenty feet before stopping again.

"I'm sorry. I just wasn't expecting all of this, ya know? God, this is so aggravating that I honestly can't remember anything."

"Honestly, it's probably better that you don't." She gave me a pointed look as she glanced over her shoulder at me.

"No one died, right? Like no one that I care about, anyway."

Groaning in protest, she let out a heavy breath and pinched the bridge of her nose. "No, they didn't."

"Well, that's good then," I said with a sigh of relief. "So what exactly is it you wanna tell me before you shimmer me back to wherever I came from?"

Taking a deep breath, she paused for a slight moment, as if collecting her thoughts. "Technically, you're not going anywhere. You're simply waking up."

"Waking up?"

"Yes... your body never left property. You have been asleep for a very long time, but now it's time for you to wake up."

"Oh, okay then. Well, let's get to it."

"You're so impatient," she groaned again. "Look... before you go, you need to know that not everything is as it was. Things have changed... people have changed. Your absence cause small havoc to rip through your family and in the future it may cause problems. There is one person who will fight against you at every turn, but you mustn't give up on them."

Was she talking about the guys?

"You don't have to worry about that. Me and the guys are going to finally be able to have the life that we always wanted."

"I wasn't referring to your mates," she sneered, rolling her eyes dramatically.

"OK then, who are you talking about?"

"I'm talking about Castor. Things will never be the same. You've missed out on a lot already, and even though she's still young, you're going to face challenges between her and her brother. They're not like the others, nor will they ever be like those who will come in the future." I didn't understand for one second what she was talking about.

My children weren't different. They were normal, and happy... thinking about them made my heart hurt, wondering how much time I had missed out on their lives.

"No matter how different Castor and Pollux are, they are my children. I will never, ever, under any circumstance, turn my back on them. I'm their mother." I had to make her see reason.

She stared at me for a moment, her eyes boring into mine, as if she was trying to judge my sincerity. However, considering the fact she could read my mind, she should have been able to tell I was being sincere.

"You have no clue what awaits you in the future, not to mention the deal that has been made. You have to hold your part of the bargain. Even if it wasn't a deal that you particularly made yourself."

Now she was talking about deals.

Last time I checked, I had made no deals, and God forbid if my mates had made some kind of proclamation while I had been away. I couldn't believe they would do something to upset me like that. They were the men who swore to protect me and the children.

Perhaps Anna simply hit her own head and has lost her mind.

"Okay, I promise. I will fulfill whatever end of the bargain I made or that someone else made for me, even though, of course, there isn't anything like that," I said with little enthusiasm as I gestured to her to continue with getting me the fuck out of here.

A smile crept across her face as she nodded her head and then waved her hand opening a door in the middle of a white void that didn't even exist.

It was literally like the white void had opened itself and became a door.

I was astonished.

I could not fucking believe it.

This entire time, there had been a magic door somewhere there, and maybe I could have just waved my hand and open it.

"Remember your promise, if you do not follow through, Castor's life will never be her own. She needs that end of the bargain in order to survive."

Stepping forward, I stopped for a moment and glanced back at Anna. Her words lingered in the air as I watched her concern gaze watch me leave. "I will protect her with my life. Anything she needs, she will have."

"Good," she replied softly. "Because one day what she needs will break your heart.

CHAPTER THIRTY-SEVEN

Returning Home

~~One year since the fall~~

James

One year.

It had been one year since the fall of the war, and Ivy still was not with us. My heart longed to see her again, and every day I passed where she slept on the bed, I contemplated if we would ever get her back, if the gods would ever release her from the prison she was in.

That was right. I blamed them.

They allowed her to do this and they could have helped her out of this, regardless of what anybody said. Her mind needed rest, yes, but a fucking year.

Something was wrong, and she needed help.

What killed me the most was that I couldn't help her.

Standing in the kitchen, I grabbed the rest of the towels from the basket I had washed and slowly folded them. It was time for the twins' bath, and even though Hale had just come down and said they were perfectly content in the crib, staring at Ivy,

I couldn't help but feel slightly jealous they seemed to know something we didn't.

"I don't know why you're always such a pessimist, James. You used to be so happy all the time," Talon growled with irritation at my latest comment.

"You're not treating them right on the training field, and you know it. The war has been over. You have to give those men a break every now and again."

"Last time I checked, you weren't in charge of training anymore. You were playing Daddy because you didn't want to get a nanny," Talon snapped, causing anger to soar through me.

"Go fuck yourself, Talon. Those are our children. How dare you fucking say something like that?"

"Yeah, I know they are. But you know what... we each have to have time for ourselves, too. You're literally up there fucking killing yourself day and night, and even at night when they're sleeping, you don't sleep because the only thing you do is sit in the chair and watch them and watch Ivy as if you're hoping she'll actually fucking wake up. She isn't coming back, James! We should have laid her to rest already!"

Talon, suggesting Ivy was dead, pissed me off more than anything. I knew he was only lashing out because he was angry, because he was hurt. He prayed in the beginning to the goddess all the time to bring her back and cried at her bedside.

But day after day after day, he was let down because she still wasn't back.

I could feel his pain through the bond. A pain I wish I could end for him. But Talon was the most messed up out of all of us.

At least he was until Damian woke up again.

Casting my gaze towards the small sitting room that led off of the kitchen, I watched Damian sit in the chair, his eyes staring out the window exactly the same as it was every day.

We were on our own now.

Ivy's mother had returned to her pack and mate months ago, mourning the loss of a child who wasn't dead. Kate had gotten pregnant, and now with the new baby around, she was back home with her mate being a mother.

Everything was continuing on as if Ivy wasn't lying upstairs, missing out on life.

Knowing that upset me, because she deserved to be here.

"I'm going to go ahead and get the twins in the bath. We promised movie night tonight and we're going to keep that. It's what Ivy would have wanted. Now, if you don't mind, please finish setting it up."

Talon sighed, nodding his head. The conversation was over and as I headed up the stairs, I couldn't help but think something about today was different.

Something about today that would change everything.

I just wish I knew what the fuck it was.

Ivy

Panic flurried through me as I felt myself gasping for air. I had to escape break free of the water holding me back. My mind trying to break through the surface of raging waves that pounded against me.

That is until I found the right moment and jolted my way to freedom. My eyes opened wide as I sat up, gasping and sputtering for air. A sense of joy and wonder filling me as I took in the surrounding room. Through the dim lighting of the room, I took in the fresh flowers and the smell of fresh cut grass that lingered through the air.

Someone had obviously been airing out the room often.

It wasn't until I cast my eyes to the right of me I saw the celestial orbs of Castor staring back at me with an excited expression. Her tiny hands clapping together frantically as she looked behind her to the dark-haired boy with pitch black eyes.

Pollux.

Both of my twins were standing there staring at me, but they weren't the same small babies I had left behind when I went to save Damian. Instead, they looked well over a year old, and realized that my heart hurt.

"Oh, my sweet babies."

I tried to move to get up from the bed, but unfortunately, my legs refused to cooperate. My time laid in bed caused the muscle mass in my body to weaken. It didn't matter though, because I was determined to find a way.

As I stared back at my children, I saw Castor look towards the bedroom door and get excited again before she turned to her brother, who seemed to be indifferent to the situation.

"Okay, you two... whose ready for a bath—"

James stepped into the room with a stack of towels in his hand, and as his eyes latched onto mine, he froze in his step. The only sound was Castor laughing and clapping her hands at the reaction before her. "Hey, James."

"You're awake," he mumbled as he glanced from the twins to me, and then back to the twins. "How—"

"Do you really wanna know how, or are you going to give me a kiss?"

He didn't waste a second before he was across the room, pulling me into his arms, pressing his lips to mine in a slow, deep, passionate kiss. To me, it was only yesterday I had kissed him, but to them... it had been much longer.

Pulling away, I smiled softly, wincing at the pain in my side. "How long have I been out?"

"It's been a year, Ivy," he whispered, his eyes falling to my lap as he seemed to try and hold back the tears. "No one thought you would wake up... but I didn't give up. I couldn't."

Running my hand over the side of his cheek, I kissed him again with a smile.

"Well, why don't I surprise the others?"

Furrowing his brow, he smiled at me. "What do you mean?"

"Hand me my children and I will show you," I laughed.

"Oh, shit... sorry, sweetie," he said, jumping to his feet and striding towards the twins. They were both eager at this point to get out, and were trying their hardest to escape him as approached the bed.

As their sweet faces came closer, they crawled onto the bed. Their arms wrapped around me as they snuggled into my chest, laying their heads against my breasts. They had missed me just as much as I missed them, and as the tears streamed down my cheeks, I thought of the others.

'I'm home.' I said through the link, causing James to smile.

It didn't take but a second before I heard the thundering footsteps of the men racing up the stairs, heading down the hallway straight for me. My door burst open as Talon, Hale and Damian stood before me.

The twins had smiles upon their faces that brightened my own and as they rushed to me, kissing the side of my head while they held me, I couldn't stop staring at Damian.

The last time I had seen him, he died in front of me.

Loki had slit his throat, and his body laid lifeless upon the ground. A sob left my throat as my red-rimmed eyes filled with more tears stared at him. "You're alive."

Never once had I really ever seen Damian show so much emotion as he did in those two seconds after my words left his lips. He nodded his head in silence as he approached me. Almost as if he was waiting for me to disappear again.

"Ivy—" he whispered. "I'm so sorry."

"For what?" I laughed through my tears. "It wasn't your fault."

"All of this is my fault. I should have done things differently from the beginning, but for so long, I kept you at arms length and didn't realize what I had until it was too late."

Looking to Hale and Talon, they moved over so I could get to Damian. He came close, sitting on the edge of the bed so I could wrap my arms around him the best I could with the twins still stuck to me. "You don't have to apologize to me. I'm your mate forever and always. I love you, no matter what."

It was a touching moment for us and having them all back made my heart swell with happiness. The time ticked on as the men told me about everything that had happened since I was asleep, including the twins' first birthday I wasn't present for.

"We didn't do anything big for them," James said softly. "Maybe we can, now that you're awake."

The guys all looked at each other in approval before looking at me. As my eyes drifted down to my now sleeping twins on my chest, I smiled. "I think that's a great idea. But maybe in a week or so, once I have gotten my strength back."

"Of course, Ivy. Why don't we celebrate it during the upcoming festival?"

"Festival?" I asked Hale. "What festival?"

"The lunar festival to celebrate the gods," Talon replied with a sneer. He wasn't too happy about the festival, but as soon as I laid a soft hand on his arm, he seemed to calm under my touch.

"None of this was their fault," I said to each of them. "We mustn't hold grudges."

"That's easy for you to say, Ivy," he replied with hurt in his voice. "We watched you basically wither away over the past year and wondering if that was the day you were going to stop breathing. It killed us."

My heart hurt for them, but I could understand what they meant.

I, myself, hurt because of all the time I had missed with them, but now I was awake and that was all that mattered. "Everything will be okay now. I just need to get my strength back."

Nodding, they all agreed, even Talon, who was reluctant.

I wanted everything to be perfect, and I wanted to pack to know I was still here for them. I was still their Luna, and would protect them no matter what.

"The festival is then. Let's let the pack welcome back their Luna."

CHAPTER THIRTY-EIGHT

Park Time Memories

Damian

The moment I walked into the room and saw Ivy awake, I was blown away. I didn't think it would ever be possible, and I had slowly started to lose hope, but the moment I heard her voice through my mind, I knew it couldn't be real.

How many times had I actually contemplated hearing her?

More than I can count, that's for sure.

For a moment I thought I was losing my mind, but when Talon and Hale took off running up the stairs, I knew it must have been real and the possibility had made my heart soar.

I thanked the gods for bringing her back to me, but I just prayed it would be forever this time. I couldn't survive losing her again.

A few days had passed since then, and with every moment she was awake, I slowly found myself going better and better. I didn't feel hollow and empty anymore. I didn't feel like I was the reason she was gone.

Instead, we spent every moment together as if nothing had ever happened.

As if the war and everything else had only been a dream.

Sitting in the living room with Ivy and the twins, I watched her sit on the floor as the twins handed her various toys. I had waited so long to see this, and now that I could, I wanted to hold the memory forever.

The twins had their mother back, and from the looks in their eyes, they were happy..

She was the love of my life, and I hated it took me so long to realize. But now she was back, and I was going to make sure I showed her just how much she meant to me. Just how much she meant to this family.

There was no way in hell I was ever walking away from her again. I would never keep a secret from her again. Those days were long over.

I'd learned my lesson just as my brothers had learned theirs.

"How are you feeling today?" Hale said to Ivy as he stepped into the living room.

"I'm feeling better than I was before. My strength is almost back completely, but I will admit that it will take some time before I'm running laps around you guys."

Her comment caused both Hale and I to laugh. The twins glanced up at the two of us with curiosity before slowly going back to their toys. "They're happy that you're home."

She glanced at me for a moment before looking back at the twins; her smile brightening knowing what I said was true. "I'm happy that I'm home as well. I have already missed out so much."

"We have plenty of time to make new memories," Hale replied, causing her smile to fall slightly as she nodded her head.

"I know, but still, I missed out on so much already. Some of those memories are ones that I should have been part of that I will never get back."

I knew full well what she was referring to. She'd missed the first time the twins had crawled, eating solid foods, those very first steps that they took. Those were memories she wanted, but she would never have because of what had happened.

Regardless, though, she didn't hold a grudge because of it. She accepted what was and moved forward with what would be. Ivy was by far one of the strongest women I have ever met in my entire life, and I was lucky to call her mine.

"I was thinking maybe today we can take the children outside, take them to the play in the park. They've been going there and playing with the other children for the past few months."

As Ivy stared at the children for a few more minutes, her eyes connected with mine again, and she slowly nodded her head. The pack knew she was awake again. They knew the moment she awoke, how strong the bond with her had grown.

The problem was we had kept everybody at bay for the time being, wanting to make sure she was ready to see everyone before they tried to force themselves upon her, eager to win her favor once again.

"I would really like that. It's been a while since I've seen everyone. Of course I was pregnant at the time, but if the children have been going there, then I want that to continue. It's about them, not me," she replied cheerfully.

"That's settled then. I'll go ahead and tell James to pack their bags and we can head out here in just a bit." Standing to my feet, I moved from the room to give Ivy time alone and drug Hale with me, who looked confused why I made him follow.

"What?" he asked as soon as we were out of the room.

"Because she deserves time alone with them. Instead of one of us always hovering."

Nodding his head, he sighed as he followed me to find James. I was excited about the prospect of being able to show her off to the pack again, being able to get her outdoors out into the fresh air with the children and for her to see the progress we've made over the past year within the pack.

One of the things I, myself, took head on was an idea she had given when she first came here. The night we had dinner with her father and Allison.

She wanted us to create a library for the children, a place where they can study, where pack kids could be tutored and get them excited about learning, but to also get them excited about who they are.

Surprisingly enough, we never had a library in our pack, which I had never really considered being an issue until I started researching what other packs did and noticed a library was actually very common within packs.

Which, of course, made me feel like a complete idiot.

Ivy was going to be excited. I knew she would.

The new building finished only just over a month ago and was filled with so many unique books. Not to mention we had requested books from the citadel and they had been more than happy to give them to us to educate younger pack members.

There was no fight anymore with the council as they had replaced their entire staff at a majority rule of the packs, so with the new council instilled, changes could be made. However, it didn't stop us from worrying to an extent.

There were still rogue players around we had to be careful about.

Ones that weren't happy with the changes we made, and the damage we caused.

The moment I had told James Ivy wanted to go out towards the play group with the children, there was a burst of excitement across his face as he started rambling on about packing a picnic and making sure we took the blanket, making sure Ivy had enough water, making sure the twins had their snacks.

It was literally one thing after another as Hale and I stood stunned by the way James was acting. "Dude, calm down," Hale laughed.

"Hale's right. You're acting crazy right now."

It didn't matter what we said, he just kept mumbling as he went around taking care of things. I wasn't sure what his damn issue was, but it was probably best we stayed out of his way.

By the time we actually left the house and made our way towards the park, Ivy was laughing hysterically as she watched James and Talon try to carry the items James packed while managing one twin. Talon had Castor, who smiled happily, but Pollux was a handful and that boy didn't want to be held.

"Is it always like this?" Ivy asked, looking up at me with a smile.

"Not exactly. James went way overboard today compared to how we normally go to the park. I'm sure that's just because he is trying to impress you."

"Go fuck yourself, Damian," James snapped, having heard what I said. "One can never be too prepared."

His comment caused a commotion of laughter to spill from us as we approached the usual shade tree the twins loved to sit under. The low-hanging branches would one day be a place I had no doubt the twins would climb, and as James sat everything down, he left Talon and Hale in charge of the twins.

They were excited and unwilling to listen to anything being said.

Then again, they were the only one so who could blame them.

"Pollux, no!" Hale shouted as Pollux tried to scamper off near the swings, almost getting taken out completely by another kid who couldn't stop if they tried. Hale reaching Pollux just in time to snatch him out of the way, but to end up getting kicked in the back by the little kid who looked as if he wanted to cry.

"Oh, poor guy. It wasn't his fault," Ivy said softly. "Hale, leave that baby alone. He didn't mean too."

Hale turned to look at Ivy in disbelief, but she narrowed her eyes and shook her head instead. "It's okay, sweetie. Don't let that big bad Alpha worry you. Go play with your friends."

The way she took charge and made that little boy feel better as he wiped his tears away was amazing. It was another Luna quality about her I loved.

"Good job," I said, smiling sweetly at her as I pulled her towards me on the blanket.

"Well, it wasn't the kid's fault. Hale should have been watching Pollux better."

"Pollux is fast," I chimed in laughing, to which she hesitated and gave me a confused face.

"Yeah, how is that? They are one... they shouldn't be moving like that so quickly."

Shrugging my shoulders, I looked to James and Talon, who held Castor. We had wondered the same thing ourselves many times, but we didn't have the answers. Even Priscilla didn't and just chalked it up to the good genes they had.

"Who knows? Every kid grows at their own pace, Ivy."

Nodding her head, she sighed with a content smile. "I suppose... oh, I was going to ask... what's this festival I keep hearing about? I want details."

James' smile grew as he went into a rant about the festival and all the party details he had, even down to the damn bonfire I was completely against. Ivy seemed intrigued though, and even threw in a few suggestions of things to do with the younger kids.

"I say we celebrate the festival, and our family. We can do something big. Maybe have Kate and my mom fly in?"

"If that's what you want, then you will have it," Talon replied quickly, stealing the words straight from my mouth.

It wasn't going to be exactly easy sharing her between us all, but the more and more we spent time together, the easier it became. I just hoped it would last this way forever.

There was no telling what would happen when I told her about Kara's visit.

I just wanted to wait a bit for her to recover completely before telling her everything, because I had a feeling she would not take it very well.

CHAPTER
THIRTY-NINE

Sexual Reunions

Ivy

Almost two weeks had passed since I had woken up, and I was excited with the preparations for today's bonfire. Over the past two weeks, I had taken slow steps towards getting my strength back, and spending as much time with my children as possible. Tonight, though, was going to be a huge step for me. I'd be putting myself back out into the light of society.

The event was massive, from what James was explaining. He had even called Kate and my mother, ushering them to come up for the celebration. To come up, and celebrate the twins', and our family. Of course, there was no way either of them would pass that up.

So, although the twins' birthday had already happened, we were still going to do something small. Something that I could be part of which made me excited, considering I had missed out on so much already.

Not to mention James wanted to give the pack an event to show that we wanted them involved in our children's lives. All of it was rather magical in a way, but completely overlooked in the moment as I found myself more entertained watching James run around his room, freaking out over preparations.

"James, will you calm down? You're literally freaking out over nothing. Everything is set up and perfect. I don't know why you're overreacting."

This was the third time this morning I had told James to calm down. He literally was making a fuss over everything, and I wasn't sure why.

"Ivy, my stress levels are literally through the roof right now. How the fuck am I supposed to calm down when everything is so chaotic at the moment?" he replied with furrowed brows and a dramatic expression.

"Uh, because you're overreacting," I said, breaking out into a fit of laughter. "Do you have an OCD outbreak every time we plan something?"

James turned to me with a shocked expression, his mouth wide and his eyes glaring. It took everything in me not to laugh, but before he could say anything, Hale stepped into the room with his hands in his front pockets, leaning against the door frame.

"I see that James is in one of his moods again."

"Fuck off, Hale," James snapped with irritation. "You can't make this shit look half as good."

"Is that right?" He hummed as his eyes slid to me. "Entertainment for the day, then?"

"Something like that?" I laughed. "Did you need something?"

"I hoped that I might be able to steal you for a moment."

The smirk that quickly lined his face made me think it could have been sexual in nature, and considering I hadn't had a rendezvous with them in the sheets since I had awoke, there was no way I was going to pass up the opportunity.

Standing from the chair I was sitting in, I playfully bit on my lips as I fluttered my eyelashes, sauntering towards him. "Sounds like something fun."

"Not exactly," he laughed, shaking his head. "I was just hoping that you might be able to step into my office with me."

Of course, it wasn't what I thought.

With a heavy sigh, I kept the smile on my face, and gestured for him to lead the way. I may not have been getting laid, but spending time with any of my mates was something I would not pass up.

Following him down the stairs towards his office, I took in the beautiful array of flowers that had been placed around the home in preparation of the day's festivities. People were up to their elbows in early morning preparations, and knowing the pack came together like this was something that touched me.

Team work makes the dream work and all that jazz.

As soon as I stepped into the office, he closed the door behind us and made his way over towards his desk. My eyes lingered on every curve of his muscles through his tight black t-shirt, down toward the rock hard cock I knew wanted to play with in his pants.

"So what was so important to pull me away from watching James act crazy?"

"That was funny, wasn't it?" He chuckled to himself.

"It was, but seriously... what's wrong?"

Letting out a heavy sigh, he placed his hand on his chin and thought for a moment. "As you know, Damian has refused to take back over his Alpha and has requested I take over permanently. But part of me just thinks Damien is scared to be the Alpha again. Even though I'm doing it, it was his title to hold, not mine."

Since I had been awake, I had learned everything that had happened, and this had been one of them. It was obvious Hale was unsure of being the Alpha and wanted Damian to take it back, but something about Damian was different now.

I couldn't blame him, though. He fucking died.

"You told Damian you don't want to be Alpha?" I asked him, watching him nod his head.

"Yeah, I have, but he just keeps assuring me I can do it."

"Well, it isn't like you're doing it alone, Hale. Yeah, you're technically the Alpha of the pack," I said, using my fingers to make air quotations. "But at the same time, you and your brothers each run a distinct division of this pack."

"I know. I just feel like I'm out of place. It wasn't a position I was elected to, or I inherited. This is Damian's right. Not mine."

"I know, but he sees something in you, just like I do. Someone who was made to be the man he can't be for us," I replied as I slowly walked behind the desk until my legs were standing between his own. "I have faith in you."

Resting his hands on my hips, he pulled me closer. "I just don't want to let anybody down."

"You won't let anyone down, Hale." I bent over, pushing him back in his chair. "You're too amazing for that."

"You're too good for me, you know that. You're honestly too good for any of us."

"I don't know about that, but if you're looking for a way to repay me, I might have an idea." My words seemed to trigger something in him. His eyes slightly darkened as he cocked a brow. "What would that be?"

"I don't know. Maybe dinner? Flowers..." My words were cut off as he quickly lifted me up and placed me on his desk as a giggle escaped me. "What are you doing?"

"You said dinner, but I was thinking about breakfast. I'm ravenous."

"Oh, are you now? Why don't you show me how ravenous you are?" I replied, as he quickly pushed me back onto the desk. His lips hovering over my own before gently kissing me as his hands slid my dress up to my waist.

"Are you sure that you're ready to have that kind of fun again?"

Grabbing the back of his neck, I bit playfully on his bottom lip with a smile that earned me a growl of approval. "If I wasn't, I wouldn't have made the comment I did. Now why don't you get down there and show me how hungry you are?"

Hale's eyes widened a little as his smile grew. Without wasting another moment, he dove between my legs, ripping the cotton panties I had been wearing and latched his mouth onto my core like the hungry wolf he was.

My back arched in pleasure as I moaned for him. "Oh, fuck... yes, right there... oh my god, Hale."

The more I moaned, the faster his tongue intruded into my core and his lips sucked on my clit. I didn't know how long I would last, but the office door opened quickly and looking upside down, I watched Talon walk into the office with a smile on his face, before locking the door behind him.

"Looks like I'm missing all the fun."

Glancing down at Hale, I watched him raise his eyes to his brother as a wicked grin crossed his lips. "I don't think she has tasted you in a while, brother. Why don't you enjoy her mouth while I enjoy her pussy?"

"Sounds like a plan to me."

The way they talked about me as if I wasn't there and my body was their possession turned me on like nothing else. I watched with anticipation, my mouth salivating as Talon slowly undid his pants and let his fat, thick cock flop out into his hand as he stepped closer towards my mouth.

"Do you want this, Ivy?"

"Yes... please." I gasped as Hale made me arch even more, a soft moan escaping at the same time Talon shoved his cock into my mouth.

"Open that throat up and let me fuck that pretty little face of yours."

I didn't bother to argue. God knows I wanted every fucking inch of both of them.

With every stroke of Hales tongue, I felt myself coming closer, but the way Talon's cock was shoved down my throat, I couldn't help but scream against him as Hale sucked on my clit one more time, tipping me over the edge.

It was at this point his mouth removed from me, and I felt the thick head of his cock line up against my tight cunt, pushing softly until he thrust his full length inside me making my gag and scream on Talons dick as he stilled letting me adjust to his size.

"Are you okay?" Talon asked, brushing the hair from my face as I slowly nodded. "We're going to fuck you like you deserve. Are you sure you can handle this?"

"Yes—" I mumbled just before they both thrust into me like I never had been. The sensation of Hales cock against my g-spot was just as amazing as the way Talon moaned every time I took inch by inch of his cock into my throat.

I wasn't sure how long I could hold out before cumming again, but it didn't take long as I screamed out in pleasure, only to have Talon finally free himself inside my throat. Soaking up the cum, I swallowed it, polishing him clean as he watched with a smile on his face.

"Fuck, you're amazing." He kissed me.

"My turn to finish," Hale growled before pulling me forward, so I was bent in half. His cock hammering into me like a piston.

"I want to swallow you, too," I whimpered against him as he held me close, unrelenting in his venture to make me cum.

"You want to take my cock in your pretty little mouth too?"

"Yes," I moaned as my eyes rolled into the back of my head, about to cum for the third time in one morning.

As the wave of orgasm split through me, he pulled out of my tight cunt and pushed me to my knees. My mouth opened and my tongue out, I lapped up every drop of cum that he spray into my mouth. His hand holding my head back as he aimed, making sure not to miss a single drop.

"Fucking hell, Ivy," Hale whispered as he looked at his brother. "I don't know about you, but I have wanted that for so long."

"Damn right," Talon replied with a smirk, fully dressed back in his clothing. "I say we do it again later tonight."

Adjusting myself, I wiped my face with a smile and fixed my dress, my eyes gazing down towards my shredded panties. "I'm fine with that, but if you keep tearing my underwear, you're taking me shopping."

"Just don't wear any?" Talon replied, looking for at Hale with a shrug.

"We have children now," I laughed, rolling my eyes as I headed for the door. "Enough fun for one morning. I'm going to take a shower. You boys need to finish helping James."

"Not a fucking chance!" Talon yelled as I left the office laughing.

It was moments like this I cherished the most. Loving how normal my life was slowly becoming. Nothing could ruin the moments I had with my mates, and I was excited about the many more that would come.

CHAPTER FORTY

Celebrating the Family

My time in the office with Hale and Talon had been exactly as I had remembered it being. Absolutely intoxicating. The only difference was their Lycans could no longer play, and honestly, I preferred it.

I preferred knowing the aggression they had for me was their own, and not the influence of a beast inside them. They were my mates, and it was them I fell in love with.

Not the Lycans that once possessed them.

Making my way downstairs, freshly showered and ready for the night, I was stunned when I walked down the stairs only to find Kate, Angel, their new baby, my mother and my mother's mate all standing in the foyer waiting for me.

"Oh my God, what did you guys get here?" I squealed with excitement as I cleared the last few steps and ran over to them, giving them all hugs.

"We've been here for about the last hour or so. They said you were upstairs taking a shower, so we settled into our rooms," Kate replied as she turned around and showed me the car seat with the newborn baby fast asleep.

"Oh, my goodness. She's so beautiful," I cooed as she set the car seat down and picked the baby out of it, handing her over to me. "What's her name?"

"Her name is Dalia." The name was just as beautiful as the child who slept peacefully in my arms. This was the size I had remembered my twins being before everything that had happened, and holding her now almost brought tears to my eyes as I thought about it.

Pushing those emotions back, though, I handed her back to Kate as I turned to my mother and the mysterious Dr. Blake. "I'm glad to see that you're back, mom. And you, thank you so much for taking care of her."

"It was a pleasure," he chuckled as he pulled my mother close. "I would take care of her a hundred times over if I could."

"Oh, you..." she cooed at him as she kissed his cheek. "He is so sweet, isn't he?"

"Yes, he is," I replied with a smile.

It was strange to see her happy like this because I had never seen her happy with any man. Even my father. Those were memories I didn't remember, and seeing my mother taken care of and loved more than anything, warmed my heart.

"With everything going back to normal, I hope that you guys will come more often. I even spoke with Damian about possibly building more accommodations."

"You mean to this house?" Kate asked, as she looked around.

"Actually, I have spoken with the guys and we are going to be constructing a new manor, a new pack house. This one will actually hold the younger generations, those who are mateless, and just starting out. Freshly graduated, almost like a dormitory where they will be able to reside until they are ready to move out on their own."

The idea lit smiles across their faces, and I was pleased they liked it. It was something I had taken on passionately, and even though it was just a fresh idea, I knew in time, it would be very beneficial.

Not to mention a welcome addition to go right alongside the beautiful library Damian constructed in my name for the pack.

"That's going to be absolutely lovely, my dear. When do you start on the new house?"

"Well, the plans are still in the works of being drawn up, so we're hoping that they can break ground on it in about a month. But the new pack house is going to have about twenty bedrooms. There's going to be the main living area for us with a second floor for our guests and then, of course, the bottom floor, that is going to be the common areas. So it will be three stories, but it's going to be a masterpiece."

I was excited about the fresh changes and from the looks of my friends and my family, I could tell they also were excited for us. There was a lot that was going to happen, but most importantly, we were making these changes for the fate of not only our pack, but for the future of our children.

After a few more small conversations, we all headed out front to where the pack members had gathered. Music was playing, and a variety of stations were set up for kids, and also crafts that some pack members made. Sort of like a small market.

As my eyes scanned the crowds, I spotted the twins with Damian, Hale, and Talon. Their happy faces laughing as Hale and Talon danced with them to the beat of the music. Castor loved music from what I was told, and often cried if the guys tried to turn it off.

As if knowing I was there, Damian turned and his eyes connected with mine, and as they did a smile crept across his face till he made his way towards me. "Well, hello gorgeous," he said, wrapping his arms around me pulling me close.

"Hello to you as well." I blushed.

"You look absolutely delicious tonight," he whispered in my ear. "Almost makes me want to take you home to finish more of what my brothers had earlier."

"Well, if you behave, perhaps later you and your brothers will enjoy more of me."

The comment was an invitation, and as I made it, a low growl echoed from his throat as he pulled me tighter against him. The feeling of his quickly hardening cock against my thigh was a welcome feeling indeed. However, for right now, there wasn't any time for that kind of fun.

We had things to do and the twins to celebrate.

As the sky quickly darkened, the bonfire was lit; we sang Happy Birthday to the twins who clapped merrily while the pack's children and other pack members stood around singing Happy Birthday, watching them blow out their candles.

Of course, we had told everybody no presents, but they wouldn't hear any of it.

The tables were piled high with gifts for the twins, and knowing that the pack loved them as much as we did was an emotional feeling. They were the future of this pack, and hopefully they wouldn't be the only ones. It was just a matter of time before things settled down further and with the new house, there would be plenty of room to grow our family.

"How do you like everything?" James said to me as he walked over from the gift table where Hale and Talon were trying to wrangle two very messy children.

My mother watching as she laughed and took pictures.

"It's beautiful. You outdid yourself, James. You honestly really did. I'm so pleased with it all." Through all the events, James wouldn't let me have a hand in anything. Instead, he took it upon himself, with the help of his brothers, to make today as perfect as he could.

Stepping forward, I brushed my lips against his, showing him the affection he deserved. The affection I had longed to give him all day. It was moments like this I was glad I actually had more than one mate, because each one of them had a unique characteristic I absolutely loved.

"I don't have time for this right now," James said with a strained voice, obviously wanting more. "We've got other things that we're doing and if you keep it up, I'm not going to be able to control myself."

He was hungry for me, and I could see it in his eyes that he wanted more of what I had to offer him. "Where is the fun in restraint?"

My teasing remark seemed to perk his ears, and as it did, he grinned. "Good things come to those who wait."

I wasn't sure what he meant, but I was eager to find out. Quickly, with a peck to my cheek, he turned and made his way off through the crowd, disappearing from sight.

He was right, though.

There was still a lot he had on his agenda of things he wanted done for the night, and I would not be the one to burst his bubble and stop him.

Instead, I made my way over to where my mom was standing with the twins, who were getting cleaned up, and watched as she cooed over them, absolutely delighted by her grandchildren.

"They've gotten so big," I said softly, her eyes casting towards me as she nodded.

"I know you missed out on a lot, dear. But there are plenty of other things to worry about. Your health being one of them."

"I know, mom," I said with a sigh. "It's just moments like this I realized I've missed out on so much. I know eventually it'll get easier, but for now, I just have to work with it one day at a time."

She knew exactly what I meant, and wrapping her arm around my shoulder, she pulled me close to her, kissing the side of my face just as she had always done since I was little.

"Well, now that you're awake, you can start working on making me more grandchildren." The comment she made caused us both to laugh as I raised my brow.

"Well, there are four of them, and considering the fact they are not interested in naturally knowing which children belong to who, I can guarantee you that with their sexual appetites, I will be pregnant more than once."

Even though this was my mother, we hid nothing from each other and as my comment made her laugh, she looked over to Damien gestured for him to come over.

I could see the hesitation in his eyes. According to Talon, he was terrified of my mother. Although I didn't understand why she was such a sweet lady. Nevertheless, he walked towards us with caution.

"Yes, ma'am," he said quite quicker than I had expected, making me laugh.

"Now that my daughter's awake and she's looking marvelous, by the way, I do expect to have more grandchildren, so considering she says you have a very large sexual appetite, I hope by next month she's pregnant again."

"Mom?" I exclaimed with wide eyes as I stared at her. "Come on now, our personal life's personal. You'll get more grandchildren when they come. We're not rushing into anything."

"Don't mom me. I want more grandchildren," she scoffed, rolling her eyes. "After all, I only got to have one child of my own, and now I'm too old to have any more. I expect to have loads of grandchildren that I can spoil."

"Oh, my goddess! Mom, stop." I laughed, looking at Damian apologetically.

"Okay, okay." She smirked. "I'll go find Blake and leave you two alone."

As soon as she was away, I stepped closer to Damien and sighed. "I am so sorry about that. She can be a little eccentric."

"Oh, I know she can. You should have seen her while you were asleep."

Cracking a smile, I shook my head and turned my gaze to where she had disappeared. "She isn't wrong, though. I do want more children. I just really want to wait until we have more room because even though the pack house is big, it's not big enough for us to have more children right now."

"Don't you worry about the house situation. I'm taking care of that. As for making more children, we could always start by practicing tonight," he said in that deep, sultry voice I loved so much.

I wasn't sure what he had in mind, but as I glanced in the direction he was looking, I saw James walking towards the house as Hale and Talon quietly handed the twins over to my mother and Blake, who were more than happy to oblige whatever they said.

And from the knowing look on my mother's face as she glanced at me, full of mischievousness, I knew exactly what they were talking to her about.

And there was no way in hell she would decline that offer.

CHAPTER FORTY-ONE

Taking All Four

I wasn't sure what to expect as I walked back towards the house with Damian, Hale, and Talon. However, the moment I stepped into the darkened corridor of the house, I was wrapped into the firm muscular arms of James, who held me back as Hale stepped forward, a smile on his face. His deep blue eyes caused my heart to race as he raised a brow.

"You look surprised."

My heart raced as my gaze fell upon the three of them. "Can you blame me?"

"Don't worry... we won't bite—hard." Talon chuckled, causing Damian to roll his eyes as he stepped forward.

"You held out on two of us earlier, Ivy," he said in a dark seductive voice as he cupped my chin in his hand. "That wasn't very nice, was it?"

"No," I whispered in response as I took a deep breath, the feeling of his hand cupping my aching cunt making my mind flood with images of what they were going to do.

"No, what?"

"No, sir." I gasped, the feeling of his finger sliding beneath the fabric of my panties was more than erotic, and as he teased my clit, I wanted to come undone. "Don't tease me if you won't finish it."

I wasn't sure where the comment came from, but the moment it left my mouth, I regretted it. The looks the guys gave me were dangerous... devious, even. I knew whatever they had planned was going to leave me completely off balance.

Before I knew it, I was lifted off my feet. James wrapped me in his arms even tighter as he dragged me backwards down the hall towards God knows where. It wasn't until we made it towards the basement door I questioned what exactly they had planned. They honestly had done nothing like this, but seeing this side of them turned me on more than anything.

"Are you sure you are prepared for what we have planned for you?" Hale asked in a sultry tone that seemed a dive right into the depths of my core, making me ache for him.

"Well, I can't honestly answer that, can I? Because you haven't exactly told me what you had planned." Sarcasm laced my tone, enough to make Talon scoff with laughter. Hale, however, didn't seem pleased and taking two steps closer, he grabbed my face tight, forcing me to look at him as he leaned down, running his tongue across my lips.

"Such a pretty mouth to be so sarcastic. Perhaps tonight we'll see just what that mouth can do."

Normal girls more than likely would have been terrified of what was about to happen: four strong men, ripped to no end, taking you down into a dark basement, manhandling you, tossing you around. It would have been like something off of a crime document.

For me, though, this was absolutely fucking hot as hell.

"All talk, and no bite." Again, with my mouth opening without thinking. Part of me was talking this way, wanting them to be bad to me. But the other part, the more rational part of me, was asking the insane side of me if I preferred duct tape as a means to shut up.

At the end of the day, though, both sides kind of said, fuck it.

James didn't hesitate to toss me over his shoulder, dragging me down to the basement in the dark. Hanging over his shoulder like this disoriented me, and as I moved, he smacked my ass hard, causing me to yelp, which in turn caused the other men to chuckle.

"James... when did you decide to go from perfect dad to dominating wolf?" I teased, earning me another smack as I felt him shake his head against my side.

"It's called balance, Ivy. We have been holding back on you with a lot of things we enjoy, and after months of you having what you wanted... well, you're finally going to see what we want."

"Sounds dangerous..." I muttered as I was quickly put on my feet, the light flickering on causing me to shield my eyes so they could adjust.

As I took in the room, I was shocked by what I saw. At first, I hadn't understood why they had brought me down into the basement. It was supposed to have been turned into their man cave, but it was clear that while I was knocked out upstairs, they had other plans.

Plans that highlighted every aspect of the kink world you could possibly think of.

Paddles, robe, chains, hooks, you name it. From furniture to more elegant features, they lined the walls and decorate the floor. It wasn't thrown together hurriedly. It seemed they had spent a lot of time taking every bit of their interest into account in creating this room.

Four corners—four mates. That meant there were four different flavors of fun.

"Jesus Christ, you guys really were busy when I was asleep."

Hale and Talon shrugged their shoulders with their arms crossed over their chests as they turned their gaze to Damian, who seemed to take charge in the situation. Even James had stepped back only for me to calculate that no matter what I did, it was going to be them who decided what I would get tonight.

"Here's how this works," Damian drawled as he slowly unbuttoned his shirt. Every slow movement of the buttons coming undone allowed me to see a part of his ripped muscles hiding beneath too much fabric. I was practically drooling with anticipation, but as he spoke again, I glanced up, trying to pay attention. "...are you listening to me?"

"Trying, but you're being very distracting right now."

Letting out a heavy sigh, he slid his shirt off and tossed it aside. "You will spend time in every corner with each of us, and as you do, we will send your mind reeling with fantasies."

I was enticed. I'll give him that. My body was practically giddy with excitement, because before the meet-and-greet with the twins earlier, I hadn't had proper fun with my mates since I had been awake. My body, now completely healed, was ready to be taken.

Ready to be treated like their perfectly good cum slut... or so I have heard Talon call me before.

The thought of each of them filling me. Each of them taking me was exactly what I wanted. I wanted to please each of them, and I wanted each of them to fill me with their cum until their balls were empty and I was dripping with their satisfaction.

"Sounds delicious—" I went to say before James grabbed me from behind by the throat and pulled me close.

"I'm glad you think so, Ivy. Because I'm going first."

Glancing over at Damian, Talon, and Hale, they all smiled at me. "Youngest to oldest, Ivy."

I didn't have time to question anything until I was turned around to face James. A dark, sinister look in his eyes gleamed before his lips were against mine, and his tongue was fighting with my own. The kiss was heated, far more heated than anything I had ever had with him—and I loved it.

Pulling me towards a four-poster bed, I was pushed against the post, my left arm quickly brought up as he shackled me to a spreader bar that was hung from hooks on the post. The tightening of the restraint caused me to glance up with a racing heart. I was excited, but nervous about what was in store.

As soon as my other hand was shackled, he slid his finger down from my lips over the curves of my breast, straight towards my aching core. His fingers slowly massaged my sensitive clit as I moaned softly against him. "I know we said we would do this, but I can't help but wonder if she would prefer to take all four of us at once."

Hearing him say that caused me to groan in pleasure as he moved his fingers faster against me. My head tilting back as my lips parted, my eyes rolling back in agonizing pleasure. "Yes, please."

"Did you hear that?" Talon chuckled, "she's begging for it."

"I don't know..." Damian replied. "That might be too much for her."

"Only one way to find out." Hale added.

They were tormenting me with their words, and as they did, I placed my gaze back on them. "You won't know what I can take until you stop being a pussy and find out."

Before the others could say anything to my comment, James grabbed my throat again and smiled. "Have it your way."

I didn't realize what I was signing myself up for, but before I knew it, the chains to my restraints were loosened, and a weird skinny brace was placed below my hips as I was bent over the object. Shackles on it were attached to my ankles, and with confusion, I watched as they made sure that I would be able to move.

It wasn't until a fanning breath on my aching pussy made me realize that one of them was aching to taste me, and as his tongue slid across my clit I gasped.

"God, you taste so good." James' voice from behind me was enough for me to smile, and as my eyes slid up, I watched two very naked twins standing before me, stroking their thick cocks.

"Look, she's practically salivating," Hale murmured to Talon as I opened my mouth and licked my lips.

"Don't be shy," I teased, only to have Talon grab my hair and yank my head back with a smile on his face as he rubbed the head of his cock against my lips.

"You want it?"

"Yes," I whispered as I stuck my tongue out to lick the pre-cum from the head of his cock. A soft moan escaped him before he shoved the full length of his cock into my throat. I gagged for a moment, but slowly he thrusted, giving me a second to breathe and then diving him back in.

All the while, my eyes drifted to Hale, who had a devious smile on his face as he stroked his full length, and James, who ate my pussy like a Christmas feast. The sensations building in me from that caused soft gargled noises to escape me as Talon fucked my mouth just like he wanted too.

The sensations were overwhelming, and as my mind reeled, I couldn't help but wonder where Damian was. That was until a quick sting crossed my ass and I yelped in surprise. "Did you like that, princess?" Damian said, causing my heart to race as I tried to concentrate on what I was doing.

"I think my brother asked you a question," Talon snapped with a smile as he slid his cock from my mouth.

"Yes!" I squealed as another smack came across me. It hurt, but the pain felt so good. My pussy was throbbing, and as he did it again, the sensation from James made me cry out as the first of many orgasims swept through me.

"Your turn Hale," Damian ordered as Talon stepped back, letting Hale take his place. "—and James... fuck that tight cunt of hers. Make her scream again."

They didn't waste time in doing what Damian ordered, and as Hale slid his cock into my lips, I moaned only to have my tight pussy filled with James' thick cock. The rapid thrusts he produced, slammed me forward just as Hale thrusted into my throat.

To make matters more insane, I watched Talon out of the corner of my eyes pick up a massive white wand with a gigantic head, and push a button, turning it on. I wasn't sure what the hell it was, but as he walked towards James, I had a feeling I was about to find out.

A rush of vibrations blasted across my sensitive clit, sending me forward as I tried to move. Another wave of pleasure coming from my throat as I came hard against it. With Hale in my throat, and James in my cunt, I couldn't control them.

The rippling waves of pleasure tore through me one after another until I felt James leave me and the shackles slowly come undone. It was Damian, though, who took me in his arms as I used him to lean against. The smile he gave me wasn't as dangerous as it once was, but the words he whispered into my ears sent a rush of heat through me I wasn't expecting.

"I want to knot with you tonight, Ivy. I want you to carry my child, but, take James and the twins at the same time. Do you think you can do that?"

I hesitated for a moment. They had already made me weak, but the fact that Damian wanted to knot with me and have me carry his child was something that spurred a fire in my soul. "Yes."

It was the only answer he needed, and I was quickly carried over towards the bed where my three other mates were waiting eagerly for me. James took my arm as Damian climbed onto the bed. His thick cock waiting to take me, and as I climbed up to straddle him, I cherished the feeling of his fingers running across my sides.

Slowly, I lowered my aching tight cunt over his cock, and as I did, I gasped softly. "Fuck, it's so thick."

"Mmm..." Damian groaned. "I'll never get tired of how amazing your pussy feels."

Pulling me forward, he took my lips in heated passion. James came behind me and dripped something thick and cool over my puckered ass before the feeling of his finger intruding me caused me to whimper as I slowly relaxed.

"Good girl." He said as he stretched my ass before lining the head of his cock up slowly, pressing it into me inch by inch.

"Breath, Ivy," Damian whispered as he kissed me again.

Stilling for a moment, I relaxed around them both, and as I did, I nodded, the slow movements of their cocks inside of me causing me to groan in pleasure. "Open your mouth, Ivy." Hale said as I glanced to my left to see his cock ready and waiting.

I did as he asked and as the sensations from Damian and James possessed every inch of me, I let Hale slowly fuck my mouth until his pace quickened and I knew he wanted to cum.

"Fuck, her ass is so tight. I won't be able to go much longer," James moaned as he picked up pace, and quickly stilled, spilling himself inside me.

"Knot her, Damian," Talon cried out. "I want to watch her cum undone with you."

"Me too," Hale replied as he slipped his cock from my mouth. "Fuck her hard."

As James removed himself from me, I was quickly flipped over onto my back. Damian hovering over my body as he thrusted savagely into my tight cunt. The force of his thrusts caused me to whimper as he took my lips again.

The swell of his knot was coming, and as it did, I glanced to each twin who stood on either side of me. Their eyes locked onto my face as they slowly stroked their thick cocks, picking up pace as Damian pounded away at me.

When I didn't think I could take anymore, I came hard, my tight pussy clasping around Damian like a vise as he came hard just as the warm spray of cum crossed my chest from the twins.

It was the first time we had ever all fucked like this, but the sensation and moment was something I would never forget. I was taken with them. Captivated with my mates in every way, and as the moment was over, they didn't hesitate to tend to my every need.

"You're such a good girl, Ivy," Damian whispered as he stroked my bottom lip with his thumb.

CHAPTER FORTY-TWO

News of the Future

I wasn't sure what I was expecting when they took me into the house but one thing I did know was whatever they had had planned for me; I was going to enjoy it.

Damn was I right.

When they took me down into the basement, they had absolutely blown my mind with the things they had done to me. They touched every inch of my body and every bit of my soul. I loved them more than anything, and nothing in the world would ever complete me more than they did.

Except my children, of course.

By the time the night was over and they carried me upstairs toward my bed, I was exhausted. They had made sure after everything they had done to me I received the proper care I needed, from them cleaning me up to caressing my body to kissing me gently, showing me nothing but affection.

Every bit of it was sweet and romantic, after I gave them the pleasure they wanted, they tended to me as if I was everything to them, which I was, in a way. I wasn't just their mate. I wasn't just their Luna. I wasn't just the mother of their children.

I was the love of their life.

They had shown that to me more than once and looking back at everything we had gone through, I wouldn't have changed a thing. We wouldn't be here if it wasn't for the trouble we had gone through to get to where we are.

All of the trials we faced together ended up strengthening us, strengthened our love, made us unbreakable. And at the end of the day, we never gave up. We never gave up on the hope one day our family could live as we always wanted.

In peace with everything we had built.

Laying in between my mates, their arms and legs entangled with my own, a massive pile up on my bed barely big enough to contain us all—I laid awake. I listened to the steady beating of their hearts, and the slow rhythm of their breathing.

They were just as worn out as I was.

The only problem for me though was I was no longer sleeping. My mind wandered over everything, wondering if there was something I was missing and when I couldn't take it anymore, I slipped from the bed and made my way downstairs towards the kitchen.

It wasn't until I was deep in the fridge searching for a snack, absolutely famished from all the exercise I had gotten from the guys I realized I was no longer alone in the kitchen. Turning slowly, I came face to face with a familiar set of eyes I had not seen in a very long time.

"Kara, what are you doing here?"

She stood before me as she always did, a brilliant warrior outfit decorated upon her body, her sword against her chest as her wings folded behind her back. An elegant headdress of feathers and jewels upon her head as her silver eyes stared at me with amusement as a small touch of a smile crossed her lips.

"It's good to see that you're awake." She stepped forward. "Word spread, in the realm that you had finally awakened. The others were eager to know if the rumors were true. So they sent me to check on you."

"That was very kind to them. I'm sad that I missed out on so much of my children's lives. It would have been nice had my father helped me along in the journey to waking up sooner."

My comment was sarcastic and slightly unneeded, but I was allowed to feel the way I did after everything I had been through. Kara seemed to know this as well and raising a brow, she shook her head. "Yes, I do apologize for that."

"Why is it that he waited so long, Kara, to tell me he was my father? I know there was no way to make it through, but I had met Frigga and you in the dream realm and never once did he approach me."

She stood there in silence unsure of what to say, as she tried to formulate words multiple times, but her mouth opening and closing vocalized nothing. After a moment of silence between us, I looked at her curiously to know why she had absolutely nothing to say and what she said next shook me to my core.

"It isn't easy being Odin. He has done things in his past that he regrets. But you were not one of them and trust me when I say he had wished many times to be here. That is why he's going to give you the gift that he is. That is why he is going to train them and protect them."

Train them and protect them? What in the hell was she on about?

"I'm sorry, I'm not following. Train and protect who?" I asked her with a narrowed gaze, trying to understand what she was saying. Even though, deep down, I had a feeling I already knew who she was referencing.

Standing up straight she adjusted herself, her eyes widening in surprise as her smile fell. "Your mates didn't tell you, I take it?"

"No, they obviously didn't. So why don't you enlighten me on what it is you're talking about?"

"Well—" She said with hesitation. "A prophecy was read when your children were born. Within that prophecy, it deems Pollux and Castor as the saviors of our realm."

"The saviors of your realm? You mean the realm of the gods? That isn't possible. They're just babies." I laughed, trying to shake off whatever she was trying to say.

"Ivy, this is not something we would joke about. Your children are special. Gifted even, and they have an important future ahead of them that demands they be present in our world." I could tell that she was trying her hardest to get me to understand what she was saying, but the only thing I heard from that sentence was 'in their world'.

"We can't all move to your world, Kara. That is impossible. We have people here to take care of," I replied, angrily.

Yet, when my gaze met hers once more I could see clearly I was misunderstanding her. "Ivy, that isn't what—"

"No, absolutely not," I snapped, cutting her off. "Over my dead body."

My reply was firm and as her lips tightened into a thin line, she took a deep breath and exhaled trying to force a smile on her face, as if she was talking to someone who didn't quite understand. "I hate to break it to you, but the terms have already been set."

"And I hate to break it to you, but there are no terms that have been set with me."

Even though I expected my comment to anger her, a smile spread across her face from ear to ear. I wasn't sure what she found funny. There was no way I was agreeing to this.

Unless....

When she said the terms have been met, it meant an arrangement had already been agreed upon. More than likely while I was asleep. "No..."

"From the look in your eyes right now, Ivy, I have a feeling that there are thoughts running through your mind over your mates possibly agreeing to something."

"They wouldn't do that. They know how much my children mean to me," I replied in disbelief.

"That they do, which is why they actually had made a counteroffer to benefit you," Kara added as she pulled a small knife from her pocket as she began picking at her nails.

"What kind of counter offer would benefit me? You're talking about taking my children. There's no way in hell that's going to fucking happen," I shot back at her as I tried to keep my tone at a low whisper. The last thing I wanted were my mates waking up to this conversation. I wasn't ready to see them if they had agreed to this.

"Unfortunately, Ivy, you do not have a say in this any longer. You were outnumbered, your mates agreed. What is going to happen is going to happen whether you want it to or not," she said, causing my blood to boil as panic set in.

"No, that isn't fair!"

"You're overreacting, Ivy." Kara sighed. "I could have taken them at six months old before you even woke up. I am on your side of this... they won't go till they turn eighteen."

"On my side? Are you fucking serious right now, Kara? These are my children."

"I know they are, but they will need guidance on how to use their powers, Ivy. Guidance that you never had, and look how well that went." She countered, giving a low blow to my self-esteem.

She wasn't wrong. I hadn't even known what I was, and I had made a terrible mess of things. I couldn't let that happen to them. I couldn't allow them to not know who or what they are.

Powers. My children had powers.

Wrapping my head around the idea was impossible. I was still an immortal when I had them, and those genes passed down to them at birth. Immortality I gave up to save Damian, and would still do even if time was returned to that moment.

"There has to be another way."

Shaking her head, she gave me a sad look. "I wish there was, but there isn't. We aren't even sure when they will start using their powers."

It took everything in me to leave that thought out of my mind in front of Kara. I had known the answer to that statement, and that was because of Castor. It was because of her I woke up. The being inside her brought me back, and if Kara knew it may have changed her mind.

She may have forced them to leave now.

"Please," I whispered with tears in my eyes. "You can't do this, Kara. They can't go through what I went through."

Low heavy footsteps on the hardwood floor behind me caught my attention and as I turned, I saw Damian stepping forth from the shadows of the hallway, his arms crossed over his chest as he looked between Kara and I before letting out a heavy sigh.

"This wasn't how I wanted you to find out. I was planning to actually have this conversation with you tomorrow," he said. "I need you to understand that this is for the best. It will help them."

"How could you?" I snapped at him, not understanding why he would ever agree to give her children away. "They are mine too, and you didn't even speak to me about this. You didn't even ask my opinion."

"How were we supposed to have asked your opinion, Ivy? You were unconscious for a year. What we did, we agreed upon in unison. We grew up not knowing how to control what we were, and it took over us until we were old enough to understand what was going on–"

What Damien was saying made sense. He didn't even need to finish that sentence for me to know exactly where he was going with it and nodding my head, tears continued streaming down my face.

It wasn't Kara's fault. She was simply doing as Odin, my so-called father, told her to do.

"Okay," I hissed. "Eighteen."

Kara seemed pleased with my response and nodded her head. "I will leave you two for now. I will be back in a few years to check on them. If you need me, you know how to call for me."

I didn't know, but I wasn't about to tell her that.

Watching her go, I turned to Damian who looked at me surprised. "You are actually agreeing to that?"

"Are you fucking kidding me? Absolutely, not."

"But–" he stammered with confusion.

"Damian, I know that you guys were just trying to prolong it. I'm not angry at you... it wasn't like you had a choice in the matter. However, if they think they are going to take my children they are sadly mistaken," I exclaimed as I smacked my hand upon the counter.

Stepping towards me, he wrapped me into his embrace kissing the top of my head. "We have till their eighteenth birthday to find a way out of this. To find a way to keep them safe. Let us just focus on that, and our family. Don't let Kara's words upset you."

I was silent in the end. Thinking over everything going on, and the fact the gods thought they were entitled to my children, when in reality, they were not. I may not have been an immortal anymore, but I was still the creature I had been before.

I could feel her beneath my skin. Not as strong, but still very much alive.

If they thought they were going to ruin my family, and take my children...

Well, I'd find a way to destroy them all.

The End.

Acknowledgments

Cover Design by Natasha Art
Editing Services by Aimee Ferro
Interior Header & Breaker Design by Leigh Cadiente

Lightning Source UK Ltd.
Milton Keynes UK
UKHW021600130123
415295UK00016B/1402